"*I'm to be married!*" *she gasped. "Oh, please let me go!*"

Micah transferred his grip from Lady Sherry's wrists to her shoulder's—lest he be condemned as a brute, it should be noted that she made no appreciable effort to escape—and gave her a little shake. "The deuce with Viccars! You don't love him!" he announced. Sherry stared at him, lips parted in mingled dismay and astonishment. There was nothing for it then but to kiss her, and he proceeded to do so. . . .

Other Fawcett Books
by Maggie MacKeever:

LADY IN THE STRAW

LADY SWEETBRIAR

STRANGE BEDFELLOWS

LADY SHERRY AND THE HIGHWAYMAN

Maggie MacKeever

FAWCETT CREST • NEW YORK

A Fawcett Crest Book
Published by Ballantine Books
Copyright © 1986 by Maggie Mackeever

Library of Congress Catalog Card Number: 86-90888

ISBN: 0-449-20805-2

Manufactured in the United States of America

First Edition: August 1986

Chapter One

All of London loved a hanging. The city was as festive as on a holiday. Vehicles of every description clattered over the rough cobblestones of the narrow streets near Newgate Prison. The air was stifling in the August heat and noisy with the cries of vendors doing a brisk business in baked potatoes and trotters and eels, lemonade and hot wine and ginger beer. It had been many years since Londoners had taken a highwayman to their hearts, and they had been gathering since the early-morning hours waiting to see Captain Toby hanged.

Through this noisy crowd Lady Sherris Childe rode on her skittish dappled mare, munching on a piece of gingerbread, absentmindedly scattering crumbs down the front of a riding habit that, like Sherry, was past its first youth. Not that Lady Sherry, even at the advanced age of twenty-seven, could be fairly called an antidote. Her person was slender and shapely, her features quite unexceptionable; her hair was a lovely red-gold color and her eyes a vivid, startling blue. Most often those eyes held a lurking twinkle, as if their owner found the world around her a source of infinite amusement, or an abstracted glaze, as if she had withdrawn altogether from the external sphere.

Sherry sighed and glanced around for her groom. How poor the people looked in this part of town, poor and hungry and resentful. And who could blame them?

Times were hard. The long years of war with France had at last drawn to an end. Napoleon had been banished to Saint Helena, and a Bourbon monarch again decorated the French throne. But peace had brought with it a slump in the prices fetched by crops, and with no more war contracts, many small manufacturers were dismissing workmen. Sherry remembered that she'd been looking for her groom, but he was nowhere in sight. She must have lost him in the crowded streets. It didn't surprise her especially; she was forever misplacing things. But it was a pity the groom had to miss the hanging, which he'd been looking forward to as a rare treat. Perhaps he'd given up looking for her and had found a place for himself in the throng, which was even denser now, so close to the prison. Sherry stared at the great, forbidding gray-black hulk of Newgate: the arched gateway and narrow windows, the sheer walls and heavy cornices, the statues of Justice and Plenty in their deeply shadowed niches. She gazed with morbid fascination upon the moveable gallows that had been erected outside the debtors' prison door. Twenty-odd people had been crushed to death in this very street, within sight of these gallows, several years before. Lady Sherry congratulated herself for having arrived safely at her desired destination instead of losing herself yet again in the confusing London streets, a habit that caused some of her intimate acquaintances to remark with exasperation that she had no more town polish than a newborn babe. Secretly, Sherry nourished no especial desire to acquire town polish. She longed to return to country life. And though she might frequently become lost, she almost always found herself again, thus admirably bearing out her personal philosophy that, given sufficient time, things generally worked themselves out for the best.

The workmen had finished their hammering on the gallows. Bow Street officers and patrolmen paced alertly about the open space between the prison and the barriers that kept the crowd from the scaffold. Eager spectators amused themselves with jokes and jibes, the latest ballads and broadsheets. They gazed out through shop windows that had been hired out for the occasion long before, shimmied up lead pipes to perch on ledges and roofs of the slum houses where wealthy families had once lived, and jostled one another for better vantage points. Fair cyprians rubbed shoulders with ladies of fashion, pickpockets and gamblers and street urchins, sporting gentlemen, and well-breeched swells. Pinched-faced poor and ragged, unemployed workmen, demobilized sailors and soldiers, gazed wistfully, resentfully, at store displays of goods they could not afford to buy.

The great bell of St. Sepulchre's began to toll at last. The black prison door opened, and the crowd roared in response, causing Lady Sherry to concentrate very hard for several moments on her skittish mare. She calmed the nervous animal and looked up in time to see a small procession pass out of Newgate. Yeoman, sheriff, executioner, man of God . . . The crowd roared again as the highwayman appeared. His hands were bound behind his back with rope. Captain Toby had captured the public imagination as had few criminals in recent times. He was said to be of good birth and education but with a ruinous liking for the good things of life. One tale claimed that, like many another son of the rich before him, he had turned to highway robbery because he knew no other way to pay his gambling debts. The more popular explanation was that he was an ex-soldier, newly returned home from the French wars to find no legal means of putting food on the table for his family and himself.

Sherry had no notion which version of the highwayman's history was true. The rogue did look like a gentleman, with his air of breeding and his fine, manly physique. If so, he was a very angry gentleman at the moment, Sherry thought as she watched him mount the gallows. She flinched as the hangman adjusted the noose. This was Sherry's first execution, and she suspected she wasn't going to enjoy it overmuch. Death by hanging was seldom instantaneous. The condemned man would expire horribly of slow strangulation, struggling for breath as his feet scrabbled for a foothold in the air. Sherry wondered whether this excursion was perhaps not one of her better notions. But since she was here, Sherry urged her horse forward through the throng. She wanted to miss none of the highwayman's last speech.

The highwayman was mounted on the scaffold now, standing on the moveable platform that would fall away from under him within mere moments, leaving him hanging by the neck. It was a pity, Sherry thought. He was a handsome rogue in the manner of the father and patron saint of all highwaymen, Robin Hood. Easy enough to imagine Captain Toby accoutered for the road in cocked hat and lace and crepe mask, pistols at the ready, astride a prancing steed; outwitting hated sheriffs, humiliating arrogant nobles, redistributing wealth, consoling distraught widows. Sixteen String Jack, who'd had a taste for good clothes and bad women; Dick Turpin, who'd had the honor of robbing Alexander Pope and almost made off with the *Essay on Man*; Captain Philip Stafford, who'd established a tradition when he stopped the executioner's cart at a tavern on the way to the Tyburn gallows and quaffed a last drink, promising to pay on the way back: gentlemen collectors all of them, who had in time danced the Paddington frisk—preached at Tyburn cross, dangled in the sheriff's picture frame.

But now Bow Street patrols had severely cramped the style of the bold knights-errant who had once made London their mecca, and consequently the heyday of the

4

highwayman was past. Sherry glanced without appreciation at the alert patrolmen who mingled with the crowd.
She was not the only member of the fairer sex present
to bear testimony to a feminine weakness for handsome
rascals blessed with swarthy complexions and dark curls
and wicked green eyes. In a moment of intense passion,
one of Captain Toby's female admirers flung a bouquet
of posies at the highwayman's feet. Alas, the damsel's
aim was not the best, due perhaps to an overindulgence
of a potent beverage known as Blue Ruin. The posies
struck the gallows with only a glancing blow and then
fell smack onto the muzzle of Lady Sherry's horse.

Sherry calmed her startled mare. Then she looked
back at the gallows. She was very close to Captain Toby
now, in her progress having made enemies of a great
number of people who'd been jostled by her horse. Indeed, so very dense was the mob, this near the barriers,
that a man could keep his feet only with difficulty.

The highwayman began to speak. Sherry listened with
approval as Captain Toby damned his prosecutor and
the jury as corkbrains and paperskulls, and then con-
signed the entire British judiciary system—nay, the entire government—to blazes. The crowd responded to this
eloquence with a resounding cheer. Screams and howls
rent the air. "No starvation!" the crowd shouted.
"Lower prices!" "No foreign corn!" What had started
as a hanging and a holiday had abruptly turned into yet
another demonstration of public anger against the grind-
ing poverty that was the working people's lot. Sherry
heard the sound of breaking glass, saw rioters attacking
houses and shops. The Bow Street men, greatly outnum-
bered, made a valiant if abortive attempt to control the
mob. Sherry ducked a flying brickbat and wondered if
Newgate was going to be stormed. The angry mob filled
the whole space before the prison and all the avenues
from which the scaffold could be seen.

Sherry's mare took offense at all the noise: the screams and curses and shouts. Had there been an open space, she would have bolted into it. Lacking that opportunity, she reared up into the air. Fortunately, Lady Sherry was an excellent horsewoman; otherwise she would never have kept her seat. She brought her frightened animal under control and looked about with some dismay at the full-scale riot that was underway. Then she remembered the highwayman whose hanging had been so fortuitously interrupted and glanced at the gallows. It was empty. The rogue was no longer there. Doubtless he had taken advantage of the general confusion to make his escape. Sherry decided that she should follow the highwayman's excellent example. She urged her horse into the nearest unblocked alleyway.

The narrow passage between the tall, ramshackle buildings was dark and malodorous with the stench of rotting garbage and other foulnesses best not too closely investigated. The mare was as eager to leave behind the melee as her rider and as offended by this new stench; Sherry was hard-pressed to hold the animal to a walk. Mere moments later, she wished she'd let the mare set her own pace, even at the risk of breaking both their necks. A man stepped out from the shadows between the two buildings. In his hand was a pistol, which was aimed at Sherry's breast.

Sherry was not accustomed to this sort of thing. Before today the closest she had ever come to life's grimmer realities had been between the pages of a book. Therefore she may perhaps be forgiven if her thoughts on this unprecedented occasion were not precisely coherent. As she stared at the pistol in the man's hand and struggled to control her frightened mare, Sherry thought of the storming of the Bastille, of the troubles that had taken place not so long ago in France. What in her appearance had alerted her accostor that she was a member

6

of the Quality? Certainly not her shabby clothes. And a neat figure and trim ankles, red-gold curls and vivid blue eyes weren't attributes limited to the upper class. She wondered how the angry mob would compensate for the absence of a guillotine.

This was no moment for such gruesome speculations. "I mean you no harm!" she protested hastily. "No matter how it may seem. In truth, the upper classes don't have money to spare, either, though I don't expect you to feel particularly sympathetic because we have to curb an extravagance here and there. Oh, pray don't hurt me! It won't help you put food on your table if you put my head on a pike! Although I do see that it might make you feel better about things in general, at least for a little while. But I assure you, the feeling wouldn't last!" She paused for breath. Her throat was dry, her gaze was fixed on the muzzle of the pistol, which had for her something of the fascination of a cobra posed to strike. Perhaps there was still hope; the rogue hadn't shot her outright. Sherry fumbled for her reticule. "Here, take this! It's all I have with me, but if you let me go, I promise I shall bring you more!"

"Blast you!" The man brandished his pistol in a manner that made Sherry's throat grow drier yet. "I'm no thief."

Sherry knew that voice. Just moments past, she had heard it raised in eloquent denunciation of all things British. "The deuce you aren't a thief!" she retorted none too diplomatically as she looked finally from the pistol to its owner's face. "You're Captain Toby. I almost saw you hanged."

The man swore a good round oath, then looked over his shoulder. Sherry realized that the shouts of the crowd were drawing close. The highwayman grasped her horse's bridle. "What the deuce are you about?" she asked, gasping, as he swung up behind her on the mare.

"I'm not about to get my neck cricked!" the man retorted roughly as he took a firm grasp on Sherry's slender waist and pressed his pistol into her ribs. She was not even briefly tempted to argue with him. Absentminded Sherry might have been, but few could outthink her when she chose to concentrate her mind; and, as has been noted elsewhere, nothing forces one's faculties into so sharp a focus as the threat of imminent demise. Sherry's faculties were very sharply focused just then. She gathered up her reins and urged her mare into a canter just as the crowd burst into the alleyway. Sherry heard confused cries and shouts behind her. A shot rang out.

'Get us the devil out of here!" the highwayman shouted.

Sherry needed no further urging. Nor did her mare. A second gunshot put paid to the mare's severely strained composure. She bolted. Sherry clung to the saddle, only peripherally aware of the mean alleys and narrow courts through which they raced; of the sheep that scattered in fear at the mare's wild approach, thus guaranteeing themselves some fate other than being hurled, broken-legged, into an underground slaughterhouse; of the donkey laden with firewood that collided with a jingling costermonger's cart in their wake, resulting in a tangle that involved a pieman, a chandler, and the ragged window blind of a cheesemonger's shop. Even as she rode hell-for-leather through the narrow streets, Sherry's mind continued to function very clearly. This outing had certainly exceeded her expectations. Indeed, it almost exceeded belief. She had set out to witness a hanging, an undertaking that, though hardly laudable, was surely not sufficiently reprehensible to land her in jail. And now here she was, showing the law a clean pair of heels. Very well she'd done it, too, judging from the absence of additional gunshots and shouts.

The mare slowed, chest heaving, laboring for breath. Sherry felt winded herself. She glanced cautiously out of the alley—less malodorous now, in this better part of town—and was relieved to discover herself in the vicinity of Soho Square and her brother's house. Her relief faded quickly when she realized what the consequences would be were she to be recognized in this rogue's embrace. A strange word to use, perhaps, but so tightly did he clutch her, so heavily did he lean against her, that it did almost seem like an embrace. He had the luck of the devil, first to escape death by hanging and then to avoid being dashed to the cobblestones from the back of a galloping horse.

But now what she was to do with him? The man was queerly silent, considering his earlier loquacity. Perhaps it was the imminence of hanging that had loosened his tongue then. Sherry turned in her saddle as best she could, no easy task in light of his grip on her waist. "Will you please unhand me?" she inquired. "This is a very awkward business, and we are luckier than you deserve to have brought it off safe. But pray spare me your expressions of gratitude! It is a little hobby of mine to help convicted felons escape their just deserts. I vow I disremember when I have had so excellent a time as this afternoon. However, all things must come to an end, even such rare treats as this, and so I bid you good day!"

It was an excellently withering speech, one that would have caused any proper gentleman to grovel at Lady Sherry's feet in mingled remorse and shame. The highwayman did nothing of the sort. Not that Sherry had expected a proper response. She *had* expected some response, however. None was forthcoming. Exasperated, Sherry drew back on the reins and uttered a good round oath—the same good round oath that the highwayman had uttered earlier, which she had immediately and un-

9

consciously added to her vocabulary, so greatly had it appealed to her ear. Forcibly, she pried loose his hands from her waist, in the process gaining possession of his gun. "Pray get off my horse!" she repeated, brandishing the pistol. "If you should not object!"

Captain Toby voiced no objection. He slid off the mare's back and crumpled senseless in the alley near the nervous horse's hooves.

Chapter Two

Sir Christopher Childe dwelt in a large, late Stuart house in Soho Square, an area that was still respectable, though no longer a brilliant social center. The same could also be said of Longacre House, which boasted three floors above a basement, and an attic under the roof. The venerable structure was embellished with such amenities as paneled rooms, carved shutters, fine moldings, floors inlaid with woods of several colors, carved swags by Grinling Gibbons on the drawing-room chimney-breast, and an oak stair with delicately carved balusters that climbed up from the stone-paved entry hall to the first floor. It also boasted a backstair so steep that the servants periodically refused to set foot there for fear of a broken neck.

Lady Sherry made her way up those stairs furtively, as if she were a cracksman embarked upon a burglary. She paused not at the second floor or the third but continued all the way to the attic. The floors here boasted no varying types of wood. Indeed, they boasted not a speck of polish or a scrap of rug for warmth. Not that additional warmth was desirable at this time of year. All the heat in the old house rose, turning the attic into a close approximation of Beelzebub's paradise. Lady Sherry paid no attention to the oppressive heat, save to wipe beads of moisture from her brow as she walked quickly down the bare and shabby hallway. She had grown accustomed to the quirks of Longacre House. The attic was very quiet at this time of day, all the servants being busy elsewhere about their tasks. Not that Lady Sherry slept with the servants in the attic. She was no poor relation but a valued member of her brother's family and as such claimed a perfectly respectable bed-chamber on the floor below. At least, Sir Christopher valued Sherry. Of the sentiments of Sir Christopher's new wife, there was considerable doubt. Due to this unhappy circumstance, as well as to several other ex-cellent reasons, Sherry had wheedled from Sir Christo-pher a book room in the attic to which she could withdraw at whim.

Never had Lady Sherry wished to withdraw more than at this moment. She paused outside the door of her re-treat, fumbled in her reticule for her key, and inserted it into the lock. Then she flung open the door and, with a keen sense of relief, stepped into the large, dark room. It was far from a luxurious chamber, but it suited Sherry well. A small window that overlooked the garden was set high in one of the walls, which were almost entirely covered with bookshelves. The few remaining bare spaces were hung with old and somewhat moth-eaten tapestries. Many curiosities crowded the room, among them an inkstand with borders of reed-and-tie design; a carved and gilded Venetian chest; a library table with supports in the form of sphinxes and decorated lavishly with Egyptian waterlilies, lion supports, crocodiles and serpents, hieroglyphics, and a pair of nodding mandar-ins. Drawn up to the library table was an Egyptian chair painted black with gilt ornaments in a similar vein. But most curious of all, to Sherry's eyes, were the two fe-males seated so comfortably on her high-backed reading chairs. The intruders were so enrapt in their cozy gossip that they had failed to note the opening of the door.

12

"Pray don't let me interrupt!" said Lady Sherry ironically.

The trespassers broke off in mid-sentence and stared at Lady Sherry with uniformly guilty expressions. The younger female ducked behind the elder with an alacrity that set the scarlet ribbons on her cap atremble and dislodged the towering confection of a wig that the older woman wore atop her own hair. Lady Sherry was very cross to see her abigail exhibiting all the earmarks of a servant terrified of her mistress's wrath. The most violent act Sherry had committed in all her life had been to hurl an inkwell at the wall, and that only because her sister-in-law had goaded her beyond human bearing. She sought relief for her irritation by slamming the door.

It was as if the slam of the door released the others from a spell. "Ye Gods!" ejaculated the older woman, readjusting her unstylish wig. "Must you give a body such a nasty start? I thought her highness had actually climbed the stairs to make sure you weren't hiding here. As, in all fairness to her high-and-mightiness, you *have* been known to do!"

Sherry didn't care to discuss her sister-in-law. Her thoughts were wholly occupied by the highwayman she'd left hidden beneath a hedge. If Sherry were the swooning type of female, she might have found respite in hartshorn and vinaigrette. Since she was not, she removed several books from a shelf and withdrew a decanter of port. "So the pair of you decided to make free of my hiding place without so much as a by-your-leave?"

"Told you she'd cut up stiff!" muttered the younger female, Daffodil by name and Lady Sherry's abigail by current profession. She peered out at her employer. Since it seemed unlikely that Lady Sherry would choose this moment to hurl an inkwell, Daffodil ventured a comment. "Lady Sherry, it weren't my idea— Cor! Begging your pardon, milady, how'd you come by that barking iron?''

Lady Sherry glanced at the pistol, which she still gripped, half hidden by her skirts, and hastily set it down on the library table. ''Never mind that now! You must help me, both of you. I seem to have rescued Captain Toby. And now I don't know what to do with him!''

This stark announcement titillated the interest of Lady Sherry's companions—or, rather, their disbelief. Daffodil expressed her disapproval of Lady Sherry's lack of truthfulness; though the abigail might herself tell whoppers on occasion, for the Quality to do likewise didn't suit her notions of what was right. Aunt Tulliver—who was, in point of fact, no blood kin to Lady Sherry—was even more outspoken, giving an opinion that the shock of seeing a handsome scamp hanged had unhinged Lady Sherry's brain. The controversy raged for some moments, even rousing the extremely fat dog who lay snoozing at Daffodil's feet. Prinny—the dog, not the regent, so named because his remarkable girth put one forcibly in mind of royalty—opened a curious eye and cocked his ears. Finally, Lady Sherry thought to inquire acerbically how, if the highwayman lying at this very moment under a garden hedge were a figment of her imagination, she had come by his pistol. Having gained her companions' attention she further pointed out the possibility that while they were brangling, he might either bleed to death or regain his senses and make his presence known, in which case some very difficult to answer questions might be asked.

Daffodil was willing to lend her assistance. The highwayman was a handsome rascal, after all. ''I don't mean to shove my oar in,'' she said apologetically, under the impression that Quality should be better at problem-solving than a mere abigail. ''But there's more than one way to skin a cat! We can't leave the poor man in the garden, and we can't think where else to take him, and that just shows that we aren't really *trying*, because we have a nacky hiding place right here! The fact is,'' Daffodil continued in a breathless voice, ''we could do it easy as winking! No one durst come into this room without your permission, Lady Sherry.'' Lady Sherry cast her abigail a pointed glance. Daffodil had the grace to blush. ''Well, nobody but us! He'd be safe as houses.'' She giggled. ''Wouldn't Lady Childe be mad as hornets if she found out!''

The three women looked at one another. If their expressions were not precisely reminiscent of pussies who'd gotten into the cream pot, it was obvious that they considered the reward of their mutual venture—to wit, putting one over on Lady Monstrous-High-in-the-Instep—to far outweigh the risks.

Determining how to smuggle a highwayman into Longacre House successfully was not so easy as winking, but neither was it monstrous difficult. The ladies had the port to lend them inspiration, as well as the tantalizing prospect of the starched-up Lady Childe with the wool pulled firmly over her eyes. Even Prinny roused from his nap to lend to the proceedings an occasional whuff and snuffle and tail wag. Indeed, it was Prinny who sparked in Daffodil the plan of action that would ultimately be used. Several others had already been brought forward and abandoned, it being thought unlikely that the highwayman could boldly walk—or limp—into the house. That Lady Sherry had done so without attracting notice was quite a different matter, as Daffodil pointed out. ''Begging your pardon, Lady Sherry, but folks are *used* to seeing your skulk about!''

It was in that moment that inspiration struck. Daffodil was bending over as she spoke, scratching Prinny's belly with her foot. She gazed upon that vast expanse of white

15

fur, then at Lady Sherry. "Crickey! That's it! Folks ain't used to seeing just *you*!" she crowed.

Lady Sherry looked somewhat doubtfully at Daffodil, then told herself that in the future it might be prudent to refrain from inviting her abigail to share the port. In point of fact, it might be even more prudent to abstain altogether from alcohol. "You want to disguise the highwayman as *Prinny*?" she inquired.

Daffodil giggled. "Not Prinny, milady." She nodded meaningfully at Aunt Tulliver, who was currently indulging in one of the little naps that she considered a perquisite of her advanced age. Even while she was dozing the old woman's sixth sense alerted her to peril. "All my eye!" she snapped on general principles.

Controversy again raged briefly. Daffodil pointed out that Aunt Tulliver was taller than most women, broader of shoulder and all else; Aunt Tulliver retaliated by suggesting that Daffodil was not only next to nothing in stature but also had precious little in the nous-box. Aunt Tulliver had lived a great many years without striking an acquaintance with the inside of a jail, and she didn't care to risk doing so now, not even for the handsomest of rogues. "Never mind!" Lady Sherry responded. "Daffodil's idea does have merit. Perhaps if you could provide us with a gown . . ."

Aunt Tulliver looked unhappy. "I've heard of many a queer start in my day, but stab me if this ain't the queerest of them all! If the lot of us are dragged off to jail, milady, it's on your head!"

So it was, and the danger of arrest grew greater with every passing moment. Lady Sherry pointed out this circumstance. Though Aunt Tulliver continued to grumble and make dire prophecies, she retired to her bedchamber and returned with a gown. Holding this item bundled under her arm like dirty clothing, Daffodil led the way down the narrow backstairs. At the bottom, she peered

16

with great high drama into the hallway and then gestured frantically to Lady Sherry that the coast was clear.

Lady Sherry followed, feeling somewhat foolish. She suspected that at her age she should not be engaging in such cloak-and-dagger stuff. Accompanying her was Prinny, who was made very happy by this intimation that he was to be taken for a walk, an undertaking for which the servants generally drew lots, the dog's mass being so considerable and energetic that the walker inevitably became the walkee.

Nor was today an exception. Prinny was ecstatic to be taken into the small garden, where he was seldom allowed, his high spirits in the past having not proven beneficial to fruit trees and flower beds and antique statuary. Consequently, the rescue effort was severely hampered by Prinny's exuberance and his determination to play fetch with Aunt Tulliver's wig. It was further hampered by the discovery that Captain Toby was no longer where Lady Sherry had left him. Stunned, the women stared at the empty space beneath the hedge.

Chapter Three

Daffodil was the first to speak. "He's sloped off!" she cried, her disappointment so acute that even the gay red ribbons in the jaunty cap perched atop her dark curls seemed to droop. She looked suspiciously at her mistress. "Unless you was bamming us all along, milady, in which case—"

"Oh, hush!" Lady Sherry was becoming very cross at these constant doubts. She pushed away Prinny, who seemed determined to wash her face with his great tongue, and straightened up from her inspection of the ground beneath the hedge, on which, to her secret relief, she had found traces of blood. "He can't have gone far. He had a nasty wound in his leg. He must be here somewhere, and we had better find him before someone else does!"

The search continued. Anyone looking out upon the garden from Longacre House just then would have seen a very perplexing sight as maid and mistress combed the area, peering under hedges and into trees; slapping vainly at Prinny, who considered it great sport to leap at their heels; and in general affording considerable perverse satisfaction to Aunt Tulliver, who was observing their progress from the book room window.

Amusement was the furthest thing from Lady Sherry's mind. She was much too warm, and much too worried, and feeling sadly out of curl. She was even beginning to wonder if she'd lived with her head in the clouds too long, as numerous people had suggested, and for that reason found herself in this horrid predicament. "Oh, do get down, you wretched beast!" she cried in exasperation as the dog leaped upon her once again. But Prinny was deaf to such remarks, even when delivered in much louder tones. So softly delivered was Lady Sherry's reprimand that he considered it an invitation to further play. He leaped upon her again. Unfortunately, Lady Sherry had bent down at that particular moment to peer beneath a hedge and Prinny's assault knocked her smack to the ground.

"Lady Sherry! Are you all right?" Daffodil ran to her mistress, then yelped as she barely escaped tripping over Prinny, who was delighted to join in this new game.

"No, I'm *not* all right!" Lady Sherry gasped, attempting simultaneously to push Prinny's great weight off her chest and to fend off his very wet tongue. "Oh, do get this wretched beast off me, Daffodil!" The abigail didn't obey immediately. Sherry shoved at Prinny's furry white bulk. "Daffodil!"

The abigail did respond then. "Lawks!" she said. There was a quality in her tone that inspired Lady Sherry to greater efforts. With a mighty shove, she freed herself of Prinny. The dog looked at her reproachfully. Lady Sherry had neither the time nor the inclination to soothe Prinny's hurt feelings, and so ignored him. Prinny knew when he was unappreciated. He heaved a great sigh and set about to be ingratiating, sticking as close as a court-plaster to Lady Sherry's heels.

Sherry tried to avoid stepping on the dog as she looked around for Daffodil. The abigail was nowhere to be seen. Where could she have gone? The gardener's shed stood not far distant. Sherry made her way toward the structure, past a barrel on wheels that could be trundled about to distribute water, and a lemon tree in a terracotta tub.

19

She paused on the threshold of the shed. The interior of the small building was dark as Sherry stepped in from the sunlight. It was also cluttered with shovels and spades and rakes, displanter and dibbles and wheelbarrow, sieves and pots and shears and ladders, and other paraphernalia of the gardener's trade. It was further cluttered by one very irate-looking highwayman, who held a trembling Daffodil with one hand and a wicked pruning knife in the other.

His expression grew even grimmer as he gazed at Lady Sherry. "I'm not going to hang!" he said grimly. "So if you value your lady's life—"

The threat was never finished. Prinny, bounding into the shed at Lady Sherry's heels, took in the scene at one glance. There was a stranger in the gardener's shed. Prinny knew what to do about strangers. He leaped.

Prinny's weight was sufficient to overset a person in good pin, which the highwayman was not. Captain Toby groaned as his wounded leg gave way, and he fell to the ground. Though Prinny was disappointed to find the newcomer such a paltry playmate, he indicated his lack of hard feelings by planting his front paws on the man's shoulders and giving his face a great damp lick.

Lady Sherry's first thought was that the rogue had fallen on the pruning knife, so much blood there suddenly seemed to be in the small shed—and if it would have been difficult to explain the presence of a highwayman on the premises, what the deuce were they to say about a corpse? "Off!" she ordered Prinny, and tugged at his plumed tail, which was violently awag. The dog awarded her with a severely wounded look. Lady Sherry bent over the fallen highwayman, ignoring the hound's reproachful glance. In a huff, Prinny withdrew to another part of the garden to play an enthusiastic game of toss-and-fetch with an intimidated under-gardener.

"Lawks!" Daffodil sighed, her hands pressed again to her breast. "It's a right good thing you showed up when you did, milady. I don't mind telling you I was all of a muck of sweat!"

Sherry found the pruning knife on the floor beside the highwayman, who appeared to have taken leave of his senses once again. The knife was miraculously free of blood. But the wound in his leg had begun to bleed again. Though Lady Sherry was far from expert in such matters, she knew the bleeding must be staunched somehow. She looked at Daffodil, who was gazing wide-eyed and somewhat wistfully at the fallen highwayman. It was a trifle lowering to recall that the abigail had been mistaken for the mistress while Lady Sherry had been mistaken for the maid. Not that the highwayman's misapprehension had been without foundation. Daffodil's high-waisted gown with its short, puffed sleeves—rose-pink in color—was all the crack. Lady Sherry wasted no time in lamenting the deplorable condition of her own riding habit, which had not benefited from exposure to hedges and Prinny and gingerbread. She lifted her skirt, removed her petticoat of thin India cotton, and began to tear it into strips. "Here!" she snapped at Daffodil. "Help me with this."

Cautiously, awkwardly, Daffodil knelt on the other side of the fallen man. Her modish gown was not fashioned for such maneuvering. Also, she did not trust the highwayman not to awaken suddenly and manhandle her again. "*Prime* and bang up to the mark!" she observed as she stared down into his unconscious face. "I wish it'd been *me* he made off with!"

This remark put Lady Sherry further out of patience. Daffodil, at some years younger, had obviously not passed the age of indulgence in romantic high flights. Nor, apparently, did she considering anything amiss in nourishing a *tendre* for an inappropriate object. Lady

21

Sherry, whose sensibilities were far too mature to be overset by the sight of a handsome face, felt like shaking the minx.

But she mustn't fly into the boughs. There was no time for such things now. If only the man didn't bleed to death! But although the wound in his thigh was a nasty one, he didn't look in imminent danger of popping off, at least to Sherry's admittedly inexperienced eyes. "There!" she said as she tied off the improvised bandage. "Hopefully that will staunch the bleeding until Tully can take a look." And hopefully the wound would not be beyond Tully's healing abilities. But Sherry could not ponder corpses now. "Here, Daffodil! Pray stop airdreaming and help me get him into that dress!"

It was not an easy task to garb an unconscious highwayman, the two women soon discovered, although perhaps the task was less difficult than if he had been able to protest. Daffodil set about it with a tenderness that made Lady Sherry recall irritably all the garments into which she'd been thrust willy-nilly by her abigail. Had she done the right thing in bringing the man here? Sherry mourned the loss of her earlier clarity of mind. "One can't blame him, not really," she said aloud, "for taking to his heels when he had the chance. The man could hardly relish the prospect of being hanged. And he didn't do anything so truly dreadful in the first place. He didn't hurt anyone other than in their pocketbooks, and he didn't rob anyone who couldn't bear the loss. One might say he wasn't so much robbing unwary travelers as expressing his discontent with the way things are."

Daffodil wasn't at all discontented with the way things were, not at this particular moment. She relished the notion of a handsome highwayman hiding in the book room, where she could go and flirt with him whenever she was bored. "Just like Robbing Hood!" she said approvingly as she smoothed Aunt Tulliver's gown over his muscular chest.

Robin Hood? Lady Sherry was not prepared to go as far as that. True, she had indulged in similar thoughts earlier, but that was before the highwayman's intrusion into her personal life. He groaned, reminding her of the need for haste. Sherry draped Aunt Tulliver's shawl around the highwayman's head and shoulders.

The women surveyed their handiwork. "I suppose he'll do," Daffodil said without conviction. "So long as no one gets a good look at his face."

Lady Sherry gazed gloomily at the highwayman. Her doubts about the wisdom of this undertaking were increasing with each passing moment. But it was too late now to cry craven. One must sleep in the bed one had made. She couldn't just abandon Captain Toby. It would have been prodigiously unfair to turn him over to the law after he'd made so miraculous an escape. And it would also be prodigiously stupid, since that escape would not have been made without her assistance. Sherry's errant memory presented her with an old statute still on the law books that stated very clearly that every person or persons who should comfort, aid, abet, assist, counsel, hire, or command any person to rob another would be hanged without benefit of clergy. Sherry very much wished that she might have benefit of clergy just now. Or preferably assistance from on high.

No such help was forthcoming. Very well, then. The moment was upon them and they would accomplish nothing by further delay. Sherry removed the stopper from the vinaigrette she'd borrowed from Aunt Tulliver and held it under the highwayman's nose. He choked and coughed, then opened his eyes and stared at Sherry. "You!" he gasped.

How weak his voice was, thought Sherry, how pale his cheek. And his eyes were certainly a vivid green.

23

And she was as bad as Daffodil, mooning over a handsome rogue. Abruptly, Sherry turned and peered cautiously out into the garden, half expecting to find a bevy of Bow Street officers outside waiting to take the guilty trio before a magistrate. But she saw nothing more exceptionable than the under-gardener at work in the distance and Prinny sprawled dejectedly outside the doorway. At the sight of Lady Sherry, he apologetically thumped his tail.

Lady Sherry turned back to her companions. "It's time," she murmured. Between them, she and Daffodil managed to get the highwayman to his feet. The man seemed dazed. Lady Sherry knew he must be in pain. Well, there was nothing she could do for him now. And were he in a better frame he might well prove less tractable. Sherry grasped the pruning knife more tightly and took a firmer grip on the highwayman's arm. On his other side, Daffodil gasped as he leaned heavily on her.

"Now!" Lady Sherry said grimly.

"Right, milady!" Daffodil replied. Together they stepped forward. The highwayman, who had not, swore. It took some time to learn the knack of moving in unison, supporting the man's weight. But before much time had passed, anyone gazing out the windows of Longacre House would have seen nothing more exceptionable than Lady Sherry and her companion, accompanied by abigail and hound, embarked on a gentle stroll.

Chapter Four

The next few moments seemed the longest of Lady Sherry's life. So weak was the highwayman, so unsteady on his feet, that it took the combined efforts of Sherry and Daffodil to keep him upright. Prinny did not lend his assistance to this project. Quite the opposite. Prinny knew perfectly well that a stranger was garbed in Tully's gown, a fact his canine brain immediately translated into an invitation to play hide-and-seek. That his friends did not enter enthusiastically into this game mattered not at all to Prinny, who was finding this day, with all its unexpected happenings, a rare treat.

This viewpoint Lady Sherry could not appreciate. She saw nothing pleasurable in hiding in the water closet to avoid being caught. Nor was she particularly interested to learn that Daffodil vastly mistrusted the earthenware vessel that was constantly washed by rainwater from a cistern on the roof. Even less did Sherry relish their encounter with Lady Childe's superior butler, Barclay, to whom she ruthlessly blackened Aunt Tulliver's character by explaining that the old woman's unsteady gait was due to having once again shot the cat.

All in all, Sherry was little steadier on her feet than the highwayman. Not much farther now, she told herself. Once in the safety of her book room, Sherry could indulge in vapors to her heart's content. She concentrated very hard on climbing the stairs. And then the greatest of all this day's disasters—thus far—struck. Lady Childe's voice arrested Sherry in mid-stride.

"Sherry!" the voice said. Sherry grimaced, though Lavinia's voice was not unpleasant in quality. Sir Christopher was even prone to claim, in moments of husbandly excess, that it was soft and melodious and soothing to the ear. On Sherry, however, Lavinia's voice had the effect of fingernails against slate.

"Now we're in for it!" Sherry murmured. "Can you support him, Daffodil? Go on, then. I'll stay and do the civil." She disengaged her arm. The highwayman's expression, as he looked at Sherry, was puzzled. Goodness but his eyes were green. As Aunt Tulliver's were not. Hastily, Sherry turned to confront her sister-in-law. If Lavinia glimpsed that swarthy face, those disturbingly green eyes, the fat would be in the fire.

Lavinia was flushed from her exertions. She was not used to dashing up so many flights of stairs. "Sherris, where have you been?" she cried. "I have been looking for you high and low. Then I saw you in the garden. Whatever were you doing? It certainly looked queer!"

Sherry took a firm grip on Prinny so that his furry bulk helped block the stair. "Looked queer?" she echoed vaguely. "I was only taking the air."

"In your riding habit?" Lady Childe surveyed that well-worn garment critically and repressed a sigh. If Lavinia had told Sherry once, she had told her a dozen times that it simply didn't do to go about looking like a dowd. Yet here was Sherry, her unstylish habit embellished lavishly with leaves and twigs and gingerbread crumbs as well as some very nasty-looking damp spots. Sherry's red-gold curls were even more dishevelled than usual; whatever she had been up to, in its course she'd lost her hat. "Perhaps," Lavinia suggested tactfully, "you might wish to change."

What Sherry wished to do was remove her sister-in-

26

law as far as possible from the vicinity of a certain highwayman. "Oh, no! I am perfectly comfortable, thank you!" she said, and began to descend the stair. Since she maintained a firm grip on Prinny, the dog accompanied her. There being scant room left in which to maneuver, Lady Childe likewise stepped back. Truth be told, Lavinia had scant liking for Prinny, whom she considered too large and rough and altogether rude. She could hardly admit to these sentiments, however, since the beast had been a present from her doting spouse. Prinny, on the other hand, was constitutionally incapable of understanding that all who made his acquaintance were not necessarily immediately smitten with affection for him. He looked upon Lady Childe as a surrogate mama and had done so since the memorable day when Sir Christopher had brought him home and deposited him in Lavinia's silken lap. The fact that Prinny had immediately christened that silken expanse may have partially explained why Lavinia most often responded to the advance of her pet by beating a hasty retreat.

Today, Prinny appearing even more than usually exuberant, Lavinia descended the steep stairs at such a reckless pace that Sherry feared a nasty tumble might ensue. Sherry did not dislike her sister-in-law so much that she wished for her to suffer a broken neck. She grasped Prinny's collar and held him back, thus enabling them to continue their descent with some semblance of dignity.

Lavinia drew a deep breath and sought to calm herself, then awarded Sherry a grateful glance. Sherry—who'd no notion that Lavinia suffered recurrent nightmares in which Prinny pursued her to a spent standstill and then licked her to death—in return merely looked blank. Lavinia wished Sherry were not such an oddity, going about so preoccupied with her own thoughts that

27

she was hard-pressed to render the observances of civility. Though Sherry's freakishness might not have raised eyebrows in the rural area where she used to live, here in London she was out of her element. Clearly, it was Lavinia's duty to bring her sister-in-law up to snuff. Sometimes Lavinia quailed at the task she had set for herself. But duke's daughters did not turn tail at the first setback. Lavinia would persevere. "You are very quiet, Sherris," she observed as they walked together down the hall. "Is anything amiss?"

Amiss? At the thought of all that was amiss, Sherry could have wept. She wished suddenly that she could confide in Lavinia. Of course she dared not. If Lavinia only knew what she had done this day . . . Sherry glanced at her sister-in-law and was smitten with remorse. Lavinia meant no real harm. If only she had not been the daughter of a duke and very conscious of her superior breeding, Sherry might have liked her very well. Or if she had not been such a generous little soul, so determined to share with Sherry her superior knowledge of how best to go on in the world. "Nothing is amiss," Sherry lied valiantly. "I was merely thinking. Pray do not tell me that I think too much, Lavinia, because I have already heard that today from Aunt Tulliver!"

Lavinia might well have expressed such a conviction had not Aunt Tulliver been before her. "Noodle!" she responded archly. "As if I would!" Since one observation had been frustrated, Lavinia then permitted herself another. "It was very shabby of you to forget that Viccars was to call!" Lavinia pointed out gently. She wondered once again how Sherry had contrived to have so suitable a match as Viccars dangling at her shoestrings. "An earl is nothing to sneeze at, after all! Nor is an income of ten thousand a year. Although you, of course, needn't worry about that! Still, my dear, you mustn't keep him on tenterhooks too long, lest some conniving female snatch him right out from under your nose!''

Sherry wished someone would perform that service for her as regarded Lavinia. Unkindly, she released her hold on Prinny, who immediately pressed closer to his surrogate mama, lavishly embellishing her pretty gown with dog hairs and paw prints and inspiring her to a frightened squeal. ''Prinny! Bad dog!'' scolded Sherry as she gave him a pat.

Lavinia brushed crossly at her skirts and withheld comment. Sometimes she thought Sherry liked that accursed dog better than she liked Lavinia herself. It was a very lowering reflection. Lavinia couldn't understand what there was about her to dislike. It was a question she had posed to any number of her acquaintances, all of whom professed themselves at an equal loss. In appearance, Lavinia was certainly pleasing enough, with pale gold hair cropped to cluster in curls around her face in the current mode and eyes of china blue. And her plump little person was always very pleasingly gowned, today in white cambric muslin with flounces of broad lace around bosom and hem and alternate bands of lace and muslin down the arm.

Ah, well. Lavinia supposed there was no accounting for some tastes. She glanced at Sherry, who appeared lost in the clouds once more. To ensure that Sherry did not once again wander absentmindedly off— thus dashing Lord Viccars's hopes once more, as well as Lady Childe's because she could not help but think that life would be more pleasant if Sherry dwelt elsewhere than in Longacre House—Lavinia took firm hold of her arm.

Sherry's thoughts were not pleasant. She could not help but anticipate the disaster that would result were

Captain Toby caught masquerading in Aunt Tulliver's clothes. Daffodil must be given time to convey their houseguest safely to the attic. To this end, Sherry let Lavinia lead her into the drawing room. Cravenly or perversely, she kept firm hold of Prinny, who was not generally allowed admission into this part of the house.

The drawing room was a spacious chamber with polished wooden floors and furnished very elegantly in the latest style. Equally elegant were the trio of people who broke off their conversation as Sherry and Lady Childe entered the room. With a sinking feeling, Sherry recognized her sister-in-law's dearest bosom bows. The Countess Dunsany was very fine today in a round gown with braces of colored satin and a white satin hat; Lady Throckmorton was equally grand in ruby merino over a cambric petticoat and a flower-ornamented bonnet of moss silk. Both were further rigged out with fans and parasols, scent bottles and handkerchiefs. And both gazed at Sherry with the expressions of grand dames about to condescend. Sherry gazed meekly back at them and released the hound.

With astonishment, the ladies watched Prinny stroll into the drawing room, give a cursory inspection to the furnishings before collapsing with an exhausted sigh beneath a table supported by luxuriantly carved legs. Then the ladies turned to Sherry, who was immediately and uncomfortably aware of how shabby she must look, particularly in contrast to Lavinia. Not only was Lavinia complete to a shade, but her pale coloring always left Sherry feeling vulgarly vivid. She raised one hand to push the hair off her forehead, thus displaying tan gloves that were shockingly stained—displaying also, to the room at large, the item she still clutched. "Sherris!" Lavinia gasped. "Whatever are you doing with that pruning knife?"

Sherry looked blankly at the knife. A large number

of lethal weapons were certainly passing through her hands of late. "I, er, had an urge to prune!" she said.

"Pruning! How original!" murmured Lady Throckmorton as if she found this a singularly novel—and perhaps a trifle vulgar—idea.

Before Sherry could retort, Lady Childe interrupted. "You wretched beast!" she cried. "Stop that at once!" Lady Throckmorton looked extremely offended. Lavinia hastened to explain that her remarks had been addressed to Prinny, who left off gnawing the table leg and looked abashed.

During this brief distraction, the only gentleman present in the drawing room had made his way to Sherry's side. Lord Viccars was a very pleasant-looking gentleman of some forty years with enviable side-whiskers, cropped sandy hair, and merry eyes. "Pruning, were you? Trying it on much too rare and thick!" he murmured into Sherry's ear. For a heart-stopping moment, she wondered what he knew or had guessed about her possession of the pruning knife. He smiled at her, then raised his voice. "Depend upon it; Lady Sherry has been plotting out her next hair-raising adventure."

The ladies twittered. Sherry regarded Lord Viccars reproachfully. Now that he had introduced the subject, the ladies would feel free to quiz her mercilessly. "Jacobs will be in a tweak when he discovers his knife is missing," she ventured. "I must return it straightaway!"

"Oh, not yet!" wailed Lady Throckmorton as Sherry turned toward the door. Sherry wavered as both Lavinia and the countess added their voices to Lady Throckmorton's pleas. Uncomfortable as she was as the focus of so much attention, Sherry did not wish to be rude.

The ladies took quick advantage of her indecision, speaking all at once. One so seldom had an opportunity to chat with Lady Sherris, she being of so very different a temperament from Lord Byron and those other literary sorts who put themselves forward to be lionized. *Not* that one could advocate such conduct, of course; just look what had happened to Byron, who'd had to flee the country in disgrace. One positively wondered what the world was coming to. Byron exposed as a libertine; Brummell living in exile from his creditors in Calais; Sheridan dead, as much from fear of debtors' prison as anything else; prices dropping and crowds rioting until it seemed that the whole of the manufacturing districts were out of work; old Grenville dead and his title up for grabs, shocking in a line as old as God. In times such as these, Lady Sherris was virtually a national treasure because she helped one to *escape*!

These last words were painfully close to the mark. Lady Sherry flushed. Then she was visited by a sudden, horrifying vision of the condition in which she'd last seen the gardener's shed. Blood everywhere and remnants of her tattered petticoat—heaven only knew what the gardener would think when he came upon the grim scene. Sherry could hardly hope that he'd fail to raise a hue and cry.

Obviously, no one had yet entered the shed. No officials of Bow Street were at the door, demanding to search the house. Sherry must do something. If only these wretched women would stop chattering at her so she could think! "You refine too much upon my small talent," she said with great sincerity.

"No, my dear, we do not!" protested the countess in the tone of one who knows indisputably what is what. "You are a genuine celebrity. As you would be aware, had you not rusticated for so long. There's no need to look embarrassed! You are to be commended for your selflessness. Lavinia has told us how you tended your invalid mama for so many years. It was for her amusement that you began to make up your little stories, was it not? No, do not fidget! You must learn to accept compliments.''

Prey though Sherry was to numerous anxieties, they almost disappeared in the force of her rage. How dare Lavinia discuss Sherry's mama with these cats! ''Pray tell us about your next!'' Lady Throckmorton gushed. ''So that we may steal a march on the rest of your fans!''

Fortunately, Lord Viccars was an astute gentlemen, or else Lady Throckmorton might have stolen a greater march than she wished. He plucked the pruning knife from Sherry's restless fingers, thereby interrupting her very vivid fantasy of mayhem enacted in Lady Childe's drawing room. ''Lady Sherris never gives away a plot,'' he said. ''It does no good to nag at her about it, because she will not budge.''

''Nag!'' Lady Throckmorton looked extremely offended. ''I'm sure I never did!''

Sherry did not quibble with this clanker. She was deep in thought. How was she to extricate herself from the drawing room with sufficient politeness so that no suspicions were aroused, yet with all possible speed? Her frantic glance fell on Prinny, who flopped dejectedly at her feet.

Surreptitiously, Sherry moved closer to the dog and poked him with the toe of her riding boot. Poor Prinny came to attention with a yelp. Heartlessly, Lady Sherry gave him a pinch. Prinny jumped, then looked beseechingly at her. Instinct told him that his friend must have good reason for her queer antics, but he couldn't fathom what that reason might be.

Nor could the other ladies fathom why the dog was jerking about in that very odd way. Lady Childe drew back, remembering the ruination of a silken gown. Oh, why had Sherry brought the brute into the drawing room? He obviously couldn't be trusted in polite company. "Sherris, pray do something with that beast!"

Sherry needed no second invitation. "So much excitement has been too much for him, I fear. Pray excuse me while I take him for a walk!" She grasped Prinny's collar and dragged him toward the door.

Chapter Five

Thus it came about that Lady Sherry ventured into the garden of Longacre House for the second time that day. And if Sherry had been angered by the knowledge that Lavinia had discussed her mama, the conversation that followed her departure from the drawing room would have made her sorely regret that she had refrained from bloody mayhem with the pruning knife. 'Twas a great pity, Lady Throckmorton ventured, that Lady Sherry's mama had been so inconsiderate an invalid as to linger on so long, thus selfishly preventing her daughter from jostling for position in the marriage mart. Leaving her, to use the word with no bark on it, an ape-leader, at her last prayers, on the shelf. With these sentiments, the Countess Dunsany murmured agreement. Visited by a vision of herself saddled for the remainder of her days with an unmanageable sister-in-law, Lavinia looked mournful. It was left to Lord Viccars to point out, none too gently, that Lady Sherry was hardly in need of anyone's sympathy, being a celebrity in her own right of whom the Regent himself had allowed that she spun a rousing good yarn.

The celebrity, meanwhile, made her way toward the gardener's shed. She did so with no appreciable speed. Though Sherry's impulse had been to take to her heels the moment she stepped out of the drawing room, she bore in mind that she might be observed. Were Lavinia to see Sherry running through the halls like a hoyden, there'd be no end to the questions she would ask or the lectures Sherry would receive.

For the same reasons, Sherry kept a firm grasp on Prinny, her excuse for this stroll. But Prinny had strolled around the garden with her once this day already and was in no mood to repeat the exercise. What he had wished to do more than anything was remain in the drawing room with his mama, a wish with which Lady Sherry had interfered. Consequently, Prinny was very much out of charity with her. As a result, his pace was very slow. Lady Sherry found herself practically dragging the great beast. She decided that they were far enough from the house now that she could release him. She did so. Prinny immediately sat down with the air of one determined to budge nevermore from the spot.

Sherry couldn't have cared less if Prinny passed the remainder of his misbegotten life beneath the lemon tree. Cautiously, she approached the gardener's shed. So stealthy were her movements that Prinny's interest was roused. He lumbered to his feet and trod stealthily in Sherry's wake, causing her to think for a dreadful moment that she was being followed by an officer of the law, and then to award the dog an irate glare. But scant protection was better than none, and Prinny was very large. Together they crept up to the doorway of the gardener's shed.

Tentatively, Sherry pushed open the door. It occurred to her belatedly that she might find someone within. What should she do then? Boldly enter and feign surprise at what she found there? Or simply, cravenly, slip away? There is scant doubt that Sherry would have settled on this latter alternative if not for Prinny's interference. The dog pressed forward. Since Lady Sherry was standing in front of him, she pressed forward also. She stumbled across the threshold, righted herself, and looked somewhat wildly about. The shed was very neat and tidy. There were no bloodstains on the floor, no shreds of torn petticoat. Sherry stared at the corner where she'd found the shawl and was relieved not to see it there again.

She leaned against the wheelbarrow. Had she imagined the entire incident? Had there been no hanging and no highwayman, no wild ride through the London streets, no pistol and no pruning knife? Was Sherry still asleep in her bed? In a spirit of experimentation, she pinched herself, then winced. She was awake, alas. Yes, and now that she looked more closely, she saw damp spots where someone had scrubbed the floor. There was even the scrub bucket by the door. But who . . .

At this point, Lady Sherry's ruminations were interrupted by a great racket in the garden. She moved to the doorway and peered out. Prinny, disappointed to find nothing of interest in the shed, had continued his investigations out-of-doors. Now he was frolicking exuberantly around Lord Viccars, for whom he had a partiality, his lordship having once brought him a nice bone. Though his lordship had never repeated this signal mark of approval, Prinny had never ceased to hope for its recurrence. He leaped up and placed his front paws on his lordship's shoulders and attempted to salute his cheek.

Lord Viccars had no wish to wrestle with an obese hound, though his innate good manners prohibited him from manhandling the furry brute. It was with relief that he saw Sherry emerge from the gardener's shed with a water bucket in her hand. Lord Viccars leaped back as she emptied the bucket over the dog's head. This treatment was the final blow to Prinny's dignity. He yelped, then fled. "I am so sorry!" Sherry cried as she brushed dog hairs from Lord Viccars's exquisitely cut frock coat. "There is simply no controlling the beast. Lavinia ignores him and the rest of us spoil him, and now it is you who suffer the results!''

Lord Viccars caught her restless hands. "Don't concern yourself," he said. "I consider it well worthwhile to suffer the beast's abuse if it gains me a few moments alone with you." Sherry blushed and sought to free herself. He made no attempt to detain her but held out the pruning knife. "I am curious, my dear," he murmured. "Perhaps someday you may tell me what has inspired this sudden interest in things horticultural. But you forgot this. You wished to restore it to its proper place, did you not? Hadn't you better do so now? We wouldn't wish to put Jacob in a tweak."

Lady Sherry grasped the knife, then fled into the shed. Once safely out of his lordship's sight, she pressed her hands to her hot cheeks and took several deep, steadying breaths. How foolish she was being. But Sherry had long ago accepted her spinster state. She had not thought to marry, and it was a circumstance she had accepted with only slight regret. Sherry had been genuinely devoted to her mama and grieved when that frail but valiant lady had breathed her last. Then she had been further dismayed to discover that her well-ordered life as a consequence must change. Used to a large amount of freedom, as befit an independent female accustomed to running her own household, Sherry found it an irksome necessity to dwell under her brother's roof. Even more unsettling, she found herself with her first beau at twenty-seven years of age. Once life had been simple. Now it was nothing of the sort.

What must Lord Viccars think of her disappearance? Probably that she was being tediously missish. Sherry brushed vainly at her unruly hair and stepped back out into the sunlight. "I quite forgot that you had promised to call today," she said shyly. "And then I come to you in all my dirt. You will think me shockingly shatter-brained. The truth is—'' She broke off. Though sadly unskilled in the art of flirtation, Sherry knew instinctively that Lord Viccars would not admire her more for discovering that she had a highwayman hidden away under the eaves. Sherry didn't want Lord Viccars to think less of her, even though his admiration left her feeling both embarrassed and confused.

That Lady Sherry was currently suffering confusion, Lord Viccars could hardly fail to note. That she frequently suffered that condition, he was ruefully aware. Lord Viccars was not accustomed to ladies who regarded him with something of the fascination they would accord to a traveling-show freak. Lady Sherry's response left him both humbled and amused. But Lord Viccars was no slow-top and he realized that Lady Sherry was more than usually distracted today. ''My dear, you can never look anything less than lovely to me,'' he said. ''Something is troubling you. I wish you'd let me help.''

Lord Viccars's perspicacity was unnerving. Sherry could not meet his concerned gaze. How tempting was his suggestion that she should seek his help. She wondered what advice he would give. Not that she'd ever know, because pigs would fly before she confided her folly to him. ''I doubt that anyone can help me,'' she said gloomily.

''Does your highwayman still refuse to cooperate with you?'' inquired Lord Viccars with a timeliness that gave Sherry a very nasty start. Then she realized that he spoke of her current work in progress, which had been inspired by the exploits of a certain green-eyed rogue. ''Oh!'' Sherry responded faintly. ''It goes well enough, I suppose.''

Conversation with Lady Sherry was *not* going well today. Lord Viccars was pleased to have sparked even so tepid a response. ''You concern yourself too much

39

about it," he said kindly, under the impression that Lady Sherry was dispirited because her current work in progress was not proceeding as quickly as she would have liked. "As my wife you needn't ever write another word, if that is your wish."

He didn't understand the seriousness of the situation. For Sherry to cease to write her novels would have been on the order of a meadowlark who abruptly ceased to sing. "And if I *do* wish to continue?" she inquired somewhat belligerently.

How prickly his lady love was today. "Then of course you must!" Lord Viccars responded with laudable patience. Perhaps a new topic of conversation might distract Lady Sherry from whatever had caused her spirits to sink so low. "They hanged the highwayman today. It's a pity you couldn't have spoken with him first. He might have provided you with some useful details."

He still might, mused Sherry. The highwayman owed her something, after all, for her efforts on his behalf. Perhaps his escape from the gallows might make an interesting chapter for her book. Perhaps a study of his character might enable her to overcome her problem with her current hero, who was disagreeable and brooding and Byronic in true romantic style; who displayed raven hair and wicked features, dashing mustache and muscular limbs. Unfortunately, he also displayed a stronger tendency toward clever conversation than dramatic action, which was all well and good in some instances, but a highwayman prone to flowery speeches lost a certain degree of credibility.

Captain Toby was not prone to flowery speeches. Sherry wondered what the rogue would say to her when they next met. "You are fortunate Lavinia cannot hear you encourage me to rub shoulders with highwaymen," she said dryly, leaving Lord Viccars to enjoy his ignorance regarding Captain Toby's demise. "How she would scold us both."

"Is it so very hard for you?" Lord Viccars suspected that he'd hit upon the source of Sherry's blue devils. He claimed one of her hands and drew it through his arm. "You must not allow her to oppress your spirits. She means well, you know."

"I do know!" Sherry smiled ruefully. "Lavinia is a repository for all the cardinal virtues, and one can only respect her for it, but she has a tendency to make life difficult for those of us who are not! Frankly, Lavinia is so concerned with my reformation that she inspires me to act contrary-wise. I cannot even take the air without listening to a peal rung over me afterward, as though I had a total want of common conduct." It occurred to Lady Sherry that perhaps Lavinia had some foundation for her strictures. Sheltering a highwayman hardly argued a respect for the proprieties.

She glanced covertly at her companion. Lord Viccars had not called today to listen to her complaints. Sherry must try to make herself more pleasing. What would be an acceptable topic of conversation? Not religion or politics. Or escaped highwaymen. Gracious, she could think of nothing else. And now Lord Viccars would think she had no conversation. Sherry would be well served if someone did snatch him out from under her nose. Indeed, she was amazed that someone had not already done so. What on earth had possessed the man to toss his handkerchief to a hayseed like her?

Lord Viccars wondered why his companion had fallen silent. If he could have been aware of her thoughts, he would have been surprised. He saw little of the provincial in Sherry. She was an original, certainly; he admired her intellect and was refreshed by her lack of social artifice. Which is not to say that he was so besotted that he was incapable of fair criticism. "I dislike to see you stand on bad terms with Lavinia,'' he remarked.

"That is because you've known her forever and she doesn't rip up at you!'' So much for good intentions, Sherry mourned. She wondered if she'd admire Lord Viccars better if he admired Lavinia less. "Oh, we refine too much upon it! I merely find Lavinia a trifle high in the instep, while she can't rid herself of a secret suspicion that novel-writing sisters-in-law aren't quite the thing. She wishes to understand me and cannot, and will not accept that she cannot and so continues the effort, which puts us both out of patience. I sometimes wonder how it came about that members of a family are expected to like one another, because the truth is that frequently they do not!''

They had, by way of gentle perambulations, now arrived at the garden gate. Lord Viccars paused and took Sherry's hands in his, then looked down into her face. She lowered her gaze. He frowned. Courting Lady Sherry was a humbling experience for a gentleman who had been the quarry of matchmaking mamas ever since the death of his first wife several years previously. But that marriage, on the surface an admirable match in all respects, had not been a happy one. Not until recently had Lord Viccars even briefly considered stepping again into the parson's mousetrap. And now that he *did* consider it, the object of his affections was as changeable as a weathervane. One day she was perfectly at ease with him and the next prone to regard him as something akin to an amiable ogre. She had agreed to marry him but could not be persuaded to set a date. The situation was as diverting as it was deflating to his self-esteem. What would be the outcome, Lord Viccars could not guess. He would give Lady Sherry time to discover the truth of her affections and meanwhile serve as best he could to buffer Lavinia's reformatory zeal.

But there was more troubling Lady Sherry today than Lavinia's criticisms or his own courtship. Deliberately, Lord Viccars refrained from taking advantage of this private moment to press his suit once again. "What's plaguing you, my dear?" he asked. "You may trust me, you know."

Shyly, Sherry looked at him. Lord Viccars cut a fine figure in his dark frock coat, and high neckcloth, striped waistcoat, well-fitting unmentionables, and gleaming boots. She should come down from her high fidgets and cease shilly-shallying, she thought. There was little doubt that Lord Viccars would make her a good husband. He was very pleasant company. He had the knack of sympathetic listening and didn't try to argue her out of her feelings, whether he agreed with them or not. And thus far in their relationship, he'd inspired her to hurl no inkwells.

Sherry realized suddenly that Lord Viccars had made no mention of marriage today, had pressed her to set no wedding date. Had he changed his mind? Did he no longer wish to marry her but was prohibited by honor from crying off? How the deuce was she to know his true sentiments? If only she were not so green! "I know that I may trust you," Sherry said in an agony of uncertainty. "You are very good."

She did not trust him enough to confide in him. Lord Viccars told himself that it was foolish to experience her reticence as a rejectful blow. He did so all the same, and above all wished that she should not know. After the exchange of a few more pleasantries, he took his leave. Sherry stood at the gate and watched him out of sight, then turned unhappily back to Longacre House.

Chapter Six

As he went about his usual business for the remainder of that afternoon, Lord Viccars's mood did not improve. He paused at Weston's to inspect the progress of a coat he was having made, at Hoby's to order a pair of fashionable Hessian boots with a tassel dangling from their V-shaped front, and at Lock's to inquire about a *chapeau bras*. These acquisitions failed to cheer him, so he repaired to White's, the most exclusive of all the gentlemen's clubs, with its bow window from which Brummell and his cronies had used to sit and stare. He passed some time playing whist and listening to *on-dits* concerning falling prices and the Elgin Marbles and most especially the highwayman who had escaped the gallows that morn. Lord Viccars placed a wager in the betting book as to how soon the rogue would be found and then left those Corinthian pilasters, that handsome and well-proportioned facade, behind to sally forth next to Gentleman Jackson's boxing salon, where he was privileged to go a round or two with the champion himself, thus vastly increasing his knowledge of the noble art of self-defense. Feeling slightly better for this exercise, he then withdrew to the Clarendon Hotel, where he kept a set of rooms, finding the Clarendon more to his taste than the town house in which he had not set foot since his wife's funeral. The food was superb at the Clarendon, his bed was several mattresses thick and large enough to hold three people easily, and the other accommodations were equally luxurious. The Clarendon even boasted a menagerie attached to the garden for the edification of those guests who were curious about elephants and llamas and other such beasts.

Lord Viccars had little interest in elephants and llamas and the like. His slight curiosity about such things had long since been satisfied. Lord Viccars's mind was not of an inquiring nature, and his pocketbook was plump enough to satisfy his every whim. Consequently, he was frequently bored. Or had been bored until making the acquaintance of Lady Sherris. She might easily have bored him as well, because Lord Viccars was well acquainted with the various strategies and ploys utilized mercilessly by the weaker sex in hopes of bringing a gentleman up to scratch. He had been diverted to find Lady Sherry seemingly without artifice, had set out to discover if she was truly what she seemed or merely more clever than the majority of her sex. He was not amusing himself with her, despite her doubts. Or if so, then with serious intent. But Sherry gave not the least sign of realizing how very flattering and particular were the attentions that he paid her, and so, ironically, he was caught. Not that he lamented the circumstance. Lord Viccars wondered if he would wish to cry off if Sherry suddenly became eager to have the knot tied. He hoped not. She was unlikely to give him an honorable excuse to cry off.

But these speculations were without basis and did nothing to elevate his spirits. Lord Viccars gave a last critical glance at his reflection in the large standing looking glass. He looked well enough in evening dress. Long-tailed coat and Florentine waistcoat, frilled shirt and intricately tied cravat, knee breeches and silk stockings and gleaming pumps . . . Lord Viccars might have reached the advanced age of forty, but few younger men could boast a more shapely calf, a more muscular thigh. "I'll be late, Williams," he said to his valet. "You need not wait up." The valet bowed and then hastened to open the door.

Lord Viccars's carriage was waiting outside the hotel. Dusk had fallen and the lamp lighters were making their rounds. The air was thick with a rich mixture of fog and chimney smoke, smuts and pulverized horse dung. "Marylebone," Lord Viccars murmured to his driver as he took his seat.

The driver needed no further instructions. He took up his reins. Like the valet before him, the coachman knew that Lord Viccars was setting out this evening to visit a certain little ladybird he kept in very comfortable lodgings in Marylebone. Nor was this the first ladybird to occupy the pretty little villa constructed in the Italian style, and neither Williams nor Briscoe, the coachman, fancied that she would be the last, whether or not their master stepped into the parson's mousetrap. About Lord Viccars's prospective venture into matrimony, both loyal retainers had mixed feelings. They wished their master to be happy, naturally, but lamented the curtailment of their freedom, for both knew well that matters would become a great deal more prim and proper when a female took a hand. Williams would no longer be able, in his master's absence, to carry on his very ardent flirtation with a Clarendon chambermaid; nor would Briscoe be able to execute the occasional commissions that enabled him to enjoy luxuries not generally available to persons of his station, an earl's coach being above suspicion and therefore admirably well suited to the conveyance of various questionable items.

Not only Williams and Briscoe lamented Lord Viccars's prospective marriage. This sentiment was shared by the lovely lady who awaited his arrival in the drawing room of the pretty Italian villa in Marylebone. Indeed, the subject of Lord Viccars's prospective marriage was a matter that much occupied her mind and made her wish to gnash her teeth. But Marguerite was not so foolish as to give voice to any rancor. "*Mon cher* Andrew," she murmured huskily as she pressed herself into his arms. "You are very cruel to leave me alone so long. I have missed you dreadfully."

"Have you, my dear?" Lord Viccars stepped back to inspect his *chère amie*. She was stunningly beautiful, as always, with her auburn curls and brown eyes and pale perfect skin, with her voluptuous body, which she was prone to drape in dampened muslin so that not a single curve was left to the imagination.

Marguerite wore no dampened muslin this evening but a wrapper with a décolletage that drew even Lord Viccars's knowledgeable eye. Experience had taught him that this generous display presaged a request of some sort. "What is it this time, I wonder?" he murmured. "Or, perhaps, how much?"

Marguerite pouted. It was an expression that she had practiced long before her mirror and that suited her lovely, roguish face well. "Andrew!" she protested. "You make me sound like a scheming minx. Truly I am nothing of the sort—except that my pockets are a teeny bit to let, and I do not wish to make a fuss about trifles, but you would not wish to see the bailiffs camped outside the door!"

Lord Viccars was indeed experienced in the arts of dalliance, and consequently immune. "You've been plunging deep again," he said coolly. "How much this time?"

"Not so *very* much, Andrew!" Marguerite gazed beseechingly at him, allowed a delicate tear to trickle down one perfect cheek. Now he would come and take her in his arms and tell her not to worry her pretty little head about anything. And she would make pretty, apologetic promises that both knew she wouldn't keep outside of a week.

What was this? He made no move toward her. Marguerite allowed a second tear to follow the first. She knew Lord Viccars did not approve of her passion for gambling, but it was the national vice and she did not see why she should abstain. After all, she *did* abstain from granting certain favors to other gentlemen, much as they might promise and plead. Marguerite prided herself that she was no common drab such as were found in the brothels around Piccadilly and in the flash cribs near Haymarket. She was a *femme entretenue*, kept exclusively by one protector and entirely at his disposal, which was sometimes a trifle inconvenient, since it was the fashion for gentlemen to spend as little time as possible at home. But Lord Viccars did not plague her in that manner, forever underfoot until she was hard-pressed not to shout at him to go away. He was very generous, his latest present having been a fashionable landau. And he also possessed a title, the advantages of which Marguerite was not one to discount.

But he was looking very stern. He had warned her of the consequences if she continued to gamble. What would she do if he did cast her off? Marguerite had gotten into the habit of living far beyond her income. She had a passion for quality in everything and a position to maintain. "*Mon cher*, you are angry with me," she murmured as she toyed with the fastenings of his waistcoat. "It was only a mere two hundred pounds. Will you forgive me if I promise never to do it again?"

Lord Viccars cherished no illusions about his mistress. She was extravagant and undisciplined, a creature of excess; her promises had no more true value than the caresses she lavished on him. When the time came, she would go from his arms to the arms of another without regret. But he enjoyed her company. In her presence,

48

he felt no obligation to say anything other than what he felt. Seldom had he encountered one of the muslin company who trod the downward road to perdition with such élan, and he admired that in her.

And seldom had he encountered such heady perfume. Lord Viccars inhaled deeply of it. "Save your promises for someone who will believe them," he said. "I'll stand your banker this time, Marguerite, but don't ask me again. Because the next time you land yourself in the basket, you must extricate yourself. And since we both know how you will do so, it will then be time for us to say *adieu.*"

Marguerite ignored this warning with its ominous suggestion that Lord Viccars knew of the gentlemen who clamored to take his place. She flung her arms around him. "*Mon Dieu!* How kind you are to me, and what a horrid wretch I am to tease you so. I vow I will make it up to you, *mon chou.* I mean to be very, very good. *Vraiment!* You will see."

Lord Viccars had scant interest in the goodness of his mistress just then. Her heady perfume invaded his nostrils and stirred his senses. As did the warm little body pressed so ardently against his. Marguerite was never so passionate as when she'd cut a successful wheedle, which was no doubt why so many gentlemen had let her lead them up the primrose path. Lord Viccars was not responsible for all the elegancies displayed in this villa. Many of them Marguerite had brought with her. Lord Viccars gazed upon a Grecian urn. He did not recall having seen it here before. But he had long suspected that other gentlemen than he showered Marguerite with presents. Only a fool would allow himself to be certain of her. Or trust her not to plant the antlers on his brow.

Lord Viccars was no fool. He didn't trust this sweet-smelling female who was kissing him so passionately. Nor was he certain of her. If she could find a wealthier and more generous protector—she had long had her eye on the Regent, but he preferred much older women, alas—she would immediately give Lord Viccars his *congé*. Such uncertainty was curiously stimulating. Lord Viccars swept Marguerite up into his arms and strode out of the drawing room and up the graceful mahogany stair.

Marguerite's bedchamber was as inviting as Marguerite herself. It was dominated by a large canopied bed with silken curtains that could be drawn closed or left open at whim. The other furnishings were equally elegant. The walls were covered with a pretty patterned paper, and an Axminster rug lay upon the floor. Soft candlelight rendered the scene most pleasing to the eye. Lord Viccars was not paying much attention to his surroundings at that particular moment, however. For one thing, he had seen this chamber many times before. Moreover, Marguerite was whispering some extremely naughty suggestions in his ear.

He carried her across the room to the bed, and set her on her feet. She smiled roguishly and helped him out of his well-fitting jacket, his waistcoat, his . . . but the prurient details of Lord Viccars mounting his mistress have no proper place in this account. Suffice it to say that *femme entretenue* though Marguerite may have been, she could on occasion comport herself like the lowest Covent Garden nun, to her protector's surprise and delight.

Sometime later, Lord Viccars was sprawled on the rumpled sheets, lingering over a bumper of fine old brandy known as "diabolino" and savoring the view of Marguerite *in naturabilis*. "I've brought you a present," he said. "A small token of my, er, affection. You will find it in my pocket." He watched Marguerite search through his discarded clothing. At least she was honest in her avarice, he mused, unlike ladies better bred and born. He did not include Lady Sherry in this assessment, of course. He watched Marguerite fumble with a jeweler's box, her lower lip caught in enchanting frustration between her teeth, and wondered what Lady Sherry would make of his acquaintance with this un-scrupulous little minx. Not that there was anything un-toward in the relationship. It was the thing for gentlemen to have mistresses, after all. He would give up Margue-rite when he was married, naturally. Not that he wished to, any more than he wished to dwell again in his ven-erable town house. But both sacrifices were required of him if he was to take a wife.

The wretched case would not open. In a fever of im-patience, Marguerite brought it to Lord Viccars. Pout-ing, she held it out. He would miss her, he thought, and carelessly touseled her auburn curls before opening the box. Her eyes lit up when she glimpsed the diamond and emerald necklace that nestled within. Then nothing would do but that Lord Viccars should fasten it on for her and she should strike various poses for him.

So very grateful was Marguerite for her present, and so provocative were the poses she struck, that no few hours elapsed before Lord Viccars departed from the little Italian villa in Marylebone. His gait was not en-tirely steady, due less to diabolino than to physical ex-cess. His thoughts were very clear, at all events. He was quite satisfied with Marguerite's response to his gift of the necklace. He wondered what gift he might make to Lady Sherry that would rouse a similar excess of gratitude. Not similar, precisely; Lord Viccars could not regard his fiancée in the same light as a member of the muslin company.

Lord Viccars pondered these matters as his carriage rattled through the dark and foggy streets. How was he to influence a lady whose sentiments he could not antic-ipate from one moment to the next? He could not lavish

51

on her such presents as he had given Marguerite because it was not the thing. At this point, a vision rose unbidden to torment him, that of Lady Sherry clad in his diamond and emerald necklace and nothing else.

Lord Viccars banished the vision with some reluctance. Pleasant as his imaginings were, they in no way helped him to concentrate on how best to earn Lady Sherry's gratitude. At the end of several more moments, he despaired of the effort. Lady Sherry clearly needed nothing that he could provide. And what the deuce had Sherry fretting herself to fiddle strings? Lord Viccars devoutly hoped his courtship had not sparked that response. If so, could he in honor go on with it? Could he, realistically, desist? Lord Viccars didn't fancy being crossed in love. Before his patience gave out, or Lady Sherry's scruples won out, she must be persuaded against further shilly-shallying about setting a wedding date.

But, again, how was the thing to be brought off? The only thing Lord Viccars might supply Lady Sherry that she lacked was the news he'd heard this evening of the highwayman's escape, and he could not even be certain that he would be beforehand with that. Sherry had taken an almost personal interest in the rogue ever since she'd decided to base her current hero on his exploits. Personally, Lord Viccars thought that, from what Sherry had said of him, her own highwayman sounded a very rakehelly sort. Lord Viccars didn't approve of rakehells. However, the ladies obviously felt otherwise, and it was the ladies who largely made up Lady Sherry's readership. How very much of an oddity was his beloved. Although Lord Viccars couldn't enter into her feelings, he knew she set great store by her story writing and became very involved emotionally in her plots.

Sherry's readership. Rakehells. Escaped highwaymen. These ideas coalesced into a brilliant notion in

Lord Viccars's mind. He knew suddenly what he could do to disarm Sherry and at the same time prove his devotion. How perfectly simple it was. He would track down and provide her with the escaped highwayman.

Chapter Seven

Meanwhile, a family dinner was underway at Long-acre House. Only Lady Sherry, Sir Christopher, and his wife were present, Aunt Tulliver having elected to take her meal in her room—or in the book room, to be precise. Lady Childe, blissfully unaware that there was hidden in Sherry's book room anything more exceptionable than paper and quills and pots of Japan ink, could only be grateful for this unusual reticence on the old woman's part. This meal, at least, would not be enlivened by muttered but perfectly audible comments on the quality of the food or the even more distressing sounds attendant upon an ill-fitting set of false teeth.

"Devilish inconvenient!" pronounced Sir Christopher as he set aside the spoon with which he'd been making forays into a bowl of pea soup. Lady Childe glanced up from her own soup bowl, alarmed that she might somehow have been remiss in her housewifely duties. But Sir Christopher had no complaint about either his wife or the dinner she had provided for him—a formal affair of several courses that included roasted beef, fried flounder, potatoes, and French beans, in addition to the soup.

"Luddites," he said in response to her inquiring glance. "Malcontents. One can barely stroll down a street in the City without seeing some meeting or other underway. On the one hand, leading figures want to relieve the distress of the working man. On the other, the working man wants to seize the property of the leading figures. And at the same time Castlereagh and Liverpool refuse outright to entertain any notions of parliamentary reform. As a result, we have mobs rioting and smashing machinery and wearing the tricolor.'' He reached for his wineglass. Relieved that she was not at fault, Lady Childe murmured sympathetically. Sir Christopher smiled upon her as well as upon his sister, Sherry. He fancied himself very much the patriarch, but one with a liberal view of the weaker sex. He believed the ladies should not be kept in ignorance of events that transpired outside their proper sphere. And so he brought with him to the dinner table each day an accounting of current events, a treat for which the ladies were secretly not so grateful as they might have been, perhaps because Sir Christopher had a tendency to sermonize, which may have been the result of the long hours he spent in the courtroom, contemplating a vast array of scoundrels who had been taken into charge on an equally vast array of criminal offenses.

There was currently in Sir Christopher's gaze a gleam that presaged just such an outburst taking place. Hastily, Lavinia distracted him with roast beef. ''Lady Throckmorton came to call today,'' she offered. ''And the Countess Dunsany. *And* Lord Viccars to see Sherris, who was not here!''

Sir Christopher enjoyed these cozy family dinners and prided himself that he could take part as well in the conversation of the ladies as that of the courtroom. ''Hah!'' he exclaimed, regarding his sister with a fond eye. ''Sly puss! Playing hard to get!''

Lady Sherry started. She had been thinking of Lord Viccars and lamenting her tendency to greet his most casual utterance with high fidgets. Even if Lavinia did not so frequently point out Lord Viccars's high standing in the marriage mart, Sherry would have guessed that he was considered to be prodigious eligible. Why he'd set his sights on her, Sherry could not imagine. *If* he had set his sights on her. If he hadn't changed his mind.

"Air-dreaming again," observed Sir Christopher tolerantly. "I know how it is. Why, when Livvy and I was courting—"

"Nothing of the sort!" Sherry interrupted hastily. If she was forced to listen one more time to an account of her brother's extremely dull pursuit of Lavinia, she would not be held accountable for her actions. Especially if Lavinia, as was her wont, giggled and simpered throughout. "I was not playing hard to get. I merely forgot. You know how sadly absentminded I can be."

Sir Christopher knew that his sister wasn't one to relish being teased and so nobly refrained from anything other than an additional chuckle and one more "Sly puss!" Personally, he didn't see why Lavinia attached so much importance to Viccars's courtship. If Sherry wished to have him, then she would; and if she didn't wish to, then she wouldn't. In Sir Christopher's mind, whichever way she chose to leap made no never mind. He was sincerely fond of his sister and somewhat in awe of her literary abilities, and also a little remorseful that he'd left their mother to her care while he pursued his own career. "After today Viccars must also know that you are absentminded." He chuckled. "I'll warrant he don't mind."

Did he not? Sherry didn't know. The entire topic was as painful to her as a sore tooth and as impossible to overlook. Throughout this interminable meal, she had been teasing herself with thoughts of his lordship and with a foolish wish that she could be more in the common way. But she could no more change her nature than a zebra could its stripes. And perhaps, just perhaps, if Sherry had been more skilled in the subtle arts of flirtation, she would not have created nine of the most popular, and gruesome, gothic novels to occupy a place of honor on any library shelf. Perhaps, if Lord Viccars were not around to confuse her, she would have less trouble with the tenth. The very notion caused a queer little ache in the vicinity of her heart. Or perhaps it was the pea soup, which tasted suspiciously like some ingredient in it had gone off.

"You should not encourage her," murmured Lavinia, resentful of the attention Sherry was being given. "If Sherris is left unattached much longer, it will be nigh impossible to arrange a suitable match. And you know as well as I, my love, that marriage is an experience no woman should be denied."

Sir Christopher was a straightforward soul, unaware of shades of meaning and malicious nuances. He thought only, in response to his wife's speech, that marriage was an experience he was glad *he* had not been denied. Of course, he wished equal bliss for his sister. "Aye," he murmured, oblivious to Sherry's indignant expression, as he gazed dotingly upon his spouse. If the wretched table were not so long, he would have expressed his appreciation of the wedded state by patting Lavinia's plump little hand. Or by kissing her pretty cheek. Or . . . Sir Christopher pushed away his untimely impulses and concentrated on his roast beef.

For a few moments, silence reigned in the dining room. But Lavinia's words had not fallen on barren soil. Sir Christopher was aware that all was not as well as it should have been within his household. He was also aware that this circumstance had to do with the relationship between his sister and his wife. Sir Christopher glanced from one woman to the other. Lavinia was a vision in cream-colored silk trimmed with knots of ribbon. For a moment, he marveled anew that so exalted a creature should stoop so low as to enter into a marriage with him. Then he turned his attention to Sherry, who looked very nice in pale blue muslin trimmed with a narrow flounce. But the vision of loveliness created by the ladies was marred by the circumstance that they were contemplating each other as if at any moment they might come to blows. Sir Christopher realized belatedly that Sherry had resented Lavinia's comments on her spinster state. He wished that she had not. Indeed, he wished that Lavinia could be persuaded from making such comments in Sherry's hearing. Not that he would ever accuse his beloved wife of nagging. And even if she *did* sometimes come perilously close to that description, Sir Christopher could not doubt that she meant it for the best.

He cleared his throat, thus reminding his womenfolk that glaring daggers at each other across the dining table was not *comme il faut*. Lavinia lowered her gaze to the saltcellar, and Lady Sherry stared at her flounder as if in it she might read some deep plot. This was not turning out to be the most comfortable of family dinners. Sir Christopher passed so many hours among rogues and ruffians, saw so much human misery parade before him, that he preferred to be surrounded by happy faces at home. He cast about in his mind for a topic that might amuse the ladies and earn him their smiles. ''That highwayman fellow,'' he offered, thereby curtailing what little remained of his sister's appetite. ''Captain Toby. He escaped hanging today by a hairsbreadth.''

How should she react? thought Sherry. How to appear as if she didn't know? She opened her eyes wide and forced her mouth to form an astonished O. Her fingers dug into her fork.

Fortunately, no one was paying heed to Sherry, or else they would have wondered why she looked so very queer. ''Escaped!'' Lavinia gasped. Though she may

58

have been the daughter of a duke, Lavinia enjoyed a thrilling *on-dit* as well as anyone. "But how?"

Sir Christopher shrugged, delighted by the sparkle of interest in his wife's blue eyes. "No one can say for certain. There was a regular rowdy-do—a riot, in point of fact. Store windows were broken and heaven knows how many heads. It's a miracle that no one was killed."

Lavinia wasn't concerned with who had and had not been injured in the fracas. As befitted her exalted social position, she had scant interest in the hoi polloi. "But Captain Toby!" she cried. "He escaped, you said?"

A glimmer of interest was one thing, but this? Sir Christopher was startled to see such fervor displayed by his well-bred wife. "Aye, he escaped. Some fool of a doxy—er, unfortunate female—whisked him away. The whole thing was planned, I make no doubt." He glanced at Sherry, who was as noticeably silent as Lavinia was vocal. "Her hair was supposedly the color of yours, puss."

This intelligence, understandably, did not cheer Lady Sherry. She dropped her fork. Frantically, she sought to regain her composure. "Oh," she said as noncommittally as she could manage as she pushed away her barely touched plate.

Sir Christopher also pushed away his plate and reached for his wineglass. He was not feeling especially in charity with his womenfolk. Was he not trying his utmost to draw Sherry out of the dumps? And she could only offer him monosyllables in response. As for Lavinia, her reaction to the news of the highwayman's escape pleased him little more. Foolish perhaps, but it caused Sir Christopher distress to realize his wife's genteel eye could be caught by a handsome rogue. "He won't be on the loose for long," Sir Christopher prophesied optimistically. "A most rigorous inquiry is underway. Handbills and posters with his description, as well as what we know of the woman who helped him escape, will be circulated. We'll find the scoundrel, and when we do he won't be given a second chance to avoid his just fate."

"The woman who helped him escape"? Those words echoed ominously in Lady Sherry's mind. She wondered how detailed a description of the lady in question was already in possession of Bow Street. "Is this hue and cry not a trifle harsh?" she asked as silent servants set out clean glasses and dessert plates, knives and forks and fringed napkins, decanters of sherry and claret and port. "The man has already gone once to the gallows."

"Aye, and missed his own hanging." Sir Christopher contemplated the large plate of fruit on the table before him, his attention wavering between peaches and grapes and cherries, figs and plums. "He won't escape again. Not with the ruckus that's been raised." He picked up his fork and speared a lush plum. "The law is not to be trifled with, by God."

Lady Sherry had no desire to trifle with the law, to have anything at all to do with the law, in fact. She feared it was a matter in which she was not to be given a great deal of choice. "What about the woman?" she murmured.

Sir Christopher stared blankly at his sister over the top of the plum. "What woman?" he asked. "Oh, the dox—unfortunate female. It depends. Perhaps she'll be transported. Or maybe she'll hang. You may be certain that she won't go unpunished. Here, puss, you aren't ill, are you? You look like you've seen a ghost."

So Sherry had, and it was her own, dangling from a gibbet alongside a certain green-eyed highwayman. She could hardly explain this vision to her law-upholding brother. "It's nothing," she murmured. "Merely a touch of the sun."

"Ah, yes," murmured Lavinia as she indicated to Sir

Christopher that he should apply his fringed napkin to the plum juice on his chin. "Sherris was out earlier today. My dear, you told nothing of all this to-do! I suppose you didn't know. What a pity! Since you were so taken with the rogue as to put him in a book, you might have enjoyed being at hand to see his escape."

Sherry could not bypass this opportunity. She opened her eyes wide. "And you were so similarly taken with him, dear Lavinia, that you're forever after me to read what I have written about him. But as for your suggestion . . . Frankly, Sister, I am shocked! Surely you realize that for a lady to be present at a hanging is hardly proper. Especially an unmarried lady like me!"

With this unkind comment, to which Lavinia could think of no suitably cutting rejoinder, the meal came to an end. Even Sir Christopher could manufacture no oil to pour on waters as troubled as these. Lavinia retired to the drawing room in a huff, there to sulk over her coffee cup until her spouse joined her and teased her into a better humor with pretty compliments. Sherry, meanwhile, appropriated the claret and withdrew, explaining to the startled servant from whose fingers she snatched the decanter that she had a touch of the headache, which nothing but water and wine would cure, and leaving him to report to his fellow footman—who confided it to the butler, who in turn conveyed the news to Lady Childe herself—that Lady Sherris was on the way to becoming as great a secret tippler as her adopted aunt.

Happily unaware that she was about to be damned as a drunkard as well as an old maid, Sherry climbed the stairs to her book room. Her emotions were in such a turmoil that it was difficult to concentrate her thoughts. She was furious with Lavinia for discussing her unwed status in that odious, condescending way—and that there was truth in Lavinia's remarks didn't make them easier to bear. But Lavinia was the least of Sherry's problems at this juncture. She was dismayed by the intelligence that the highwayman had been seen riding off with a red-haired female. If Bow Street somehow trailed him to this house . . . Sherry quailed at the vision of herself being tried at the sessions at the Old Bailey on an indictment of conspiring at a condemned criminal's escape. She quailed, too, at the thought of what such a scandal would do to her brother's good name. She was horrified that her rash action had put his reputation in jeopardy. Obviously, her only reasonable course of action now was to go to Sir Christopher and make a clean breast of the affair. But Sherry was sadly lacking in courage. Anticipation of her brother's resultant wrath made her tremble. Even if he were able to prevent her incarceration in Newgate, he would doubtless tell Lavinia of Sherry's folly, and Lavinia would in turn tell Lord Viccars. Anticipation of Lord Viccars's resultant revulsion of feeling cheered Sherry little more. And the thought of the highwayman himself . . .

Her fingers, in kid gloves, were clumsy. Sherry stripped off the gloves, thrust her key into the lock, then glanced up and down the hallway to make sure she was not observed. This was a strange hour for Sherry to visit her book room. She normally courted her muse much earlier in the day. But she had been trying for what seemed an eternity not to think of what might be going on abovestairs, lest some guilty admission slip from her careless lips or her thoughts be read. She opened the door, backed into the room, then turned—to find herself staring down the muzzle of a pistol for the second time that day. This time the pistol was clutched by no highwayman but by Aunt Tulliver instead. Behind her, Sherry glimpsed Captain Toby stretched out on the settee, looking unnervingly like a corpse on view, as did Prinny, stretched out on the floor beside the sofa, or as corpselike as was possible for a dog so obese. He opened his eyes and observed Sherry, toward whom he nourished a grudge so severe that he closed his eyes again without so much as a welcoming twitch of his plumed tail.

Aunt Tulliver lowered the pistol. "Stab me!" She gasped. "I'd just closed my eyes for a minute and then the door opened— Well, I don't mind admitting I thought I was done for! Come to think of it, you was almost done for yourself, milady. I could have put a hole in you as easy as winking, and even you wouldn't hold it against me under the circumstances!"

"I'm sorry," Sherry said, stricken with guilt by the sight of Aunt Tulliver, wig awry, clutching at her chest. Was there no one of her acquaintance whom Sherry had not mistreated this horrid day? She walked across the room, looked down on the unconscious highwayman and the bloodstained bandage wrapped around his leg. "He looks so pale," she said.

"So would you look pale if you'd just had a bullet dug out of you." Aunt Tulliver adjusted a pillow behind the highwayman's head and picked up a bowl of bloody water and rags. The room stank of the gin with which she'd rendered him sufficiently senseless to probe for the bullet in his leg. *Her* gin, in point of fact, from her private stock; for though Tully might have a taste for most alcoholic beverages, she preferred that fiery liquor known commonly as Strip-Me-Naked or Blue Ruin.

Lady Sherry looked worried, as well she might. The highwayman, and the book room, was no reassuring sight. But Tully knew a fair bit about medicine, due to the circumstance of having nursed three spouses through illnesses that proved fatal (though that was not her fault) and to the additional fact of having a very inquiring mind. Tully was curious about everything from the mating habits of cuckoos to the latest scandals of the *haut ton* and claimed to see a distinct similarity between the two; she was interested in medicine, and in anatomy in general, and was not so very old that this scoundrel's well-knit anatomy did not strike her as very interesting indeed.

Nor was Tully so very old that she failed to see which way the wind was blowing. This rogue had made off with Lady Sherry at gunpoint and so she wished to save his neck. It made perfect sense. *In a hen's foot!* Tully thought. Lady Sherry was as great a pig-widgeon as her abigail, both of them betwattled by a handsome face. Aunt Tulliver had been in the world a great many more years than either of them and was therefore considerably more skeptical. Certainly this highwayman fellow was as handsome as Adonis. But Tully could not rid herself of the feeling that something about him was not right.

But she would not voice these doubts, not yet; Lady Sherry had enough already on her plate, and the rogue could do her little harm in his present condition. "This one won't be dancing a jig for a while," she said, shifting the bloody bowl from one hand to the other. "No, nor even walking a few steps. That's a nasty wound he has. But he'll do, milady." And then she went on to speak knowledgeably of the danger of sepsis and mortification of the flesh as result of probing for a bullet, and the theory of laudable pus.

Lady Sherry could not care for this conversation or for the bloody rags and water that Aunt Tulliver seemed bent on waving under her nose. Resolutely, she quelled her squeamishness. "I'll sit with him awhile," Sherry said. "You need to rest."

Tully did not argue. Mettlesome and temperamental as she might pride herself on being, she was also old. Sherry followed her across the room, then once more locked the door. Then she picked up the pistol from the table where Tully had placed it and set the claret decanter on a table that bore mute evidence to the fact that Aunt Tulliver, at least, had enjoyed a hearty repast. A chair had been drawn up by the settee and Sherry dropped down into it.

The book room was very quiet. Sherry leaned her head back against the chair. She looked again at the highwayman, watched the steady rise and fall of his chest. Goodness but he was a handsome rogue in a reckless sort of way, even with his current pallor and his bright eyes masked. Sherry's eyes closed also. She slept.

Chapter Eight

For some moments, all three of the occupants of the book room dozed. Prinny dreamed of chasing rabbits and Lady Sherry of being kissed in the manner enjoyed by the heroines of the books she wrote: activities that neither had experienced in real life. The third dreamer was not so far ranging in his imagination, although there is little doubt that he would have vastly preferred not to know firsthand that of which he dreamed. Micah Greene—known also in certain quarters as Captain Toby—had also passed a very trying day. Now, in dreams, he again left behind the filth and promiscuity and general unpleasantness of Newgate Prison to mount the scaffold erected outside the debtors' prison door. His dislike of the proceedings was not mitigated by the discovery that at least half of London had turned out to see him hanged. Micah stood on the scaffold, staring out at the sea of faces, seeing his life pass before him, a pageant of missed opportunities and foolish mistakes. But unwisely as he may have frittered away his days upon this mortal coil, Micah at five-and-thirty was not yet ready to write off the business as a bad job of work. The memory of standing on the gallows with the rope around his neck, staring out upon that sea of brutish, expectant faces, made him shudder in his sleep.

That movement jerked him back to wakefulness. Micah welcomed the horrid pain because it meant he was not dead. Fate—or some agent thereof—had intervened, and Micah had not been hanged. Micah's memories of his escape were fragmented. He had accosted a female on horseback, had demanded her assistance at gunpoint; from that moment onward, matters seemed to have gone quickly downhill, beginning with the unlucky bullet that had lodged in his leg. He recalled hiding in a gardener's shed, in a water closet, under a shapeless sack of a dress and a shawl and a hideously uncomfortable wig. He'd walked for what seemed like miles on his wounded leg, drifting in and out of consciousness, supported by two females. Then, as if the preceding had not been trial enough, matters had only gotten worse: he had regained his senses only to discover one female sprawled across his chest, holding him down, while another applied what felt like red-hot pincers to his leg. Another time, under different circumstances, Micah would have raised no objection if a bright-eyed lass wished to deposit herself upon his chest, might even have invited her to take whatever further liberties suited her fancy. But the liberties taken by this lass had been such that he hoped he would not set eyes on her again, nor the ancient beldame who had kept her company. How pleasant it would be, Micah reflected, to open his eyes and discover that these past few days had been no more than a singularly nasty nightmare.

Not even briefly could Micah cherish that hope. His throbbing leg told him all too clearly that this was no dream, that no overheated imagination could be held to account for his recent travail. His delirium had subsided somewhat now, at least sufficiently for him to wonder where he was. It occurred to Micah, in light of his recent ill luck, that he might be easier in his mind if he did not know. But Micah was no coward, whatever else he might have been. Cautiously, he opened his eyes.

His first impression was of a large, dark room cluttered with bizarre furnishings and books. Then he glimpsed the female dozing in a chair drawn up close to the sofa where he lay. She was holding a pistol. *His* pistol, he realized. The pistol that, during his abrupt descent from the scaffold, had been pressed into his hand. Who had given the gun to him? Had his escape been planned, that riot could not have been better staged. But there was little point in asking questions for which answers were not readily at hand. Micah looked again at the pistol and the sleeping woman. She looked familiar. Of course. He had not immediately recognized her now that she was neatly coiffed and gowned, but this was the woman whose horse he had commandeered, who had dressed him in that queer rig, who had torn strips from her petticoat to bind his wound, in the process revealing an ankle that was exceptionally neat. Though Micah should have been grateful, in his dazed mind this red-haired, blue-eyed female was associated with a great deal of inconvenience and pain. Now she held a pistol trained on him, and Micah had had quite enough of being held prisoner. Freedom seemed worth any risk. He took a deep breath and lunged.

Lady Sherry wakened suddenly to find herself staring yet once more down the barrel of a pistol and with the additional perplexity of a highwayman sprawled across her lap. Sherry had been dreaming most pleasurably of kisses, and was as a result somewhat disoriented to find herself caught up in a very different kind of embrace. "Are you going to shoot me?" she inquired faintly. "I wish that you would not!"

Certainly, Micah did not wish to shoot this female. He had not shot anyone in all his life. But he did not lower the pistol, or remove himself from the lady's lap. He could not. Prinny had leaped atop him, under the impression that the man's queer antics signified a desire to play some new game. The pain was intense. Micah

68

groaned. "Oh, you wretched beast!" cried Sherry, and swatted at the dog. Prinny removed himself from atop Micah and stalked across the room in high dudgeon, then flopped down by the door. Sherry helped the highwayman back onto the couch. He stared at her with perplexity. "You're no serving wench!" he gasped.

A serving wench? Was that what he had thought her? Sherry remembered Lord Viccars's compliments on her appearance and almost laughed. "No. I'm no serving wench," she said wryly, then frowned again as he grimaced with pain. "However did you get out from under that hedge?"

Micah did not care to recall the hedge, which had been very prickly, or his feelings when he had suddenly and painfully awakened, the horrid moment when he thought he'd been flung alive into his grave. "Was it you who put me there?" he asked as he took firmer hold of the gun that she had failed to take from him.

Sherry resented the man's suspicious expression, his unappreciative tone of voice. "Good heavens, man! *I* didn't shoot you!" she snapped. "Nor have I turned you over to the authorities as any sensible person would have done. Instead, I saved your ungrateful neck. Oh, do put that thing down before it goes off and we have the whole household gathered outside the door, wishful of knowing what is going on!"

Micah forced himself to remain conscious, to concentrate on the pistol in his hand instead of the pain in his leg. Perhaps this female had saved him from the gallows—why, he could not fathom, unless she was one of those queer, bored women who would do anything for excitement—but every instinct screamed at him to trust her not one inch. His fingers, damp with perspiration, slipped on the pistol and he wiped his hand on his thigh. "I'll just bide here a little longer and then be on my way," he said.

Lady Sherry gazed worriedly upon her houseguest. She could not like the pallor of his face, the perspiration that stood out on his brow. The idea that he should leave was ludicrous. "You're hurt," she pointed out.

Micah knew perfectly well that he was hurt. Each little movement, each breath he drew, caused his leg to throb in an agony almost sufficient to make one wish to cease to breathe. But Micah had some scores to settle first. "Fiend seize it, of course I'm hurt!" he gasped. "If I wasn't, I wouldn't be bleeding like a stuck pig. Why the devil did you have to mix yourself up in this business? I might have been clear of the city by now if you hadn't interfered!"

It was a very good thing that Micah's pistol was no longer within Lady Sherry's reach, else her tenth crime might have been other than she'd planned. "It was you who interfered with me," she pointed out with a forbearance that was possible only because she remembered she was speaking to a wounded and perhaps deranged individual who clutched a pistol in his hand. "Not the other way around. All I wanted to do was come home. I do not recall that I invited you along. But since you are here, and obviously in no condition to take yourself elsewhere, it might behoove you to keep your voice down. My brother is a magistrate, and you are currently beneath his roof—without his knowledge, I might add!"

A magistrate's sister? A magistrate's *roof*? Micah could think of no words sufficiently forceful to express his dismay. In a most unfriendly manner, he gazed upon Sherry. "The devil!" he groaned.

How ill he looked. "You mustn't worry!" Lady Sherry said hastily. "You'll be safe enough as long as we are careful and you remember not to shout! This is my room, and only Tully has a key besides me. Frankly, sir, I wish I'd never set eyes on you, but I did, and here you are and here you must stay until you may leave without running a risk of landing all of us in the basket! Oh, do stop waving that gun about. You are the worst person I have ever met for threatening people. Pistols and pruning knives—'' She frowned. ''Which is an odd thing in you, because you are said to have treated your victims so very courteously. Perhaps you are courteous only when committing robbery?''

This argument made no small impression on Micah. Even greater was the impression Sherry made when, exasperated, she tweaked the pistol from his hand. He looked into its barrel and attempted a smile. At this abrupt volte-face, Sherry stared at him in surprise. ''I must trust you, must I not?'' he asked. ''And I must also apologize. I've used you infamously. My only excuse is that I found the prospect of my own hanging a trifle unnerving. Damned if I know why you're doing so much for a curst ill-tempered brute! But since you're willing, I'm not about to look a gift horse in the mouth.''

That pretty speech cost him dear, thought Sherry as the man lay back on the pillows with which Tully—or more likely Daffodil—had softened the contours of the couch. Sherry gazed at him. The fear that she had experienced in the dining room had changed into exasperation with the discovery that her highwayman was safe. So she had come to think of him, the result of having put him in a book, although it was hardly an inspiration for which she was grateful, since the manuscript was going far from well.

But writing hair-raising adventures was one thing, living them quite another. That she *was* living an adventure, Sherry realized as the highwayman smiled at her again. ''My apologies, ma'am, for ever mistaking you for a serving wench,'' he said. ''It's clear you're nothing of the sort.''

If the rogue had been handsome when unconscious,

he was an Adonis when he smiled. "You are forgiven," Sherry said ruefully. "I fear I looked the part." How merrily those green eyes twinkled. She dropped her gaze. Cursing her shyness, aware that the highwayman was watching her with amusement, Sherry sought a diversion. She remembered the claret. "Here. I thought this might refresh you," she said awkwardly, and shoved the decanter toward him. His hand shook as he grasped the decanter, and he swore to find himself so weak. Sherry reached for the bottle as it slipped through his fingers. Her hand brushed his.

His skin was cool, almost too cool; a temperature that surely should not have caused heat to prickle up Lady Sherry's arm, throughout her entire body, to flame in her cheeks. She jerked away, almost dropping the decanter herself before setting it unsteadily on the table beside the sofa, where crumbs and dirty dishes testified to Aunt Tulliver's feast. Her eyes fixed on the man's face, she put the pistol down on the library table, out of his reach. The highwayman looked puzzled, she thought.

Micah was indeed puzzled. He wondered what had caused his benefactress suddenly to turn pink and then pale. "Wait!" he called softly. She did not heed his plea but sped out of the room as if the hounds of hell themselves were in hot pursuit. Micah heard the key turn in the lock. The huge dog remained sprawled vigilantly by the door; whether to guard him or to prevent his escape Micah could not say. Not that he could hobble far on this curst lame leg. He wished the pistol were not so far from his reach.

Micah sighed, reached for the decanter of claret, then leaned back against the pillows. Experimentally, he tested his leg. It twinged dreadfully. Micah was obviously destined for a long convalescence. He raised the bottle and drank deeply from it, his benefactress having failed to bring him a glass. Then he settled back among the cushions and drifted to sleep again, to dream not of the gallows but of a great white dog and himself astride its back, taking from the rich and giving to the poor as if he were indeed a Robin Hood.

Chapter Nine

The hour was late when Lady Sherry withdrew to her bedchamber. It was, in point of fact, the same hour when Lord Viccars was inquiring of his coachman how best to go about tracking down a criminal who'd gone to ground in London's seething underworld and consequently causing Briscoe a very nasty few moments, as result of some of the extracurricular activities to which he'd put his lordship's coach. The same hour, indeed, in which Marguerite was testing her luck once again at the gaming tables, smugly displaying her new diamond and emerald necklace to her envious intimates and announcing that she shouldn't begin to groom a replacement for Lord Viccars just yet, there being many a slip 'twixt the cup and the lip—or, in this case, between betrothal and wedlock. Marguerite didn't deem it yet time to cut her losses, to throw in the towel. She had several aces up her sleeve. Since Marguerite was wearing no sleeves worth comment, and what precious little else she wore clung to her body most fetchingly by way of dampened petticoats, it was obvious that she spoke figuratively, so no one accused her of cheating at cards. Instead, her cronies wagered among themselves as to whether or not Marguerite would succeed in vanquishing her bête noire.

Lady Sherry stepped into her bedchamber, unaware that she was being plotted against by other than an unkind fate. The room was welcoming with the soft and romantic glow of a brass lamp with a French-roughed glass globe. Sherry gazed longingly at the canopied bed. She was exhausted by the events of this long day. She hoped that a sound night's rest would enable her to contemplate her situation more clearly and to figure a way out of the predicament into which she'd been plunged. But before she could achieve that sound night's sleep, she must divest herself of this pretty dress. Sherry peered into the room's farthest shadows, but Daffodil was not there. Yet again Lady Sherry must deal unaided with hooks and tapes and myriad other fastenings. She could ring for assistance, of course, but then word would get to Lavinia that Daffodil had been remiss in her duties and Sherry would be forced to endure yet another lecture regarding the proper care and discipline of her servants. Sherry thought she must spare both Daffodil and herself that aggravation. She also thought that she would have a few choice comments to make to her abigail when next they met. It was all of a piece with the rest of this accursed day, Sherry supposed as she stood sideways in front of her circular, convex dressing mirror, and amid various contortions attempted to unhook her gown. This morning her only problem had been with her fictional highwayman. Now she had the real highwayman above-stairs and must look forward at any moment to her own incarceration in Newgate. She gloomily supposed that there was some consolation in that things couldn't be much worse.

No sooner had Sherry made this assumption than the door burst open and Tully stalked into the room with a tearful Daffodil in tow.

Lady Sherry paused in her efforts to disrobe herself, then turned away from the mirror and frowned at her abigail. "*Where* have you been?" she demanded. "I was about to instigate a hue and cry on your behalf. We had an agreement, Daffodil. You were to fulfill your duties as a lady's maid and refrain from helping yourself to things that weren't yours by right, and no mention would be made of the past. But— Oh, good heavens, child! There's no reason to take on like that. I'm not going to turn you off! Indeed, I'm grateful to you for tidying up the gardener's shed!'' Prolonged pondering had led Lady Sherry to the conclusion that only Daffodil could have performed this task.

Daffodil sobbed all the harder. "I didn't!" she wailed. "I would've if I'd thought of it, but I didn't! Oh!" Her further utterances were quite unintelligible.

"If you did not, Daffodil, then who *did* clean it?" persevered Sherry, the puzzle quite taking possession of her mind. "Aunt Tulliver?"

"Not I!" responded that venerable lady, whose wig was askew, giving her a distinctly raffish air. "Plague on't, mayhap you *should* turn off the plaguey chit. She's been like this ever since I found her hiding under my bed. Do stop tuning your pipes, gel, or I'll box your ears for you! I can't get any sense out of her, milady. Perhaps if you was to try, we might discover what she's making such a piece of work about!"

Lady Sherry wasn't sure she wished to know what had thrown her abigail into such a pucker. She could not imagine that Daffodil's nerve storm boded good. However, Sherry was fond of her abigail and could not bear to see the girl in such distress. She suggested that Aunt Tulliver release Daffodil's ear. With obvious reluctance, Tully obeyed. Daffodil sank down onto an upholstered chair. "He mustn't find me!" she gasped and broke into renewed sobs.

Lady Sherry and Aunt Tulliver exchanged glances. Lady Sherry's was bewildered, Aunt Tulliver's irate. "Who mustn't find her?" Sherry asked.

"Demned if I know!" the old woman responded. "Or care!"

Since Daffodil took exception to this hardness of heart and sobbed all the harder in response, it was some time before any sense could be made of her remarks. "Is it the highwayman you're afraid of?" Lady Sherry inquired, at a loss. "If this is the way he has chosen to repay us for our help, by frightening you half out of your wits—"

"Wits?" interjected Aunt Tulliver scornfully. "Hah!"

This lack of sympathy had its desired effect. Daffodil left off weeping to glare at the old woman, who was seated at Lady Sherry's dressing table, adjusting her sadly abused wig in the beveled mirror. "If you'd had the fright I've had, you might be a mite overset yourself!" Daffodil said indignantly. "And no, milady, it wasn't Captain Toby as scared me half to death." Tears welled anew in her dark eyes. "It was Ned!"

"Ned?" echoed Lady Sherry. Whatever could her groom have done to upset Daffodil so? Most often, he went out of his way to try to please her. "I don't understand. Has his, er, ardor cooled?"

"If so, no one could hardly blame him," muttered Aunt Tulliver as she gave her wig a last jerk and pat. "Not with Miss Saucebox here playing the flirt with every well-breeched footman who comes into her view!"

Daffodil's tears ceased as if by magic. Her woebegone expression changed into a scowl. "I never!" she said indignantly.

"Oh, no?" Aunt Tulliver turned on the bench. "I suppose you wasn't mooning about over that accursed highwayman, either, eh?"

"No, I was not!" cried Daffodil, with that degree of indignation that is possible only when a nerve is struck. In truth, Daffodil was a little bit in love with the highwayman. It was of no great consequence. Daffodil was always a little bit in love with one person or another. It was in her nature, as it was in Aunt Tulliver's nature to be crotchety and in Lady Sherry's to have her head in the clouds.

"I was not mooning after him!" Daffodil repeated, in case her earlier protest had gone unheard. "I *felt* for him, that's all. I know what it's like to be in jail!"

This claim of fellow felling did not impress Aunt Tulliver. "So both of you was in jail," the old woman said. " 'Tis nothing to brag on, gel. No, nor to try to rouse our sympathy with, since both of you belonged there!"

Daffodil thought this remark very poor-spirited. She swelled with indignation. "Well, I never!" she cried again.

"Oh, yes, you did!" responded Aunt Tulliver, equally indignant. "*And* you got caught! As you *wouldn't* have, if you weren't such a jingle-brain!"

Lady Sherry was deriving no amusement from this argument. She cleared her throat, thus interrupting her companions' brangling. "Please, the both of you!" she begged. "I still don't understand, Daffodil, why you were hiding in Tully's room. Surely you cannot be afraid of Ned!"

"Oh, can't I just?" said Daffodil bitterly. "He's gone off his hinges, milady, and that's a fact! And no, he hasn't cooled toward me. Although he's acting so queer I wish he had. I went to his room to fetch these." She held up the bundle that she'd been clutching to her chest. "Clothes, milady, for himself upstairs, because he can't keep on those dirty, bloody rags without anyone who sees him suspicioning who and what he is."

Lady Sherry suspected that anyone who saw the highwayman would have little difficulty in determining his identity no matter what he wore. "Go on," she said, tactfully refraining from inquiring into how Daffodil came to be so familiar with Ned's room. "Ned caught you making free with his belongings, I take it. I suppose he asked you for an explanation. What did you tell him?''

"Nothing." A fresh tear trickled down Daffodil's cheek. "He told *me*! He lost sight of you awhile this morning, milady. But then he saw you with Captain Toby when you was riding off. And he saw you and me come out of the gardener's shed. Neddy's no nod-cock even if he *is* queer in the attic all of a sudden. He said he wasn't fooled for a minute that it was Tully we was helping along! So after we was out of sight he went into the shed to take a quick look-see himself. And what he found confirmed what he was thinking. It was him as cleaned the place up!''

"Why didn't you say so sooner!" Relieved, Lady Sherry perched on the edge of her bed. Ned was her servant, not Lavinia's. He'd been in Sherry's service for several years, had accompanied them to London from the country. Ned was loyal and posed no threat to them. Why, then, had Daffodil burst into renewed sobs? Lady Sherry gazed at the girl with real concern. Daffodil looked the picture of misery. Lady Sherry could only think that she had suffered a disappointment of the heart. Though Daffodil might fall in love with someone new every couple of weeks, she expected her swains to remain eternally devoted to her and took it very hard when they did not. Lady Sherry thought of Lord Viccars and sympathized.

But sympathetic as Lady Sherry felt, Daffodil's sobs were wearing on her nerves. "It's all right, Daffodil!" she said. "Think in what a worse case we would be if anybody other than Ned had seen us or found the shed in that condition. As for what may have passed between the two of you—''

"Begging your pardon, milady, it ain't all right!''

79

The time had clearly come to make a clean breast of things. Daffodil sat up straight and wiped her damp nose on her sleeve. "Ned wants to marry me."

"Ned wants to marry you," Lady Sherry repeated slowly. "Forgive me, Daffodil, but I don't see what there is in that to make you take on like this."

Daffodil took a deep breath, then looked around to make sure there were no inkpots within Lady Sherry's reach. "He wants to leave service, milady, and set up in business on his own. He thinks it would be nice to buy a tavern. There's one as has caught his eye. He thinks I should go with him. He says he can see me clear as anything serving up tankards of ale. He says it would suit me to a cow's thumb."

Lady Sherry was trying very hard to follow these disclosures. Try as she might, she could find nothing in Daffodil's confession to cause her spirits to plummet so low. "I should miss you," she said, "but if that's what you wish—"

"It ain't what I wish!" protested Daffodil. "Leastways, I don't wish it that way. That tavern . . . Ned don't have the wherewithal to buy it, milady. And so . . ." She paused, gathering her courage. "He thinks you should buy it for us!"

This announcement awakened Aunt Tulliver, who'd been enjoying a short nap. She put forth the opinion that Daffodil had been into the port again because no one who wasn't a trifle bosky would make a suggestion that was so addle-brained. Lady Sherry was inclined to agree. "He thinks *I* should buy it?" she echoed, stunned. "But why?"

Daffodil frowned at this lack of perspicacity on her mistress's part. "Why? Because he thinks I'm all the crack! He says that if he can't stop me making sheep's eyes at other gents, he can at least make sure that's as far as I go. Milady, I don't know what to do! I don't want to be leg-shackled or go live in a tavern, but he vows he'll peach on us if I refuse!''

"He'll peach on us.'' Lady Sherry experienced a very unpleasant sinking sensation. "Daffodil, are you sure?''

"Yes'm.'' Daffodil looked even more mournful. "He vows that if you don't buy him off, he'll go straight to Sir Christopher and tell him everything!''

"Buy him off?'' echoed Lady Sherry. She felt faint. "How much does he want?''

Daffodil licked dry lips. This horrid fix wasn't any of her doing—she'd hardly *made* Ned fall in love with her— but she felt guilty all the same. She whispered, "Five hundred pounds.''

"Five hundred—'' Lady Sherry stood up abruptly. Was there to be no end to the troubles gathering around her head? Lacking a handy inkwell, Sherry came perilously close to alleviating her anger by hurling a pretty porcelain bibelot into the fireplace. "Oh, *bother*!'' she cried, and began to pace.

It had taken Aunt Tulliver some moments to digest this startling information. "I always said he was a bad lot!'' she remarked. "As for you, gel, that's what you get for playing off airs! That's set the cat among the pigeons, 'adzooks. Well, milady, what's to do!''

Lady Sherry wished she had an answer for that question. She paused in her perambulations and turned to Daffodil. "Perhaps you might give him a disgust of you,'' she suggested.

Daffodil looked even more depressed. "It ain't likely,'' she said. "He's proper smitten, milady. No one else will do for him.''

Sherry thought it must be very pleasant to be so certain of a gentleman's devotion. "You were going to run away, weren't you?'' she asked. Daffodil nodded. "It won't serve. Ned would hold me responsible and probably go to Christopher, anyway. And to think I trusted that damned fellow! I swear I could wring his neck.''

Daffodil, too, had risen to her feet, the better to follow her mistress as she paced. "He's not a damned fellow, not really!" she protested, catching at Lady Sherry's sleeve. Secretly, Daffodil couldn't help but feel a teeny bit flattered that someone had gone off his hinges for love of her. "It's just midsummer moon with him, that's all, I swear!"

This display of compassion earned Daffodil no similar tolerance from her companions. Lady Sherry merely yanked her sleeve away. Aunt Tulliver, however, was considerably less reticent. She made a number of unflattering comments on Daffodil's lack of character, judgment, and common sense.

To be called a clunch and to have a peal rung in her ears when her spirits were already sorely oppressed . . . After she had fetched and run errands all day, even sat on the highwayman's chest when the bullet was being dug out, although the sight of all that blood had made her think she might lose her breakfast . . . And had she protested at such mistreatment? No, she had not, even though she was no mere serving wench but a grand lady's abigail. Well, perhaps Lady Sherry wasn't all that grand, but the principle remained. Daffodil had done service far beyond the bounds of duty. And now, in addition to all that, to have to endure a trimming . . . It was more than flesh and blood could bear. "Adonedo!" cried Daffodil, and hurled herself, weeping, on Lady Sherry's bed.

Aunt Tulliver followed, then flung a pillow over the girl's face to muffle her sobs. "Plague take it!" the old woman muttered as she valiantly resisted an impulse to bear down on the pillow and stifle the silly chit permanently. She moved away from the bed, sat down again at the dressing table, and poked unhappily at her wig.

"Demned if I've ever seen such a watering pot," she said. "Looks to me, milady, like you've landed yourself in the suds."

Lady Sherry gazed upon her elderly companion with a singular lack of appreciation. "How nice to have the support of one's friends!" she retorted witheringly. "Apparently, I must point out that *your* lot will hardly be enviable if I'm taken off to jail, because the first thing Lavinia will do is turn the both of you out into the streets!"

An unhappy silence greeted this announcement. What Lady Sherry said was true. Daffodil and Aunt Tulliver would be no part of this household or any other if not for Sherry's efforts on their behalf. Daffodil's dark eyes would not have so merry a sparkle or her cheeks the rosy glow of such good health, if she were brought again before the magistrate. And Aunt Tulliver would hardly wax so stout in the workhouse.

Tully tucked in her chins and looked ruminative. "There's nothing else for it that I can see, milady. You'll have to pay up."

"If only I could." Sherry leaned against the mantelpiece. She felt sick at heart. "You're forgetting something, Tully. My brother controls my purse-strings. We could not continue to reside in the country house after Mama's death because Christopher would not allow me the funds. And now . . . Of course, he is not ungenerous. He anticipates and provides for my every need. Almost my every whim! Oh, what a curst dilemma! What possible reason can I give him for wanting five hundred pounds?"

Aunt Tulliver had no answer for this question. Neither did Daffodil, who had been following the conversation very closely from beneath the pillow Tully had flung across her face. Nor, obviously, did Lady Sherry, or else she wouldn't have asked the question in the first place. The bedchamber was quiet as the ladies waited for inspiration to strike. Then suddenly Daffodil flung aside her pillow and sat up. "I know!" she cried, triumphant at this opportunity to redeem herself. "We'll tell Sir Christopher you want the money to buy your bride clothes!"

Chapter Ten

The following morning, Lady Sherry made her way to the stables. She was desirous of having a word with Ned. She was especially desirous of discovering whether the dramatic-minded Daffodil had exaggerated the seriousness of the situation, but this, alas, was not the case. Ned had arrived at a decision and from it he would not be swayed, no matter how great an effort Lady Sherry made to turn him up sweet. Nor would he be moved by threats and pleas. Ned was sure he was very sorry to see her ladyship in a pucker, but he was very needful of getting his hands on some of the ready-and-rhino and there was nothing else for it but that her ladyship must knuckle down. The conversation, which was entirely too distressing to repeat here in its entirety, continued for some few moments. At its end, Lady Sherry conceded reluctantly that she would be granted no reprieve. She abruptly left the stables then before she fell prey to a violent impulse to wreak bodily damage on her groom with a pitchfork that leaned against one wall.

She made her way back to the house and into the kitchen, where she requested a tray to take with her to the book room as a midmorning snack. A pot of tea and a plate of seedcakes, a large serving of cold green-goose pie . . . Lady Sherry realized that she was providing this repast for a gentleman not in the pink of health and additionally requested that the cook provide her with some of the excellent restorative that she always kept on hand. Cook agreed that Lady Sherry was looking a mite peaked and immediately put a large teacupful of her calf's-feet jelly into a saucepan along with a half-glass of sweet wine, a little sugar, and nutmeg.

Lady Sherry watched the cook beat in the yolk of an egg and a bit of butter, then grate into the concoction a portion of fresh lemon peel. "I'll take it up myself," she murmured. She grasped the tray and walked out of the kitchen, leaving the servants to agree among themselves that this was a very queer household. Lady Childe was the highest of sticklers and could not be pleased. But at least with Lady Childe one knew where one stood. Lady Sherry, on the other hand, didn't seem to know her proper place and consequently threw everyone else out of kilter. The cook had the final word on the subject. "Lady Sherry is neither fish nor fowl nor good red herring!" she announced with a shake of her head.

Lady Sherry was aware that her brother's servants didn't approve of her country manners. She could not greatly care. At this moment, as she continued down the hallway, Sherry was far more concerned about her own servant and his unexpected perfidy. How could Ned be so very unreasonable as to expect her to produce five hundred pounds in the winking of an eye? Lady Sherry had no notion how she might produce so much, given an entire year. She supposed she would have to follow Daffodil's suggestion, since she could think of none of her own. Sherry wasn't impressed by Daffodil's cleverness. She had not forgotten that Daffodil's nacky notions were to a degree responsible for this wretched predicament. She detested the idea of prevaricating about a matter so serious as her own nuptials. And what was she to say to her brother when tradesmen failed to arrive with boxes containing the trousseau she had supposedly bought? For that matter, what was she to say to her prospective bridegroom, who had no notion that a trousseau was indicated posthaste? Sherry didn't suppose her brother could be persuaded to say nothing of the matter to Lord Viccars.

"Oh, what a tangled web we weave!" Sherry murmured, greatly startling a young housemaid passing by her in the hallway just then. Lady Sherry continued up the stairs. Deep in thought, she flung open the door to the book room, causing Prinny to leap alert and growling to his feet and Micah to come awake abruptly with a curse and a groan for his sore leg.

Some moments later, order had been restored. Prinny had been persuaded against savaging Lady Sherry and Micah from crawling across the room to retrieve his gun from its hiding place on the library shelf. "Oh, do hush!" snapped Lady Sherry to the pair of them as she set the tray down on the little table by the bed and dropped into her writing chair.

Micah regarded her with some perplexity. The females of his acquaintance did not generally walk into a room, plop down into a chair, and prop their elbows on a table and their head upon their hands, without so much as a word of greeting exchanged. The woman looked as if she was praying, which struck Micah as very queer. Unaware that his benefactress was a novel writer, Micah did not realize that this supplicating gesture was the attitude Lady Sherry assumed when courting her muse. But queer as she might be, he was grateful to this red-haired female and meant to be civil to her, no matter how great the pain of his wounded leg.

Discreetly, he cleared his throat. Sherry raised her head to look at him. "The devil!" said Micah, forgetting his good intentions of only a moment past. "You look worn to the bone."

Sherry lowered her chin again to rest on her clasped hands. "Thank you!" she said. "It needed only that. How kind of you to tell me that I am hagged. It is my own fault, of course. I should have known better than to go about such arduous tasks as rescuing highwaymen at my advanced age!"

Micah detected a note of sarcasm in her voice. He could hardly fail to detect it, his only physical deficiency being his wounded leg and not his excellent hearing. He recalled his determination to do the civil. "I already thanked you!" he pointed out. So that he might better reach the tray of food, he attempted to sit up. His leg pained him and he winced.

"Oh!" cried Lady Sherry, aghast at her thoughtlessness. She pushed back her chair and hastened to his assistance. "I'm sorry! I didn't think." She drew the table closer to the sofa. "There!"

Micah did not lack for acuteness, when pain and gin didn't dull his brain, and a good night's rest had done much to restore his native wit. He would not now have mistaken his benefactress for a serving wench. Furthermore, it was obvious that something troubled her. He hoped those troubles boded no further ill for himself. Before Lady Sherry could back away, he caught her hand. "What am I to call you?" he asked.

Again that tingling sensation where his flesh touched hers. It required all of Sherry's willpower not to jerk away. What strange power did this rogue possess? Even as she wondered if she should reveal herself to him or not, she was telling him her name. It was his eyes, of course. Sherry forced herself to look away, to concentrate on an ancient counting table with a checkered top where counters had once been moved about and accounts cast. She realized that the man was still speaking and telling her his name. He said she was to call him Micah. Why, then, was he known as Captain Toby? She dared to glance at him. "What?"

The woman appeared on the verge of flight like some shy woodland creature caught by the hunters unaware. Micah was not accustomed to being regarded thusly by the weaker sex. With a wry expression, he released her hand. "Don't fear; you're safe enough with me. I promise you I have no designs on your virtue, ma'am. And even if I did, I could hardly act upon my impulses." He glanced ruefully at his wounded leg.

This evidence of Micah's excellent intuition discomposed Lady Sherry even more. "Here, drink this!" she said, and forced upon him the calf's-feet broth. Obediently, Micah drank. The restorative had no pleasant taste. "What the devil is this stuff?" he said gasping. "Surely you didn't save me from the gallows just to try to poison me, ma'am!"

"Nothing of the sort." Lady Sherry wished he wouldn't call her ma'am in that odiously respectful manner, as if she were his maiden aunt. Sherry was feeling her twenty-seven years very much just then. "Frankly, sir, were you to expire now, we'd be in even worse case, because I don't know what we should do with a corpse. As for the other, I know you don't— You couldn't— I mean, I didn't think you did— Oh, dear!" Cheeks aflame, she sank back into her chair. "After all, I'm hardly in my first youth!"

Micah looked up from the green-goose pie, which he was currently sampling and which was very good. "Peagoose!" he commented none too distinctly.

Peagoose? Had the man just called her a peagoose? Sherry surveyed him with bewilderment. "I *am* past my first youth!" she protested. "I'm quite twenty-seven years of age. What a very strange gentleman you are,

Mr. Greene. If a gentleman you are! You speak like one, at any rate, yet no true gentleman would make reference to a lady's age.''

''I never claimed to be a swell,'' retorted Micah, his words much clearer now that he'd washed down the remainder of the green-goose pie with a gulp of tea. As if determined to prove his lack of social graces, he then inquired how it had come about that Lady Sherry had reached so very advanced an age without being wed.

The man was incorrigible. Sherry could not help but smile. ''Are you always so very outspoken?'' she inquired. He merely shrugged and helped himself to another seedcake. Yet, oddly enough, Sherry did not resent his question, perhaps because her sister-in-law had so frequently given it voice. Stranger still, she considered the question worthy of reply. Micah was a good listener, interjecting comments that indicated his interest, and Sherry found herself telling him much more of her earlier life than she had intended. She realized she must be boring the poor man. He was simply not so unkind as to tell her so. She fell silent.

Micah promptly disillusioned his benefactress regarding his capacity for kindness. ''So you left behind your country pleasures and came to London to catch yourself a husband,'' he commented, curiously disappointed to find her so ordinary a member of her sex.

''I came to London because I had no choice!'' retorted Lady Sherry, stung by the man's censorious tone. The highwayman, she reminded herself. How dare he judge her? But then why should he be the exception? Sherry felt as if everyone were judging her these days. She thought of Lord Viccars and her impossibly muddled romance, and sighed. ''To tell the truth, I liked country life very well. If I could, I would trade all these teas and balls and soirees that my sister-in-law so dotes on for a country fair with a traveling fiddler to play for the dances, and puppet shows, and gingerbread stalls. As for Almack's—well, I find more honest entertainment in a hasty-pudding contest or chasing a greased pig!''

Micah quirked a brow. His benefactress had redeemed herself by denigrating the temple of the *ton*. ''Did you participate?'' he inquired.

''Did I— Oh, do not be absurd!'' But perhaps she should have participated, Sherry thought. Even Lavinia would quail at introducing to polite society a sister-in-law who'd gone about chasing greased pigs. ''Life used to seem so simple,'' she murmured. ''Perhaps it didn't seem so at the time, but it certainly does in retrospect! But I don't need to tell you that, do I? Life must have been a great deal simpler for you also before you were caught and sent to jail!''

''Simpler? You might say so!'' Micah's laughter was humorless. But this subject was not one that he cared to discuss. He reached for another seedcake, only to discover that the remaining seedcakes, as well as the rest of the green-goose pie, had vanished off the tray. Prinny, stretched out on the floor beside the sofa, looking for all the world like a large, shaggy rug, emitted a gentle burp. Micah looked at the beast with disfavor. Prinny was accustomed to seeing that expression on the faces of his nearest and dearest. Apologetically, he wagged his tail.

Lady Sherry was oblivious to this byplay. She was thinking very hard, remembering what Lord Viccars had said about the highwayman and how great a shame it was she'd had no interview. Here was her opportunity, and she must go about it tactfully. As shy as Sherry was about talking of her books, she'd discovered people were even shyer of her, afraid that she would translate them somehow into a character in one of her novels, with all their foibles and follies in plain view. Micah, she had put between the pages of a book already. She had based a character on his exploits. Instinct warned her that he would not take kindly to that intelligence, or aid her struggling efforts by laying bare his soul for her to dissect.

Therefore she would not tell him. She would be subtle in her approach. "It was very brave of you," she said. "To take to the road. Not that I am commending highway robbery, of course! Particularly when it is committed by some gay young blood who takes a purse for the mere fun of the thing. But I cannot disapprove of it entirely, either. Particularly since it is merely a symptom of a greater social ill! Consider Robin Hood, who took from the rich to give to the poor."

So his benefactress *was* one of those pitiful females who would go to any lengths to introduce some excitement into their dreary lives. Micah was disappointed in her for the second time that day. Nor did he intend to encourage her wrongheadedness. "Consider Robin Hood's successors," he said perversely. "They may have robbed the rich, but not in the interest of social justice, I think."

"You are a gentleman," she prodded gently. "You must have had some other motive for what you did than pure greed."

Micah's face twisted. "No," he said. "Don't delude yourself, ma'am. Captain Toby has no conscience, social or otherwise. He does what he does for the pleasure of it and the profit. Nothing else."

How strange to hear a man speak of himself in the third person as if he were talking about someone else. His conscience pained him, no doubt. And so it should, but Sherry saw no need for the man to wallow in his guilt. "Are you trying to frighten me?" she asked in a tone calculated to indicate that she was nothing of the sort. "By reminding me that I have a hardened criminal hidden beneath my roof? Will you repay me by stealing the silver and murdering us all in our beds?"

Now he looked startled. "I didn't say that. You've nothing to fear from me, ma'am."

Curiously enough, Sherry believed him. No wonder her manuscript was giving her trouble, because her hero was nothing like this highwayman. She foresaw massive revisions. She also foresaw a pleasurable interval of plumbing the depths of this strange man's mind. Suddenly she remembered another bit of highwayman lore she would rather not have thought of just then, this concerning the miraculous powers of a body that had been hanged. The mere wood chippings from the gallows were said to cure the ague and a splinter the headache, whereas the hand of the corpse was an excellent remedy for goiters and ulcers and cancerous growths. Sherry didn't know how Micah felt about the matter, but she for one preferred that he should not benefit his fellow man to that extent.

He looked exhausted. "I've kept you talking too long!" Sherry said guiltily, and rose from her chair, then picked up the tray. Micah caught her hand again as she passed by the sofa where he lay. "You still haven't told me what has you fretting your guts to fiddle-strings," he murmured.

Sherry looked at his hand, so dark against her fair skin. Again she felt that giddiness. "It's nothing to concern yourself about," she said.

Micah suspected that what she said was untrue. Anything that concerned this lady, and this household, must concern him as long as he was kept prisoner here by his accursed leg. But he was so very tired just now, without energy left to pursue the matter.

"Come back. Later," he murmured, and released her,

then closed his eyes. Sherry gazed down upon his face. She had no choice, she told herself. The die was cast. She left behind her book room and went in search of Sir Christopher.

Chapter Eleven

Lady Childe was reclining on her sofa, a very elegant piece of furniture in the classical mode, with a boldly curved headpiece and a short armrest, a low, scrolled end and lion-shaped legs. In her pretty muslin dress, Lavinia looked lovely as always save for her expression of extreme discontent. Even a glance at her reflection in a pier glass, which assured her that she was as close to perfection as she had ever been, did not elevate her spirits.

Lavinia sighed, undraped herself from the sofa, and retrieved her needlework from a brass-inlaid mahogany chair. Lavinia was very clever with her needle. Her current project involved roses, daisies, and strawberry blossoms embellished with leaves and a realistic-looking caterpillar, all done in petit point. Alas, that occupation soon palled also, and she set it aside. Fortunately, the butler appeared in the doorway then to announce the arrival of Lord Viccars.

Lavinia set aside her needlepoint gratefully and told Barclay to show his lordship in. This eagerness on her part must not be misconstrued. Lavinia was fond of Lord Viccars, but it was in the manner of fondness reserved for those persons upon whose knees one was dandled as a child. To Lavinia, Lord Viccars was an avuncular figure. He was her confidant.

"How glad I am to see you!" she cried as he stepped

into the drawing room. "Because, if not precisely blue-deviled, I am beset by ennui! Christopher is off dispensing justice, and Sherris is deep in a fit of creativity that apparently leaves her with neither the time nor the ambition to enjoy her family's company. Oh, do sit down, Andrew! We do not stand on ceremony, you and I. But how rude I am to run on like this! Pray forgive me, Andrew. It is just that one grows very weary of one's own company. How good it is of you to call. We have not seen you for some days. But of course you will have been setting your affairs in order, and forgot about your old friends!"

Lord Viccars murmured noncommittally and conceded to her request that he should take a chair. He looked startled by her comments, Lavinia thought. But she could hardly say outright that she knew his romantic doubts had been laid to rest because Sherry had requested a sum of money with which to purchase her bride clothes. So very considerable was the sum that Lavinia concluded that her numerous comments about dowdiness had not fallen on barren soil. She wished she could feel a greater gladness that Sherris was at last to be comfortably bestowed. Unfortunately, Lavinia could not stifle a certain resentment. Unstylish, unfashionable Sherris had somehow managed to ensnare one of the most eligible and elusive gentlemen in all of London. A gentleman, in fact, who could generally be relied upon to divert one with the latest *on-dits*. Even that pleasure would soon be denied her, Lavinia realized. Sherris would be privileged to keep abreast of current gossip, for which she didn't care, unlike Lavinia, who liked to keep in touch with what was happening in her world. She inquired of Lord Viccars whether it was true that the regent had acquired the services of Marie Antoine Carême, master of the uniquely French art of *haute cuisine*. Lord Viccars spoke briefly of Carême, who had learned his art in Napoleon's kitchens, then related an amusing account of Princess Caroline, the regent's estranged spouse, who was currently embarked on a pilgrimage through the Holy Land and had astounded the multitudes by entering Jerusalem astride an ass.

Lavinia made only perfunctory responses. She was wishing, very uncharitably, that her sister-in-law had never come to town. Now she must share Lord Viccars with Sherris, as she already shared her husband and her household and even her dog. Prinny displayed a large fondness for Sherry's book room of late. Not that Lavinia wanted Prinny to dote on her similarly, but the beast had been a present from Sir Christopher to her, not to Sherris. Lavinia could not help but feel that the hound owed her some respect. As did Aunt Tulliver and Daffodil. Principles were involved. In some obscure manner, Sherris was at fault for all of Lavinia's discontent.

But Lord Viccars was looking at her oddly. Lavinia supposed she'd failed to make an expected response. Perhaps Lord Viccars might be persuaded to explain what it was about Sherris that had inspired him to toss the handkerchief in her direction after neatly sidestepping so many other matrimonial traps. *Had* Sherry set a trap for him? Lavinia realized she knew very little of her sister-in-law. She inquired whether his lordship would care to partake of some refreshment.

Lord Viccars was not in need of refreshment of the manner that Lavinia would offer him, although a bumper of diabolino would not have come amiss. However, it was obvious that Lavinia had something on her mind. First she had talked his ear off, then had subjected him to a silence so intense that she might altogether have forgotten his presence. Lord Viccars could only conclude that Lavinia and Sherris were again at odds. As he was the confidant of both, it was clearly his duty to try to pour oil on troubled waters. He agreed that he should enjoy a cup of tea.

Lord Viccars was very quiet today, Lavinia thought. Perhaps he, too, was preoccupied with the contemplation of bride clothes. It made Lavinia very melancholy to think that she would be deprived of her dear friend. Of course Sherris would interfere with the friendship once the knot was tied. Certainly Lavinia would have in her place.

But the knot was not yet tied, and Lavinia would not be denied the comfort of her friend so soon. Hoping to disarm him, she ventured a remark, and they spoke for some moments of the falling prices of iron and copper and the decline of other exports; of the unemployed colliers at Bilston Moor, the molders at Merthyr Tydfil, the Spitalfields silk-weavers, the Leicestershire stockingers, and the Nottinghamshire hosiers, all of whom were vociferous about their hunger and their discontent.

After a few moments of this conversation, both participants were understandably depressed. Lord Viccars attempted to lighten the atmosphere by inquiring whether Lavinia had read *Glenvaron*.

"I most certainly have not!" Shocked by the suggestion that she might have read that singular libel published by Caro Lamb about her family and friends, Lavinia had recourse to her vinaigrette. "I doubt that anyone would read the wretched book except to assure themselves that they are not among the unfortunate beings caricatured within! What a shocking thing! But what else could one expect from a female who pursued Byron so shamelessly that she even disguised herself as his page?" The thought of Lord Byron, suspected of all manner of abominations including homosexuality and incest, caused Lavinia to apply once more to her vinaigrette. "I shudder to recall that I actually spoke with the man several times! He and Christopher belonged to the same club. Not that Christopher had anything to do with him after the awful truth came out!'' Lavinia did not add that this rebuff had more to do with her wishes than with Sir Christopher's. He had been inclined to view the matter as a tempest in a teapot. A tempest in a teapot? It was a very good thing Lavinia wasn't the sort of female who leaped to conclusions, or else she might start wondering if her husband's affection for his own sister wasn't suspect. Sir Christopher had actually inquired whether some unkindness on Lavinia's part had caused Sherry's withdrawal from family life. Unkindness! As if Lavinia hadn't done everything humanly possible to make Sherry feel welcome in this house. ''So you are to be felicitated?'' she inquired.

Lord Viccars stared blankly at his hostess. He had no notion of what she was speaking about. But he knew what he wished to speak to her about, and this seemed as good a moment in which to do so as the next. ''You must not be so critical of Lady Sherry,'' he said. ''She means no harm. You must remember that not everyone has had your advantages, puss! Though it hardly seems the thing, Sherris has had the managing of her own affairs. It is difficult for her to play a subordinate role now. As for her eccentricities—well, we would not wish her to be in the common way!''

''Hah!'' exclaimed Lavinia with righteous anger, thereby so startling Lord Viccars that he nearly spilled the contents of his teacup onto his superbly tailored lap. ''I should say Sherris isn't in the common way! Certainly she has proven herself capable of managing her own affairs. And I will say to you, Andrew, though I should not, that you must take care lest you discover that you are *not*!'

Clearly, Lavinia was out of humor. Lord Viccars could not imagine why. Nor did he understand why she kept referring to his affairs. She had intimated earlier that they needed setting in order, he recalled. Lord Viccars was not aware that his affairs were out of order. He wondered what she'd meant.

And then an explanation occurred to Lord Viccars, almost causing him to drop his teacup for a second time. Could Lavinia have referred to Marguerite? A moment's frantic reflection reassured him that Lavinia could not possibly know of his *petite amie*. And even if she had somehow learned of Marguerite's existence, she would surely not be so unladylike as to mention it. Would she? Man of the world though he was, Lord Viccars was startled that Lavinia's loyalty to Sherris had prompted her to trespass thus the boundaries of good taste.

Lord Viccars did not wish to discuss the topic. He owed explanation to no one for the fact that he kept a high flyer for his amusement. After all, it was only human for a gentleman to wish to enjoy a bit of frolic every now and then. Not that he had had much time to frolic these past few days. Lord Viccars had not been seen in his usual haunts of late: not at Weston's or Hoby's or Locke's, not in Brook's Club or White's, not inspecting horseflesh at Tattersall's, not weighing himself on the great scales at Berry Brothers wine shop, and not disporting himself with the fair Marguerite. Lord Viccars had been inspecting quite a different part of town, of which he had hitherto been only peripherally aware: that part of London that lay beyond the boundaries of the polite world. Enlightening as these explorations had been, at the end of his investigations Lord Viccars knew little more of Captain Toby than he had when he set out to run him to ground. It was as if the highwayman had been whisked off the face of the earth. Perhaps Londoners were fond enough of Captain Toby that they'd told deliberate tarradiddles to those stalwart representatives of the law who'd set out in pursuit. Or perhaps the rogue had friends in high places who'd tucked him away somewhere safe.

Still, Lord Viccars did not despair just yet. He had come across one interesting bit of information concerning the highwayman's red-haired doxy. He thought of Marguerite and Lady Sherry and mused upon the determination of Dame Fortune to introduce red-haired females into his life.

This train of thought reminded Lord Viccars of the purpose of his visit. He wished to speak with Sir Christopher on a matter of grave importance. But first he asked, "Is Sherry in?"

"Sherris, always Sherris!" Lavinia made a moue. "What is it about her that keeps Sherris so constantly on everyone's mind? You will make me think that my company does not content you, Andrew. I should not be surprised, I suppose! In answer to your question, I'm sure I don't know whether Sherris is in or not. We've seen precious little of her since the day of the highwayman's escape." Did Andrew look sympathetic? Lavinia tried harder to rouse him to a sense of fellow feeling. "Yes, and where *was* Sherris the morning of the hanging? Her disappearance has still not been satisfactorily explained. I tell you, it is not easy to live with a writing person, Andrew. One must grow accustomed to being treated like a stick of furniture. Sherris spends hours in her book room, seldom even appearing for meals. If one could read what she is writing, it would be a different thing, but Sherris is very selfishly refusing to make public the product of her busy pen!"

Lord Viccars eyed his hostess. He had seen these little temper tantrums before. It was best to let them run their course. "Perhaps Sherry doesn't want anyone to read what she has written until she is satisfied with it," he suggested diplomatically.

Lavinia was not persuaded. Previously, Sherris had

not been so reticent—had even admitted that she profited from Lavinia's criticism and advice. Lavinia frowned. Perhaps Sherry was writing something of which her family would not approve. Perhaps the highwayman was only a pretext and Sherry was in fact penning an exposé of her family and friends à la Caro Lamb.

Lavinia would not tolerate it. As long as she had breath in her body, there would be no vile scandal attached to this family, this house. "No doubt Sherris is in her book room even now," Lavinia said. "I'm sure she'll wish to see *you*, Andrew. I'll fetch her to you myself!" Even as she spoke, Lavinia hurried from the room. She had always deplored Sherry's lack of proper manners, but now she realized that Sherry's character was as gravely flawed. Well, she would make certain that Sherris did not refuse to see Lord Viccars, thereby lending her assistance to romance. Thereby also availing herself of the opportunity to peruse the pages of Sherry's current manuscript while Sherry was safely belowstairs.

After Lavinia left the drawing room, Lord Viccars sank back into his chair. He lapsed again into thought, not of his fiancée but of the highwayman who had captured the imagination of so many Londoners. Where the deuce could the scoundrel have gotten to? Lord Viccars would find out or know the reason why. This investigation offered him a challenge the like of which he had not enjoyed for some time.

Sir Christopher walked into the room then. "Chris!" Lord Viccars exclaimed. "You are just the person I wished to see."

"Of course you did!" Sir Christopher said expansively as he clapped Lord Viccars on the back. "Lucky fellow! So I am among the first to wish you happy, eh?"

Wish him happy? Lord Viccars, still caught up in thoughts of Captain Toby and a certain red-haired doxy, was very confused. Then Sir Christopher made mention of bride clothes and St. George's, Hanover Square. A suspicion blossomed in Lord Viccars's mind, causing him to feel as though the ground had shifted suddenly beneath his feet. "Lady Sherry!" Andrew gasped.

Sir Christopher could understand his friend's confusion. He recalled his own overwrought emotional state when he had at last gathered the courage to pop the question and his Livvy had said yes. "Don't fret! You have my blessing!" he said reassuringly as he clapped his prospective brother-in-law again on the back, then bore him off to the library for a frank discussion of dowries and portions and other matters pertaining to the marital estate.

Chapter Twelve

Purposefully, Lavinia tapped on the book room door, again and then again. She heard the murmur of voices and was not deceived that no one was within. She pressed her ear closer to the door but could not make out specific words. An attempt to peer through the keyhole availed her only a glimpse of some dark cloth. She rose from her knees and tapped once more, peremptorily. "Sherris!" she called angrily. "Open this door at once!"

The door did open then, to Lavinia's surprise, just as she had decided to give it a good kick. Sherry stood in the doorway, a startled expression on her face. "For heaven's sake, have you run mad, Lavinia? Whatever is this fuss about?"

Run mad, had she? This was surely a case of the pot calling the kettle black. Lavinia was no bedlamite, though she was not certain there was not one in this house. "I wish to know what you have been doing closeted away up here!" she insisted as she peered over Sherry's shoulder into the book room, where she saw nothing more exceptionable than Daffodil and Aunt Tulliver putting together a map of Europe on the old counting table and Prinny dozing on the settee. "You are responsible for that beast's atrocious manners!" she wailed. "I won't tolerate him making messes on *my* furniture! Nor will I tolerate *you* making messes, either,

Sherris! I will not have our dirty laundry aired in public, or our names bandied vulgarly about on every tongue!''

Since Lady Sherry had no notion that Lavinia had decided she was writing an exposé, she looked in bewilderment at the hand that clutched her arm. "I wish you would tell me what has sent you into the boughs, Lavinia!"

"I am not in the boughs!" Lavinia snapped, with a great deal less veracity than might be expected from the daughter of a duke. With, in fact, very much the shrill tones of a fishwife.

Those shrill tones awakened Prinny from his nap. Even when it was raised in anger—especially raised in anger—he knew his mama's voice. Eager that she should not think him guilty of neglecting her, he lumbered down from the settee and across the room. Since Lady Sherry blocked the doorway, he contented himself with gazing soulfully at Lavinia and wagging his tail.

Lavinia gazed at that pink, damp lolling tongue and shuddered. She took a deep breath, left off shaking Sherry's arm, and sought to compose herself. "I have a right to know what you are writing, Sherris. This *is* my house. You would not have this room at all if not for me. Therefore I think it only fair that—"

"If not for you?" Lady Sherry interrupted, growing annoyed in her turn. She stepped aside, allowing Prinny to push past her, then followed the dog into the hallway as Lavinia hastily backed away. She tried not to laugh at Lavinia's expression as she attempted to fend off her pet. "Am I mistaken, Lavinia? I thought it was Christopher who provided me with this chamber for my own use. Over your objections, as I recall. Has my brother changed his mind? Am I now to be denied my privacy? Perhaps it is a matter that he and I should discuss!"

This suggestion filled Lavinia with such panic that she failed to sidestep Prinny, who took advantage of his mama's abstraction to press close to her side. Lavinia knew Sir Christopher would be angry with her for badgering his sister, for so her actions must appear. Not that Lavinia had been doing anything of the sort, but she had no doubt that sly Sherris took advantage of every opportunity to present Lavinia in a bad light.

"You mistake my meaning," Lavinia said stiffly, having counted to a hundred under her breath, thus enabling her to speak in a voice that was almost normal, albeit strained, in pitch. "I only wished to tell you that Lord Viccars has called to speak with you. He awaits you in the drawing room. But since you are determined to interpret my concern as a desire to *trespass* . . . Well, Sherris, I wash my hands of the affair!"

Sherry did not take advantage of this opportunity to apologize for her rudeness. Clearly, Lavinia would be given no opportunity to peruse Sherry's manuscript this day. But other days remained. Or nights, after the household was asleep. If only she could gain possession of a key.

But Sherry must not guess her purpose. Lavinia must feign disinterest now. She turned, head held high, to make a dignified retreat. Unfortunately for Lavinia's intentions, Prinny had placed a great paw on the delicate flounce of her pretty gown. As must happen when irresistible force meets immoveable object, something had to give way. In this instance, it was Lavinia's flounce, which parted from her gown with a loud tear.

Lavinia stared at her tattered hem. This additional frustration was more than she could bear. "Oh, you wretched beast! You brute, you oaf!" she wailed. Prinny took refuge behind Lady Sherry barely in time to escape the humiliation of having his mama box his furry ears. Lavinia gathered up the remnants of her dignity, and her favorite morning dress, and proceeded angrily down the stairs.

Sherry contemplated the dog. Prinny gazed woefully back at her. She could hardly praise the beast for having routed Lavinia, Sherry realized, but the truth was that Sherry was feeling very much in charity with Prinny. Much as Sherry tried not to stand on bad terms with her brother's wife, the sad truth was that Lavinia could drive a saint to try to swear the devil out of hell. And what bee had Lavinia gotten in her bonnet now to come pounding on the door like that, startling them all very nearly out of their wits and necessitating that their house-guest should be shoved willy-nilly into a closet? Lavinia was suspicious, it seems—but of what, and why?

Yes, and Lavinia was very likely to come back for Sherry if she did not make an appearance in the drawing room. Sherry could hardly refuse to see Lord Viccars now that she had allowed her family to think that they would soon wed. Indeed, Lord Viccars must be informed of this development. It was not an interview to which Sherry looked forward. Much as Lavinia might deplore Sherry's manners, Sherry had been sufficiently well brought up that she knew better than to do what she had done. And what she was about to do. But she could think of no other reasonable resolution to the imbroglio in which she now found herself.

Sherry looked down at Prinny, who sprawled dejectedly at her feet. "You had better come along with me," she said. Prinny greeted this invitation with enthusiasm and a great damp lick of Sherry's hand. Already regretting her generous impulse, Sherry pushed him away. But Prinny would prove a diversion in the drawing room, which might be a very good thing. With Prinny at her side, Sherry descended the stair.

Lord Viccars was not in the drawing room. Perhaps he had grown tired of waiting for her and had taken his leave. Perhaps he had grown weary of her altogether and had been relieved when her failure to put in an appearance had given him a reprieve. He *had* taken her in disgust, Sherry thought gloomily. And he would make it so obvious that she would have to withdraw her request for bride clothes. At which point they would all go to prison, because Ned would overturn the apple cart, as he was threatening to do, because Sir Christopher was taking his sweet time in handing over the money and Ned was made very cross by the delay.

Perhaps she should simply ask Lord Viccars to lend her the money, Sherry mused as she paced around the perimeters of the drawing room. He could afford to extend her credit. Hadn't Lavinia told her repeatedly that he was blessed with an income of ten thousand pounds a year? But Sherry dared not ask. Lord Viccars would want to know why she needed five hundred pounds, and she could not explain. Nor could she hope to repay the loan within a reasonable time. Bride clothes it must be. At least the money she was attempting to wheedle from Sir Christopher was her own.

Sherry had just decided to return to her book room when Lord Viccars walked into the drawing room. So she was to have no escape. Escape? Odd to think of Lord Viccars in that manner. Odd and unfair. "Prinny!" she cried. "Pray get down. Lord Viccars does not wish dog hairs all over his nice coat."

Lord Viccars wanted no dog hairs not only on his nice blue coat but on his fashionable yellow breeches and buff waistcoat as well. Nor did he wish his gleaming top boots to be scuffed and drooled upon. With exasperation, he fended off the hound and watched with disfavor as Prinny stretched out with a great sigh on the sofa where his mama had so recently lounged. Then he glanced again at Sherry. "My dear, I hope you don't mean to introduce hounds into *our* drawing room!" he said, and smiled.

"Our—" Sherry blushed. "You have spoken with Christopher."

"I have," Lord Viccars murmured as he took her hand. The conversation with Sir Christopher had left him absurdly shaken. Of course he wished to marry Sherry. Had he not been waiting impatiently these past several months for her to set their wedding date? Why, then, this sudden wish that he had discovered Captain Toby's hiding place so that he, too, could now go to ground?

Sherry was made uncomfortable by Lord Viccars's silence, his intent gaze. She withdrew her hand from his. "You are angry with me," she said, close to tears. "I am sorry. I had thought— You had said— But if you have changed your mind and no longer wish to marry me, you must say so at once!"

"How absurd you are," responded Lord Viccars as he firmly banished his doubts and a nostalgic memory of the fair Marguerite. "I was never more pleased with anything in all my life. It's just that this is all so sudden. You took me by surprise."

Sherry smiled. "I think that's supposed to be my line, Lord Viccars. I am supposed to be overcome with maidenly reluctance and the like. I owe you an apology. I've made a rare muddle of the business, haven't I? Since I have never before decided that I wished to be married, I am sadly ignorant of how to go on!"

She was sadly ignorant of many things, Lord Viccars thought. Unlike another red-haired female of his acquaintance. But one did not seek similar virtues in wife and ladybird. Sherry would learn what he wished her to. For now, he must take care not to frighten her. "Do call me Andrew," he said. "I don't think I care to be addressed as Lord Viccars across the breakfast cups, my love."

Across the breakfast cups? At the image thus conjured—intimacies leading up to seeing his lordship across the breakfast cups—Lady Sherry's cheeks flamed. "I thought you had gone," Sherry murmured. "When I came into the room and found you were not here. It was good of you to call. We have not seen you for some days."

No, Sherry had not seen him. She, too, had been subject to his neglect even though it had been caused by his efforts on her behalf. Not for diversion had he visited such locations as Petticoat Lane on the boundary of the City, where one might buy anything from shoe buckles to coffins; and the British Museum, where one could admire all manner of displays, from Egyptian mummies to Aztec turquoise mosaic work to enameled Chinese cocks. Lord Viccars had derived no great entertainment from sitting for hours in the coffeehouse across from the Bow Street police headquarters or from rubbing shoulders with such strangely named individuals as Tinker Tom and African Sal and Billingsgate Moll. But he had gleaned information of interest about which he had wished to speak with Sir Christopher, and it was for that reason he'd come today to this house. But no sooner had he stepped across the threshold than things had gotten hopelessly muddled, and the capture of a certain notorious highwayman—even his desire to help Sherry overcome her creative difficulties—now seemed of only secondary importance.

Even yet he could not believe his good fortune. He gazed ruefully at his bride-to-be. "My dear, how fine you look today," he murmured. It was true. Sherry's morning dress had puffed sleeves and pretty frills at neck and wrist. It was even free of inkstains, as Sherry was herself. Lord Viccars concluded that she had taken especial pains with her appearance today on his behalf. This effort boded well, he thought as he drew Sherry with him toward the settee, forcibly evicted Prinny, then

110

with equal masterfulness ensured that Lady Sherry seated herself by his side. "I had a most interesting conversation with your brother," he said. "But do you know, I rather wish you'd broken the happy intelligence of our forthcoming nuptials to me first instead of to him. Therefore let us make believe that you have not yet spoken with Chris. You are going to speak with him after you have spoken with me first. Now, what have you to say to me?"

Sherry wondered what Lord Viccars would think if she said nothing at all but fled the room instead. She might well have done so had not Lord Viccars retained firm possession of her hand and Prinny sprawled across her feet.

Lord Viccars was waiting for an answer. She must say something to the man. "I have a great regard for you!" she stammered. "A decided partiality! And I am truly sensible of the honor you do me in asking me to be your wife. And— Oh, Lord— Andrew! I don't know what you wish me to say!" she wailed with such anguish that Prinny roused and tried to console her by climbing into her lap. Lord Viccars dealt with this distraction by bodily evicting the hound from the drawing room and closing the door.

Lady Sherry regarded her fiancé with admiration. "Gracious! You are very strong."

Lord Viccars brushed dog hairs off his jacket, then grasped Sherry's hands and pulled her to her feet. "I am a brute to tease you so," he said, and bent and kissed her lips. It was a very gentle kiss designed not to alarm, the sort of embrace that rapidly palled, and he very quickly drew away. "Much as I dislike to leave you, I must do so, my love. You have made me very happy, and you have also given me much to arrange. I fear my sisters will be plaguing you as soon as they have the news; they'll want to know how you brought this

confirmed old bachelor up to snuff. Don't tell them anything. Let them guess! But you'll know how to deal with
them. Tell Cecilia you'll agree to one betrothal party
but with only a few hundred guests!''

"A few hundred!" echoed Lady Sherry, but Lord
Viccars had already stepped into the hall, there to
adroitly avoid a collision with Prinny, who lurked in
hopes of having his revenge.

Chapter Thirteen

Marguerite paused by an E.O. table, watching the gyrations of the little ball. She looked especially lovely this evening in an Empire gown of India gauze shot with silver, which displayed substantial areas of back and bosom, charming the beholder by revealing everything it pretended to conceal. Charming the gentlemen beholders, at any rate; the ladies tended to be a little spiteful because Marguerite had outdone them all in near nakedness. The gown was embellished with a Vandyked and scalloped hem and festoons of flowers. Marguerite carried a fan of pierced horn leaves and wore an astonishing amount of jewelry, as well as flowers in her hair.

The E.O. table did not tempt her, and Marguerite moved through the suite of apartments on the first floor of this discreet establishment in St. James's Square, which was furnished with many chairs, tables, and stands for the punters' rouleaux and their wineglasses. All around her, games of chance were underway, hazard and piquet and whist and macao. A faro bank was in operation at one end of the largest salon. Marguerite paused, then moved on. She had been punting against the bank all the evening, losing on the one side what she gained on the other so that she had merely broken even after several hours of play. She would have some dinner now and a glass or two of claret, and then return to the tables in the hope that her luck had changed.

Marguerite descended the stair to the ground-floor chamber where the dining tables had been set up. Entrance to this establishment was by invitation only. The food was tolerable, as was the wine, and the play was known to be fair. As she passed through the hallway, the butler was opening the door to a late-arriving guest. He was a slight man with shrewd, disdainful features, dark hair disheveled a la Titus, and carefully cultivated side-whiskers. The high points of his shirt collar brushed his earlobes and framed his chin. He wore a brown-spotted silk coat and breeches, pale pink silk stockings, a pale silk waistcoat with an overall pattern in rose, shiny pumps, and a frilled shirt. Marguerite smiled at this vision of sartorial elegance. "*Bon jour, mon ami!* You did not tell me to expect you here tonight."

The man turned, raised the quizzing glass that hung on a black ribbon around his neck, and subjected Marguerite to its scrutiny. Saucily, she stuck out her tongue. He let the quizzing glass fall, brought forth a small enameled box, and inhaled snuff—Martinique, from Frebourg and Freyer's—in an intricate, one-handed style that he had copied from Beau Brummell. Marguerite watched his posturings with amusement. Only when he had finished and tucked away the snuffbox did he speak. "I expected to find you in a tweak, my pet. At the very least vowing vengeance and tearing at your hair. And why ain't you? Or do you know something the rest of us don't?"

Marguerite frowned. She had no notion of what her friend was talking about. Why should she tear at her hair? She had no cause for complaint other than her perenially pinched purse. She recalled that Jeremy had a perverse sense of humor. "What are you playing at now?" she asked.

"You truly don't know?" Jeremy quirked a brow. "Sometimes the extent of your ignorance amazes me.

We can't talk here." He drew her some distance down the hallway into a small anteroom furnished with a couple of chairs, a table, and a clock. "I think you had best sit down," he said as he reached into a pocket of his brown-spotted coat.

Marguerite obeyed. Jeremy's sympathetic manner made her more mistrustful yet. He handed her a folded square of paper, then leaned indolently against the wall. Bewildered, Marguerite unfolded the newspaper announcement and squinted her pretty eyes as she attempted to make out the words—for the fact is that she did not read easily or well.

Jeremy watched her frown over the newspaper item for the space of several clock ticks. It amazed him that Marguerite was so unaware. She never read a newspaper, trusting that her friends would enlighten her regarding anything she should know. Well, this information she should know, and it was Jeremy's duty to enlighten her. He helped himself to another pinch of snuff.

Whatever might be said about Jeremy—Jeremy Johnston, self-styled man-about-town, known variously to his acquaintances as a man milliner, an encroaching mushroom, a basket scrambler—his acumen was not at fault. It *was* amazing that Marguerite had not discovered that her protector's betrothal was official now. All of London was abuzz with the news of Lord Viccars's forthcoming nuptials.

Marguerite finally finished reading the news of the betrothal and let the paper drop. "That beast! That brute! That libertine!" she shrieked. "*Coquin! Diable! Merde!* How dare he play fast and loose with me? After all I have done for him. All I have given up! And now he means to conduct himself with conjugal obligation and decorum and cast me off like an old shoe. I won't have it. Do you hear me, Jeremy?"

Of course Jeremy heard Marguerite. It was very likely

115

that every person present on those select premises heard her, so vehement was her shout. Upon this fact, Jeremy remarked. He did not think Marguerite wished to broadcast the fact of her altered status, especially to those persons who held her vowels—for Marguerite could read and write sufficiently well to set her signature, frequently, on IOUs—and who had been remarkably lenient about payment as long as she was known to be Lord Viccars's particular friend.

Marguerite saw the force of this argument. She bit her lip and fell silent. But so great was her affliction that she rose from her chair and began to walk agitatedly up and down the room in unknowing but ironic imitation of the lady responsible for the very great trouble in which Marguerite now found herself. Not that Marguerite would have believed Lady Sherris could have problems anywhere near as severe as those that she now faced. Lady Sherry did not have to contrive mightily to be beforehand with the world. Lady Sherry had a brother, a family. Soon she would have a spouse. Marguerite saw a different, bleak future stretching out before her, and the prospect turned her perfectly sick. She would be harried by creditors and have bailiffs sleeping in the house—or not, because the house was not hers and Lord Viccars would no doubt evict her. But at any rate the constant worry and depression over her perennial financial crises would make her old before her time. This thought sent Marguerite hurrying to peer anxiously at her reflection in the looking glass that hung on one wall of the small room. She was relieved to see that she hadn't aged an entire year in the few moments since Jeremy had brought her the disastrous news.

Jeremy. Her old friend. Surely *he* would not desert her now. Marguerite turned to him with a woebegone expression. "I don't know what is to become of me!" she whispered.

"Bravo!" responded Jeremy, and clapped his hands. He had enjoyed Marguerite's performance very much, watched with appreciation the tear that trickled delicately down one perfect cheek. But Marguerite looked very much as if she meant to hurl herself into his arms, and Jeremy didn't care for this idea. He was immune to Marguerite's wiles, to her heady perfume; he was unmoved by her extreme décolletage and her near-naked style of dress. She stepped toward him, and he thought merely that he didn't want tearstains to ruin his brown-spotted jacket and pink silk waistcoat. "I told you not to put all your eggs in one basket!" he said callously as he opened the door.

Marguerite followed him into the hallway. "Where are you going?" she cried. "How can you leave me alone at a time such as this? I have been treated most cruelly, and you walk away. *Mon Dieu*, I think it very hard!"

"You have been outjockeyed, my poppet, and by a bluestocking. It is really infinitely droll. There's no use glowering at me like that. *I* ain't the one who bungled the thing so completely." But despite his callous remarks, Jeremy was not entirely without heart. He stopped a passing waiter and provided Marguerite with a glass of claret.

Marguerite clutched the glass. She felt very strongly that it would not be to her advantage to hurl its contents into her friend's face. Instead, and far more prudently, she downed the claret. "You might show me a little sympathy." She pouted. "This is a cruel blow. Jeremy, what am I to do now? Without Viccars to back me, I don't know how I am to make a recovery, because my pockets are all to let."

Jeremy paused to observe the players at a game of macao, a form of vingt-et-un that called for no particular skill but a very steady nerve, since thousands could change hands in the blinking of an eye. There was nothing to keep him at the table, and he soon passed it by. Unlike Marguerite, Jeremy was not a reckless plunger who could not help succumbing to the fascination of the tables. He was not addicted to play. But play he did when the occasion warranted, and with enviable good luck that was partially accounted for by the fact that Jeremy was very discerning when he sat down to play. He had no interest in overcautious players who kept their judgment and their emotions under strict control, but in those who in the excitement of the moment would stake fortunes on a single turn of the card or throw of the dice. Jeremy was, in short, that particular sort of social parasite known as a Captain Sharp. He had never been accused of cheating yet, but he could claim a steadily increasing list of reckless young bloods whom he had led astray. Jeremy felt no twinges of conscience about his chosen profession. It was more honorable, and lucrative, than others he could name.

He turned and looked through the crowd for Marguerite. If she were to come down in the world, then he must come down with her, because it was through their friendship that Jeremy had gained the entrée to such select establishments as these, which were liberally supplied with foolish young bucks waiting to be fleeced. There she was, at the faro table, trying to resolve her pecuniary embarrassments by risking a few pounds she could ill afford to lose. Jeremy drew her away. "I think," he murmured, "that it is time to utilize the aces you have up your sleeve, my pet."

Aces up her sleeve? Marguerite passed a moment in puzzlement before she remembered her boast. "I don't *have* any aces up my sleeve," she said gloomily. "I thought of all sorts of things, but they weren't practical. I mean, I don't know who I could bribe to have Lady Sherry transported or kidnapped. And if I did, my part in it would be bound to come out and Viccars would cast me off anyway. I still do not believe it, Jeremy!'' She looked at the newspaper clipping, which she still clutched in one very smudged glove. "He said not a word of it to me. I might have been given some warning, don't you think? Instead, I have not seen him for some days, not since he gave me this!" She touched the diamond and emerald necklace at her throat.

Jeremy's interest was aroused. Lord Viccars was a gentleman and would not treat his *petite amie* like some chance-met member of the muslin company. There would be a touching farewell scene. And since there had not been . . .

"There's something dashed smoky here!" Jeremy said. "Viccars has taken quite an interest in that highwayman fellow who barely avoided having his neck stretched. He's been asking questions all over town and visiting the queerest places, like Bow Street and Petticoat Lane and the British Museum.''

Marguerite glanced up at her companion. Since their conversation was being conducted in low tones as they passed through the throng in the gaming rooms, she thought she could not have heard his words correctly. *"Comment?"* Jeremy repeated his earlier statements. She had not misunderstood. "The British Museum?" she echoed, perplexed. *"Pourquoi?"*

Jeremy shrugged. "I don't know why. He's trying to track down the highwayman's red-haired doxy, from all accounts. It don't signify.''

"Maybe not to you!" Marguerite interrupted with an expression of perfect horror on her pretty face. "But you haven't been offered false coin! So *that* is what it is! *Zut!* I have wracked my brain, I can tell you, trying to figure out what she has that I do not—and now I understand! I tell you, Jeremy, it has rather raised my

119

spleen, because never have I been so deceived in any-one!''

If Marguerite at last understood, her companion was not similarly blessed. Aware of the curious glances being cast at them, Jeremy begged Marguerite to lower her voice. He then begged her to share her enlightenment with him. Just what did it concern?

"Why, Viccars, of course!" Marguerite was exasperated to find Jeremy such a slow-top. "Lady Sherris, me, the highwayman's wench—we're all redheads, don't you see? Oh, *la vache*!"

So much of Marguerite's logic, Jeremy could follow. But he failed to see what about it had sent her into the boughs. "So you're all carrot-tops. So what?" he inquired.

"And so it doesn't matter *which* red-haired female he's with!" Marguerite cried. "When he's with one he forgets the other, and vice versa. He hasn't been to see me because Lady Sherry occupies his thoughts. And he's probably neglected her while traipsing after the highwayman's wench. Two of us aren't enough for him, apparently! *Mon Dieu,* Jeremy, don't you see?" she added in response to the skeptical expression on his face. "It's plain as a pikestaff! His memory for his mistresses is short; we're all interchangeable!"

Interchangeable, were they? Jeremy was not impressed by this extremely specious example of feminine reasoning. But one aspect of Marguerite's logic—or il-logic—struck him forcibly. Marguerite, Lady Sherry, and the highwayman's doxy were all red-haired. Jeremy was prepared to lay a monkey that he could make some good use of this coincidence.

"Listen, poppet," he said. "Viccars will come to visit you again, and when he does . . . Well, I don't need to tell you how to turn him up sweet! Don't breathe a word to him of your suspicions. Don't nag at him or scold. Act like you're happy for him. Wish him a long life and happiness. But don't act like you don't care a groat—you know the sort of thing!''

Marguerite did know. She would be a martyr and a hypocrite. But to what end? *''Alors?''*

Jeremy only laughed when she asked this question and tweaked an auburn curl. ''I can't tell you that just yet. You must leave all to me. And don't despair; we ain't in the basket yet!'' On these encouraging words, he took his leave.

Don't despair, he had said. Marguerite wished she could believe so easily that her troubles were at an end, that her creditors would not begin to hound her in earnest at any moment, and that she would be forced to sell her jewels and all else that she owned. Lord Viccars's rejection was symbolic. She did not suit his taste. Consequently, never again would Marguerite dare to aim so high. She would be forced to make her way in the world in the only way she knew and endure a series of fickle protectors, each less wealthy and blue-blooded than the last, until she was Haymarket-ware. Depressed beyond all bearing by these gloomy reflections, Marguerite swallowed another glass of claret, then retired to the faro table. If she were to be hanged, it might as well be for a sheep as for a lamb.

Chapter Fourteen

Hanging was also on Micah's mind, though in regard to his own neck as opposed to sheep or lambs. He stood at the book room window, looking down into the gardens and wondering if the furor about his escape had yet died down. His leg had healed enough now that he could hobble about, was healing so very quickly, indeed, that Tully called it a near miracle. But she could take much of the credit for his recovery. Few convalescents would be as coddled as Micah had been. Both Tully and Daffodil were forever bringing him treats filched from the kitchens, fussing over him and unbosoming themselves to him, even allowing him to instruct them in the intricacies of the backgammon board. As a result, Micah had learned a great deal about Sir Christopher's household. He knew where the family silver was hidden and of Lady Childe's attitude toward his benefactress; he knew about the three gentlemen Aunt Tulliver had married and several more she had not; and he knew how Daffodil had come to be an abigail.

Micah turned away from the window. The book room was stifling hot, so he took off his shirt and flung it into a chair. Then he limped to a bookshelf and surveyed the volumes lined up there. Though Micah wasn't much of a reader in the normal way of things, he had taken to this means of whiling away the hours when he lacked company. Thus far he had read Maria Edgeworth's *The*

Absentee, a powerful description of Irish exploitation by English landlords; Shelley's *Vindication of Natural Diet,* which traced man's evil impulses, and most wars, to the ingestion of meat; and Lord Byron's *The Giaour,* a tale of Oriental adventure, violence, and love. He had perused a number of accounts of gentlemen of the road that Lady Sherry, rather surprisingly, had on hand: *True and Honourable History of the Life of Sir Oldcastle,* who was believed to be the original of Mr. Shakespeare's Falstaff; *The Life and Death of Gamaliel Ratsey,* a rather dull volume except for a description of the highwayman's unusual mask, which covered his entire face with painted features described as extremely repulsive; and *Recantation of an ill led Life,* by one John Clavell, who was eager to tell the world how to travel without being robbed, no doubt in an effort to avoid the hangman's noose.

The hangman's noose. Micah grimaced and turned away from the shelf. He hobbled around the room in search of diversion, spent some time inspecting the worn tapestries that hung upon the walls. Then his glance lit upon Lady Sherry's manuscript. He knew now that she wrote novels and had even browsed through some volumes set aside on a special shelf. Murder and ravishment and kidnapping, ghosts and vampires and moldering castles—Micah was amazed to discover that Lady Sherry's mind was of such a lurid bent. Expecting more of the same, he sat down at the library table and began to scan the closely written pages. A moment later, he chuckled and settled down to read in earnest.

Lady Sherry found him in this posture, a half hour later, when she walked into the book room, a tea tray in her hands and Prinny trotting eagerly at her heels. No sooner did she have the door open than the dog pushed past her, prepared to leap. "No!" cried Micah. Prinny dropped abjectly to the floor.

Sherry stared, amazed, at Prinny. "However did you manage that?" she asked in awe. "The beast actually obeyed!"

"It's all in the tone of voice!" Micah gasped, still caught up in merriment. He gestured with a manuscript page. "I'd no notion you had such talent for comedy! Captain Blood! Ophelia! 'Pray, sir, if you are a man of honor, you will not ravish an unhappy lass!' " He dropped the page and burst into renewed whoops.

Lady Sherry glanced anxiously into the hallway, which was fortunately deserted, then hastily closed and locked the door. Micah was still chortling. How dare he poke fun at her story? Lady Sherry frowned. Although truth be told, she didn't like the thing much herself. "I suppose you will tell me it isn't realistic," she said with resignation, and then added, "Oh, gracious!" as she realized belatedly that she was locked alone in a room with a man who wore no shirt.

Micah realized the import of the situation in almost the same moment, due largely to the startled expression on Lady Sherry's face. He realized that he had placed Lady Sherry in a very compromising position by his current mode of dress. Or undress. "Have I offended you? Shall I put my shirt back on? It's just so accursed hot!"

"Oh, no!" said Lady Sherry. She wished no one to suffer discomfort on her behalf. Also, unusual as the situation might be, Lady Sherry was no schoolroom miss to swoon away at sight of a man half dressed. She was instead a mature novelist, aged twenty-seven, who could not help but think that so risqué an encounter—properly fictionalized, of course—might liven up her current book. "It *is* hot, and I am not offended. In truth, I would take my own shirt off if I dared!"

"Why not do so, then?" Micah was intrigued by this suggestion. "*I* don't mind!"

"You don't—" Lady Sherry elevated her gaze from Micah's bare chest to his face. He was smiling. "Wretch!" she said.

"You would be perfectly safe!" said Micah, enjoying the sight of her pink cheeks. "I am incapacitated, you will recall."

No man could be called incapacitated who possessed a chest and shoulders so muscular, so well-defined. Lady Sherry, quite properly, did not voice that thought. "What you are, sir," she said wryly, "is an arrant flirt. But you were reading my story. You don't mind, I take it. I was afraid you might."

"Mind?" Micah compromised comfort with conscience by shrugging into the shirt but leaving it unfastened. "Why should I mind? I thought you might dislike me reading your story without so much as a by-your-leave."

"Oh, no!" Lady Sherry set down the tray that she had brought, on which were arranged teapot and cup and a plate of sugar-dusted teacakes. "I meant, I thought you might not like it that I'd based a character on you."

Micah paused in the act of reaching for a tea cake. "On me?" he asked, startled.

"On Captain Toby, of course." Sherry lifted the teapot and poured. "You never have told me how you came by that name."

"Captain Toby," Micah repeated, and smiled. "No, I don't mind. It's rather a good joke. But your Captain Blood—it's all balderdash; you must know that."

"Balderdash?" Sir Christopher had voiced a similar conclusion on the sole occasion that he had read one of Sherry's books. Now Micah, too, thought her writing lacked a realistic touch. Sherry could not take this criticism too seriously, since her readers apparently did not care whether her tales were realistic or not. But she was curious. She sat down at the library table and prepared

125

for a serious literary discussion. "What is balderdash? Why do you say that?"

Micah joined her at the table. "My good girl, this is *all* balderdash!" he said. "Poppycock! People don't act like this. *Life* isn't like this. Good God, you know that! And furthermore, this Captain Blood of yours is the dullest cove I've read about in any book. Your Ophelia—and why Ophelia, of all things?—could duel him with a hat pin and win!"

"I see." But Andrew had thought Captain Blood too rakehelly. Sherry rested her chin on the palm of her hand and looked morose. "Perhaps I should just give the whole thing up as a bad piece of work." She glanced at Micah. "Unless you'd be willing to tell me what a highwayman's life is really like . . ."

"*I* tell you—" Micah broke off here to scowl at Prinny, who had inched unobtrusively forward to put his head on his new friend's knee. Since it was not his injured leg that Prinny thus favored, Micah did not push him away. "You did save my bacon," he concluded. "It's only fair that I repay you. Just what is it that you want to know?"

Hastily, Sherry set down her teacup, reached for her pen and ink and several sheets of the best paper. "Everything! How did you come to embark upon a life of, er, crime?"

"Ah!" Micah appropriated Sherry's abandoned teacup, which he filled to the brim. "I was always a bad 'un. Started spinning whoppers as soon as I could talk. Started running off as soon as I could walk! Drove my old guv'nor half wild with all the trouble I got into. And then I came of an age to discover—"

"Women and wine!" said Lady Sherry, scribbling furiously. "Of course!"

"Women and wine *and* the gaming tables!" Micah amended with a wicked leer and a flourish of his teacup.

"I drank wine like it was water, and the ready flowed through my fingers like it was the same. As for women—"

He sighed. "Ah, but I was a wild lad. The guv'nor did right to cast me out before I brought us all to ruin."

Lady Sherry was intent upon her paper, her flying pen. "Of course! As I suspected! You took to the road to pay your gambling debts. What was your game—faro? Macao? Deep basset? And how *did* you escape from the gallows? Was that riot part of the plan?"

Micah was watching her, amused by the enthusiasm with which she was writing down his words. "It was my doxy," he explained. "She arranged it all. A clever piece is Moll. She'd take to the road with me if I let her, and many's the time I escaped out her window when the law came sniffing too close to my heels."

Sherry glanced covertly at Micah's half-bared chest and experienced a pang of envy for the very bold-sounding Moll. Then Micah added somberly: "As for the other—why, 'twas backgammon as was my ruin."

"Backgammon?" Sherry saw the mischievous expression on his face. "You're telling me Banbury tales, you wretch!"

"Well, yes," admitted Micah. "You must not blame me when you rise so prettily to the bait! The truth of the matter, you see, is that I'm not a highwayman at all."

"Yes, and I'm not a magistrate's sister!" Sherry set down her pen. "What clankers will you try to tell me next? It is very bad of you. I had hoped you would help me with this wretched book!"

Micah picked up the manuscript pages and leafed through them. "What's wrong with it?" he asked.

Sherry looked at him indignantly. "What's wrong with it? You yourself said that it was balderdash just moments past. I can hardly consider that high praise!"

127

Micah shrugged, thus disturbing Prinny, who removed his head from Micah's lap and went to stretch out on the settee. "I didn't say it was *bad* balderdash! Whether or not you meant it to, it made me laugh," Micah said. "I'll tell you what I think: What's wrong isn't with your book; it's with you. Your heart's not in it, so to speak."

How strange, thought Lady Sherry, that a highwayman should possess such depths of understanding. She realized that what he said was true. This was the first book Sherry had written without her mama's participation in the process, without each evening's enthusiastic discussion of the work in progress. Of course it must seem different. Sherry wondered why she hadn't realized this for herself. How her mama would have loved *this* adventure, Sherry thought. She reached for the teapot and found it empty, so she went to her bookshelf to fetch the decanter and glasses that she kept hidden there. Micah's pistol lay there also. She picked it up and brought it to him.

"You might as well have this," she said, then unstoppered the decanter and poured. "I suppose I've been listening too much to Lavinia. She thinks I should set my pen to instructive, enlightening, and, above all, moral tales. As if what I write isn't respectable somehow. Although Lavinia seems to enjoy reading it well enough! And so I feel guilty because I cannot write other than I do, because it emphasizes my deplorable lack of high-mindedness!"

"How absurd you are!" responded Micah as he sampled his port and adjudged it very fine. "High-minded females are a bore, and so are instructive books. Look at your Lady Childe. Why would you wish to model yourself after such a prune?"

A prune? He had called Lavinia a prune? Seldom had Sherry felt so in charity with anyone in all her life. Or

128

so comfortable, she realized with surprise as she smiled at her highwayman over the rim of her own port glass. She would miss him when he was gone. Because, of course, he must go, and soon. Reticent as he was on the subject, the man had a life elsewhere, a family, perhaps even a wife. Of course a wife, Sherry decided as she gazed at his handsome face. It was a pity. If only Micah were other than a highwayman . . .

She flushed, then lowered her gaze. It was foolish to waste time with such thoughts. Even if Micah were of unexceptional birth and social standing, he would not be for her. He would have his pick of beautiful women, and among them would not be a spinster authoress. And he was *not* of exceptional birth and social standing but a highwayman and a rogue; Sherry was appalled at herself for entertaining such thoughts. Apparently, she had reached that advanced stage of life when ladies must beware of strange fantasies.

Micah watched her, frowned as an unhappy expression settled on her face, got up from his chair, hobbled around the table, grasped her wrists, and pulled her to her feet. "What the devil is it that plagues you so?" he asked. "One minute you're laughing and the next you're blue-deviled again. I wish you would let me help."

The only way Micah could help Sherry now was by releasing her, and he did not. Such was the effect of his touch, his proximity—his bare chest—that Sherry was half deafened by the pounding of her own pulse. Nor were her thought processes unaffected. Sherry knew only that Micah mustn't guess how he affected her, and therefore said the first thing that came to her mind. "I'm to be married!" She gasped. "Oh, please let me go!"

How pink were her pretty cheeks. How her lovely bosom heaved. How adorably confused she was, altogether. Why had Micah not realized it before . . . "You're going to be *what*?" he inquired.

"Married!" Lady Sherry blushed all the harder as she struggled with a most improper impulse to touch her fingertips to Micah's bare chest. "To Lord Viccars— Andrew! Soon!"

Micah transferred his grip from Lady Sherry's wrists to her shoulders—lest he be condemned as a brute, it should perhaps be noted that she made no appreciable effort to escape—and gave her a little shake. "The deuce with Viccars! You don't love him!" he announced. Sherry stared at him, her lips parted in mingled dismay and astonishment. There was nothing for it then but to kiss her. He proceeded to do so, so thoroughly that Prinny, who had been watching these strange goings-on with interest from the settee, yawned in boredom and resumed his nap.

"Oh!" cried Lady Sherry when Micah at last released her. She pressed her hands to her flaming cheeks. "How *dare* you—"

"Don't be so missish! It doesn't suit you!" Micah interrupted impatiently, and drew her closer into his arms. After a moment's hesitation, Sherry relaxed against him. Clearly, they were both lunatic. And it was equally clear that Sherry knew as little about romance as she did about highwaymen. Andrew's kiss had been pleasant, had filled her with a gentle warmth, but *this* . . .

Many moments elapsed in this fashion. At their conclusion, Lady Sherry and Micah both reposed on the settee while Prinny sprawled in a very dejected manner by the door. Prinny was feeling very jealous, because it had been made very clear that his new friend preferred someone to him. Micah, too, was not free of the pangs of jealousy at the thought that this female with her astonishing depths of passion should be promised in marriage to someone else. Yes, and if she made those marriage vows she would not break them, unlike many other so-called ladies that he'd known. But Lady Sherry was like no other female he'd ever encountered, and Micah was not inexperienced in the petticoat line. He stroked Sherry's red-gold head, which rested upon his chest.

Lady Sherry's thoughts were not so coherent. But then she lacked Micah's experience in the game of hearts and had nothing with which to compare what had just taken place. What should *not* have taken place, she reminded herself as she listened to his strong heartbeat. What must never take place again, because she was no giddy miss to toss her bonnet over the windmill. Nor was she cut out for life as a highwayman's light-o'-love, even if he wished that of her, which of course he would not. He had been bored and she had been at hand, and so . . .

And so he must never realize that she had suffered the sting of Cupid's dart. Sherry sat up, straightened her rumpled clothing, and smoothed her tousled hair. Micah watched quizzically as she unlocked the door, then brought him the key. "You are well enough to travel now, I think," she said, and dropped it onto the settee.

Well enough, perhaps, but Micah was not ready to leave. "Wait!" he called as Lady Sherry walked toward the door.

Sherry's footsteps did not falter. If she were to pause even one instant, she would disgrace herself by bursting into tears. "What just passed between us . . . It was a singular piece of folly on both our parts and I do not wish to discuss it—indeed, I wish to forget that it ever happened—and I beg you will do the same!" she said with a gasp, and then with as much dignity as she could muster stepped out into the hall.

Chapter Fifteen

Lady Sherry did not appear at the dinner table that day, nor would she open the door of her bedchamber to family or friends, claiming to be prostrated with a sick headache. And indeed she was prostrated, had flung herself down on her bed in all her clothing, stricken by something perhaps best described as a sickness of the heart.

Not surprisingly, Lady Sherry found sleep elusive. She tossed and turned upon her mattress until the sheets were in a dreadful tangle. The Montagues and Capulets had nothing on a highwayman and the sister of a magistrate, she thought. Not that she and Micah were starcrossed, because he did not love her, which was, all things considered, probably for the best. But it was a great pity, if she was going to respond to any man with such intense feeling, that it was not the man to whom she was betrothed.

What was wrong with her? She was affianced to one man, yet dreaming of another. Sherry pounded her pillow into a more comfortable shape. She could not force from her mind the memory of Micah's kiss, the feeling of his skin against her hands. Sherry shook her head as if to banish memories. Why couldn't she have fallen in love with Andrew, who was so good and lawabiding? It had something to do with Ophelia and Captain Blood, she suspected, because Micah had said

Captain Blood was dull and Andrew thought him a great deal too bold. *She* had been a great deal too bold, mourned Sherry. Never, ever again would she take a drink; the port had obviously gone straight to her head.

Oh, this was absurd! Sherry abandoned her efforts to sleep, lit the pretty brass lamp, and studied her reflection in its soft glow. She frowned at the image offered back to her by the honeysuckle-framed mirror. She looked distraught, wild-eyed. And red-eyed also, for she had not withstood her mournful thoughts without recourse to a handkerchief. Lady Sherry had fallen in love with a highwayman and sent him away in almost the next moment, and now she wished that she had not. What a pretty pickle this was! Shocking as it was in her, what Lady Sherry truly wished to do at that moment was to return to her book room. She sighed and began to effect such repairs as she could to her tear-streaked face.

Lady Sherry was not the only member of her brother's household to be awake so late that night. True, the servants slept the sleep of exhaustion in their cramped little rooms beneath the eaves. Greedy Ned dreamed of Daffodil, who in turn dreamed of the newly hired footman who possessed a most shapely calf. Aunt Tulliver dreamed of a country pleasure fair complete with puppet shows and gingerbread stalls, a pig-faced lady and a pair of dwarfs. And Sir Christopher snoozed peacefully in his great carved bed. He did so, unknowingly, alone. Lady Childe did not rest companionably beside him now. Lavinia was not even present in the bedchamber that she shared with her doting spouse. She had come into possession of a certain key ring—had in fact filched it from her butler's pantry when Barclay's superior gaze was directed elsewhere—and was at this very moment stealing down the upper hallway on tiptoe.

There it was, the book room door. Now all that remained was to discover which key fit the lock. With candle in one hand and key ring in the other, Lavinia glanced cautiously over her shoulder to make sure that she was not observed. It was rather a thrilling moment. Lavinia felt as though she was being very adventurous and brave. Dukes' daughters, after all, did not skulk about the hallways in the dead of night during the normal course of affairs.

"Ah!" A key that fit. Lavinia savored the sweet taste of triumph. But before she could turn the key in the lock, the door swung open and Lavinia very nearly lost her balance from sheer astonishment. She kept her wits about her and did not scream, not wishing to be asked to explain her presence here, with Barclay's keys, at this very advanced hour. She kept firm hold of her candle, too, not being wishful of setting the house afire, ducked into the book room, and quietly closed the door.

Once inside, she looked around her curiously but saw little more than worn tapestries and cast-off furniture and piles of books. And on the old library table were a tea tray, a liquor decanter, and a stack of manuscript pages. Lavinia tsked at the sight of the decanter. But since it was there . . . She set her candle on the table and settled herself upon a chair, then poured some port into a glass and began to read.

Lady Sherry, meanwhile, succumbed to temptation. She could not banish Micah so cavalierly, could not let him leave without a more appropriate farewell. In truth, Sherry did not know how she could bring herself to allow him to leave at all, except that she could hardly keep him prisoner forever beneath her brother's roof. She pondered these matters as she tiptoed up the stairs and down the dark, narrow hall. Sherry also carried a candle with her to light her way and clutched to her breast a pretty hot-water jug with ivory handles that sprang from two serpents and rose to a single winged head. In case Micah decided to launch a further attack upon her virtue, Sherry deemed it best to be prepared.

She paused outside the book room doorway, gathering her courage, still with no notion that anything might be amiss. Even Prinny's failure to appear and accompany her caused Sherry no second thoughts. She merely assumed that the dog had minded its manners and Micah had not evicted him. But when she placed her hand on the door handle and it opened without a key . . . Cautiously, stealthily, Lady Sherry stepped across the threshold.

She saw a figure seated at the library table reading by candlelight, its back turned toward Lady Sherry and the door. The figure was clad all in white. For a moment, Sherry thought she saw a ghost. If this is not precisely a logical deduction, she must surely be forgiven that. Sherry had passed a most trying day and was in grave need of solace, and she would have most enthusiastically welcomed a reunion with her mama, even in so incorporeal a form. Who else could her visitor be? Who else cared enough about Sherry's little stories to trouble to read them in the dead of night?

Who else? "Lavinia!" Sherry cried, realizing that the specter was merely her sister-in-law clad in white nightcap and gown. "*What* have you done?"

Lavinia started mightily at being rudely interrupted in her perusal of the adventures of Ophelia and Captain Blood—and, for the record, Lavinia thought Captain Blood most satisfactorily swashbuckling, though she found Ophelia rather too outspoken for her taste. She swung around in her chair. "Sherris! How you startled me!" she protested with that degree of indignation popular among those who have been caught in the wrong. "Why are you clutching that hot-water bottle, Sherris? Have you taken a cold in the chest?"

Sherry ignored this display of sisterly solicitude. She

135

walked to the library table and set down her hot-water bottle with an angry thump. Her first horrid suspicion was unfounded, then. Lavinia would hardly greet Sherry in this manner if Micah had been discovered and taken off to jail. "What the devil are you doing here, Lavinia? That is, aside from indulging your irrepressible nosiness by snooping into my affairs?"

"Irrepressible . . . *Snooping?*" Lavinia clutched the hot-water bottle to her own chest, into so extreme a state of consternation was she thrown by Sherry's incivilities. "Gracious, Sherris, but you are severe! *Too* severe, I think. What do you have hidden here that you do not wish me to discover? And don't bother to try to tell me that is not the case, because you aren't one to make a piece of work about simply nothing and otherwise you wouldn't be looking like such a thundercloud!"

"I am looking like a thundercloud," Sherry said grimly, "because you are a sneak, Lavinia! A gabble-grinder, a Polly Pry!" But as long as she and Lavinia were brangling, Lavinia would not leave the room so that Micah could come out from wherever he was hiding. "Oh, let us talk of it tomorrow, Lavinia! I wish to go to bed."

"Yes, and I do not!" retorted Lavinia icily. A Polly Pry, was she? A sneak? "But pray do not allow me to keep you from your beauty rest! I shall simply stay here and read. And it is hardly proper for you to chastise me for misconduct, Sherris, when you have that dreadful book upon your shelf!"

A brief diversion ensued here, which need not be described in its entirety, since it does not appreciably advance our tale. Lady Childe referred, of course, to *The Giaour,* and expressed considerable indignation at finding the work of such a reprobate as Lord Byron present in her house. Lady Sherry in turn expressed a large lack of concern for her sister-in-law's feelings and informed

Lavinia that she had no more literary taste than the mice who lived in the wainscoting. Lady Childe expressed horror at the suggestion that rodents might dwell beneath her tidy roof—although rodents might be preferable to Lady Sherry, whom Lavinia (perhaps inspired by the hot-water bottle that she still clutched) likened to a serpent nourished in her bosom and then added a rather confused comparison concerning thankless relatives and adders' tongues. Lady Sherry—who, during this exchange, had been wandering about her book room, peering surreptitiously into her closet and beneath the settee, in the former of which she found only clothing and beneath the latter a well-gnawed ham bone abandoned amid a considerable amount of dust—responded very cordially that the only viper who dwelt in this house was, alas, her brother's wife.

There is no telling how long this quarrel might have continued: Lady Childe was very unhappy to have found no trace of the exposé she knew Sherris must be writing, and Lady Sherry was even more displeased that her sister-in-law could not be persuaded to retreat. However, they became aware then of noises in the hallway outside the book room door. Running footsteps were heard, and raised voices. The ladies stared at each other with startled expressions. And then the door burst open.

Lavinia uttered a little shriek and almost dropped the hot-water bottle. Lady Sherry was more composed, having already mistaken a nightgowned figure for a ghost once this eve. "Daffodil!" she cried.

Daffodil recovered somewhat from her own surprise at finding the book room thus occupied. "Lawks!" She gasped. "You scared me out of a year's growth!"

Lavinia drew herself up. She was among those few women who could look commanding even in nightgown and cap. "What do you mean by bursting in here like that, girl?" she snapped. "Explain yourself at once!"

Daffodil was not cowed by Lavinia. She darted around the table and skidded to a stop before Sherry. "Milady! There's a proper ruckus going on downstairs! The whole household's at sixes and sevens, and Sir Christopher's threatening to call in Bow Street because her ladyship here turned up missing and then you wasn't in your room!" She caught at her mistress's arm and gestured toward Lavinia. "What's *she* doing here?"

"Snooping," said Sherry bitterly. "Prying. Meddling. But Daffodil, what's all this fuss about? Why should Christopher become so upset? What's this about calling in Bow Street? Good gracious, it's the middle of the night!"

So it was, and Daffodil shared her mistress's misgivings. She, too, glanced surreptitiously around the book room. "Oh, milady, there's been a robbery! The front door was found unlocked and Barclay's keys have been filched right off their hook!"

"A robbery?" Sherry echoed with relief. Micah had not fled the book room on Lavinia's invasion and consequently been caught. Then she and Daffodil exchanged glances, both stricken by the terrible suspicion that the highwayman whom they had sheltered and protected had chosen to repay them in this cruel way.

"A robbery?" wailed Lady Childe, having taken advantage of her companions' abstraction to hide Barclay's keys in the bodice of her nightgown. But how was she to explain to Christopher her presence in Sherry's book room? There was one sure way to win his sympathy. "A robbery!" she cried again, and gracefully swooned.

Chapter Sixteen

As matters evolved, Sir Christopher did not call in Bow Street, to the great relief of several members of his household. It seemed a trifle absurd to report a robbery when nothing seemed to be missing from the house. For this queer circumstance, Lady Childe provided an explanation: She had been drawn from her bed by noises heard in the night, had gone to investigate and in so doing had obviously frightened away the thief. She was, in short, a heroine, as Sir Christopher pointed out.

This ramification had not occurred to Lavinia, but she took full advantage of her heroic status to retire to her bedchamber, prostrated by excitement, with her worried and admiring spouse attached firmly by her side. Having secured this captive audience, Lavinia availed herself of the opportunity to complain—in the most delicate manner—about the unfortunate repercussions of Sherry's sojourn in this house. Not that Sherris could be faulted for it, dear sweet creature that she was. Indeed, if any fault could be laid at Sherry's door, it was that her heart was perhaps a teeny bit too generous, too large. Not that Lavinia would ever utter the words "I told you so," but she *had* felt that it might not be entirely prudent to introduce Daffodil into the household. Perhaps the girl did have a flair for fashion, a passion for pretty clothes; she also had an unfortunate history and background and moral character. Though others might blithely assume that the chit had reformed, Lavinia was not so gullible, and frequently reassured herself that her jewels were intact, as well as the family plate. And as for this current contretemps, Lavinia wasn't certain that Daffodil wasn't somehow involved, might even have unlocked the front door so that some of her vulgar low-bred friends might sneak into the house, heaven only knew for what purpose, perhaps to murder them all in their beds!

Clever as this ploy was, it fell on deaf ears. Sir Christopher had been stricken all aheap by his darling wife's unsuspected bravery, and was not at all surprised that reaction should now have set in and the dear creature should have become semi-hysterical as a result. "There, there!" he said, and patted her. "Least said, soonest mended, after all!" Lavinia, of course, was not appreciative of this attitude and flung herself away from her spouse across the bed, at which point Barclay's key ring fell out of her nightgown and onto the rug. Sir Christopher bent and picked it up. "By jove! Barclay's keys! How the devil did they get here?" he said.

If ever Lavinia thought quickly, she did so then. A notion brilliant in its simplicity struck her. "Prinny!" she said with a gasp.

"Prinny?" Sir Christopher looked with concern at his wife, who had apparently been more overset by her adventure than he'd previously realized. First she went into raptures about that dastardly highwayman, and now she seemed to fancy the Prince Regent as a houseguest.

"*Not* the Prince Regent!" cried Lavinia, when her doting spouse aired these views. "Prinny! The dog, the hound! You must remember, Christopher; you gave him to me!"

So he had. Now he remembered the great, frolicsome beast that had not turned out to be one of his better-chosen gifts. So it was the wretched dog who'd filched the butler's keys and caused all this brouhaha, had ruined a good night's sleep for the entire household. Who, furthermore, adorned every object with which he came into contact with spittle and dog hair.

Clearly, the beast needed punishment. Sir Christopher set out to track down the culprit, leaving Lavinia to sink back with exhaustion upon her pillows and beg in weakened tones that her abigail should fetch her vinaigrette. Not long was Lavinia left to catch her breath, however. A thorough search of the house, including Lady Sherry's room, revealed that Prinny was nowhere to be found. "Maybe he was stolen," Sir Christopher conjectured at the close of these investigations. "It *was* a valuable beast."

"Stolen!" Lavinia sat abruptly upright. Previously, when she had claimed to be a heroine, she had thought the whole business to be a hum based on her appropriation of Barclay's keys. Now that it appeared otherwise—if Prinny had been stolen, then there *had* been an intruder in the house and Lavinia had been in mortal peril—she let out a shriek and swooned.

This swoon was one too many for Sir Christopher to bear with equanimity. Sensibility was an admirable thing in a woman, but his Livvy was carrying it to excess. Never, to his recollection, had he seen anyone so sorely pulled about. No, and he didn't care for it. "Get that damned sawbones here on the double!" he snarled at Lavinia's abigail, and waved away the burnt feathers she'd brought to wave beneath her mistress's nose and patted his wife's hands clumsily between his own. The abigail sped to execute her errands and at the same time spread intimation of further disaster through the house. All waited with breathless anticipation for the sawbone's verdict, which when it finally came caused no little sensation: Her ladyship was discovered to be in an interesting condition. There was to be an addition to the household. The doctor made reference to the prospective patter of little feet. By which he did *not* refer to the footsteps of that misbegotten hound, whose salutations he was grateful to be spared this day. So saying, he took his leave.

And so, finally, the household settled down to a semblance of its usual daily affairs. The servants set about their duties and served up a tardy dinner, which Sir Christopher tenderly spoon-fed to his wife, who was nearly as overwhelmed by the glad tidings as he. In all her wildest longings for a weapon to use against her sister-in-law, Lavinia had thought of nothing so effective as this. Naturally, Christopher would not wish the bearer of his future heir to be upset. Lavinia smiled tenderly at her spouse and uttered a fragile sigh.

Lady Sherry, meanwhile, had withdrawn to her bedchamber with Aunt Tulliver and Daffodil, who had combined efforts to make her presentable for an evening party she had promised to attend. "No, milady, you shan't cry off!" decreed Daffodil as she applied her foot to the small of her mistress's back and pulled smartly on the laces of her stays. "You promised that you would go, and so you must, before poor Lord Viccars thinks you've changed your mind and wish to break off with him. Anyways, it will do you good to get out of this house and away from her highness's high flights!"

Sherry did not comment. To do so would have been difficult, lying facedown as she was upon her bed while Daffodil attempted to compress her waist into a circumference several inches smaller than nature had intended. Sherry's thoughts were not happy ones. Her highwayman had gone, leaving behind no trace, nothing to indicate that he had been anything but a figment of her imagination. She would never see him again, never know what had become of him and what he had become.

Daffodil at last tied the laces to her satisfaction.

"There!" she said, and helped her mistress to rise from the bed. Daffodil's frame of mind on this occasion was little happier than her mistress's. She knew by way of the household grapevine—by way of Lady Childe's abigail, in point of fact—what accusations had been made of her and as a consequence was very angry. Perhaps Daffodil was less than perfect and in the past had done certain things that she should not, but she had nobly withstood temptation the entire length of her residence in this house. And this was her reward for such self-sacrifice, Lady Childe saying that she must have left the door open for her friends to come and pillage the house. As if she would! It made Daffodil almost wish she had taken her highness's jewels and hid them somewhere, just for the pleasure of watching Madame High-in-the-Instep go off in a conniption fit.

Aunt Tulliver interrupted Daffodil in the midst of airing these feelings. "What a rumption!" she said. "And all over a stupid hound, because her high-and-mightiness don't know there's nothing else missing from her house. But we know better, don't we? And I'd like to know why our friend left so quick. His leg wasn't healed yet. And nary a good-bye or a thank-you did he say to any one of us." She cast a keen look at Lady Sherry. "Or did he?"

Sherry avoided meeting the old woman's shrewd gaze. She walked to her dressing table. "He said nothing to me."

"Humph!" responded Aunt Tulliver, who hadn't reached her advanced age without gaining considerable knowledge of the world and what went on in it, especially as concerned those matters that touched the human heart. But she couldn't force a confession from Lady Sherry. "I'm not convinced that it wasn't all a hum. There was something not quite right about him, if you take my meaning, and about him meeting up with you like that.''

"Not quite right about it?'' echoed Sherry, puzzled. "What do you mean? It was the most accidental of meetings. No one knew that I was going to be there. The thing could not have been contrived. And, anyway, why should it have been?''

Tully shrugged, left off fussing with Lady Sherry's party dress, and sank down into a chair. "Maybe. Maybe not,'' she said. "But I'll tell you this, 'tis never wise to bet against a dark horse!''

A brief silence descended upon the bedchamber then. No one wished to ask Tully to explain her enigmatic remark. Lady Sherry sat down by her honeysuckle-wreathed mirror, and Daffodil began to arrange her hair. "Well, say what you wish,'' muttered Daffodil. "*I* thought he was all the go!''

"*We* know, prime and bang up to the mark!'' retorted Aunt Tulliver from the depths of the chair into which her bulk had settled so thoroughly that anyone glancing at her retained an impression primarily of a pink and green turban and red shoes. "That's why he set the household by its ear!''

Lady Sherry had been involved in sufficient set-tos for one day—perhaps even for one year; she was not naive enough to think that Lavinia would not somehow take her revenge—and quickly intervened before her two retainers could come to blows. "I'm afraid I'm responsible for that,'' she interjected. "Or perhaps Lavinia is because she did not stay snug in her bed. Oh, this is pointless! Micah—the highwayman is gone now, and we can relax. It doesn't matter even if Christopher does call in Bow Street, because we've nothing to hide.''

This was a pleasant notion. Unfortunately, both Daffodil and Aunt Tulliver knew it wasn't true. Their

144

glances met above Sherry's head in the dressing-table mirror. "You'd better tell her," Tully said.

"Tell me what?" Sherry realized the answer even as she spoke. It seemed so obvious as she looked at the pert and mischievous face reflected near her own. Not only to her had the highwayman made advances; Daffodil would be much more his type. Probably he wouldn't have made advances to Sherry at all if she had not practically hurled herself at him. It was a very good thing he was gone. And she would bite out her tongue before she told anyone what had transpired between them in the book room the day before. "You mean that the man was an arrant flirt? Heavens, I knew that!"

"Oh, he weren't no flirt." Daffodil applied her brush to Lady Sherry's hair with rather more force than was strictly necessary. "Leastways, he didn't flirt with me, and I'll say as shouldn't that he would've if he was of a mind! But he was nacky company even if he didn't throw the hatchet at a girl, and for the life of me I can't figure why he left in that queer, abrupt way. Taking Prinny with him yet!"

"All my eye," muttered Aunt Tulliver. "More like the beast took himself along."

For a foolish moment, contemplating the adventures Prinny must have in the company with Micah, Lady Sherry envied the dog. She was also very curious about something Daffodil had said. Micah had not flirted with her? Could that be true? "There's no need to try to pull the wool over our eyes, Daffodil," she said. "You would be neither the first nor the last to find yourself in amours with a man who wasn't all that he should be."

Daffodil set down the brush, satisfied at last with her arrangement of Lady Sherry's curls, and reached for a pretty little pot. Then she attempted to repair the ravages of the day by the discreet application of a little rice powder and rouge. "Yes, well, that's what I was wishful of speaking to you about, milady!"

So it was true. He *had* trifled with not only mistress but also abigail. Lady Sherry was filled with sorrow and indignation at the ignominy of woman's fate. With false deceivers lurking in every bush, how could one be expected not to go astray? "Oh, Daffodil!" she cried, and turned on her stool to grasp her abigail's wrist. "I am so very sorry! Had I known that this would happen, I would not have had him in the house! I would never have gone out that morning, and indeed I wish I hadn't, because if I hadn't, none of these horrid disasters would have taken place!"

Though Daffodil was still of tender years, in some areas of experience she was almost as old as Aunt Tulliver. Therefore, she understood why Lady Sherry spoke as she did and on whose account. "Oh, milady!" she protested. "It's Ned as is the bad lot, not anybody else."

"Well, at least *that* trouble we no longer have on our dish!" Lady Sherry said briskly, pleased to have her thoughts take another, more pleasant direction. "How fortunate that Christopher is turning out to be such a miser, or Lavinia is persuading him to be so! Ned can no longer threaten us, because what can he say? Who would believe him if he went about saying we'd hidden a highwayman in the attic? There is no proof of such a thing. People would think he was queer in *his* attic, most likely." She smiled for the first time in many hours. But there were no answering smiles on the faces of her companions. "Well, wouldn't they?"

Daffodil looked at her own reflection, not wishing to meet her mistress's eager gaze, then helped herself to the contents of her mistress's rouge pot because her own healthy cheeks were unnaturally pale. "Neddy don't see it that way. He thinks you should pay up anyways. He's hinting that there's others as'll pay him for what he knows if you won't.''

Lady Sherry was being made cross by this relentless adversity. "Then let him!" she snapped. Daffodil said nothing. After further reflection, Sherry added, "Who can he mean?"

Daffodil put down the rouge pot. "I'm sure I don't know.''

"Maybe not, but you could guess!" offered Aunt Tulliver from the depths of her chair. "If you was to put your mind to it. Think on this, milady: Who do we know that's pettish and peevish and tiresome and fret-ful—and who also hasn't exactly welcomed you with open arms to this house?"

For a person who was not addicted to guessing games, Lady Sherry divined this answer very promptly. "La-vinia, of course. She *would* listen to Ned."

"Aye, and Sir Christopher would listen to *her*, and then we'd all be in the basket." Aunt Tulliver shook her turbaned head. "I don't say I blame you for ripping up at her, milady. Anyone would be thrown into a pucker by finding her snooping about like that. But now that she's increasing . . . If Sir Christopher was be-twattled previously, now her highness will truly be able to wrap him around her little finger. Devil of a business as it is, milady, you'd best pay up!"

How sad to think of her brother dwelling beneath the hen's foot. Sadder still to think of herself and her re-tainers exposed as accessories to a highwayman's es-cape from his justly deserved fate. "I'll think of something," Sherry murmured. Daffodil looked re-lieved.

Tully's expression was not so readable. "I wonder," she murmured, "if the scamp will be back on the high toby now."

Sherry's patience was exhausted. "Oh, let us hear no

more of the wretch!'' she cried. "Daffodil, do you mean to stare forever into that mirror, or will you help me dress? Andrew will be here at any moment and I do not wish to keep him waiting, and so if you do not mind—''

No more did Daffodil wish to keep Lord Viccars waiting. He'd take Lady Sherry's mind off things it had no business dwelling on. Aunt Tulliver lent her assistance also, and soon Lady Sherry was turned out, as Daffodil put it, in prime style. Chemise, drawers, stays that further constricted her small waist and emphasized the shape of her breasts, silk stockings, and a thin sarcenet slip; a gown of white French gauze striped with blue, with long, full sleeves and a lace-scalloped hem, a very high waist and a very low bodice cut into a deep V; satin slippers tied with crossed ribbons and long white gloves.

At last she was ready. Lady Sherry fastened a sapphire and pearl necklace around her throat and picked up a blue Levantine pelisse edged with floss silk, then went downstairs to await the arrival of her escort.

Chapter Seventeen

Lady Sherry might have been en route to her own execution rather than a party in her honor, so grim was her mood. Nor were her spirits elevated when Lord Viccars's elegant carriage rattled past St. George's in Hanover Square. Not that the church was not impressive, with its elegant portico and large Corinthian columns, its lofty tower terminated by a turret-crowned dome, but Sherry could not think with complacency of the wedding ceremony that was scheduled to take place there within a few weeks. She thought of Micah, then forced him once again from her mind. Idylls end, she told herself; she must be grateful that she had enjoyed one at all. And if the world seemed a great deal more flat than it once had, if she knew there was no grand and glorious surprise awaiting her around the corner, because she had already had her surprise and it was behind her now—well, that was just the idyll's price. Sherry knew that all things had their price. She was no green girl. She was to be married, and time was marching forward at a relentless pace. As was Andrew's carriage, arriving long before Sherry was prepared to face his sisters at a big, red mansion with a balustraded roof, which was approached by way of a forecourt and a prominent portico.

Within that elegant structure waited, amid a great deal of fashionable company, the Ladies Cecilia and Sarah-Louise. Lady Sherry was introduced to a great many people whose names she would not remember; she was reminded of the comment of a fellow writer who had said to her that in society he felt like a poodle dog compelled forever to stand on its back legs. Then the sisters drew her away to a brocaded sofa and seated themselves on either side of her for a comfortable little coze. They bore a marked resemblance to their brother, who looked very fine this evening in his knee breeches and striped stockings, frilled shirt and Florentine waistcoat and long-tailed blue coat. Not that either Lady Cecilia or Sarah-Louise could lay claim to lush side-whiskers—though Cecilia did have the faint shadow of a mustache on her upper lip—but both had the same sandy hair and Sarah-Louise had a familiar smile.

Lady Cecilia was a great deal less merry. The heat and dust in London at this time of year were unbearable, were they not? she volunteered as the eldest of the family. And what did Lady Sherry think of these Hampden clubs that had sprung up all around the city, many of which entertained very seditious ideas, even designs of seizing property? Lady Sherry thought she would avoid a discussion of politics with her prospective sisters-in-law—as if Lavinia were not sister-in-law enough for anyone!—and adroitly turned the conversation to the Horticultural Society, which she knew was Cecilia's consuming passion. Consequently, she was privileged to hear a dull, if uncontroversial, discussion of the experimental growing methods that produced strawberries as large as small apples and eleven-pound Providence pines.

Sarah-Louise broke into the conversation then; at five-and-thirty, she still remained the impetuous, spoiled darling of her family. "Oh, Cissy!" She pouted. "That is such dull stuff. *I* wish to know what Lady Sherris is writing now—Andrew mentioned a highwayman. I am a great fan of murder in Gothic castles and Oriental palaces myself! Ancient, *moldering* castles! Ghostly apparitions and avenging shades!''

"Oh, yes, the highwayman." Was everything to remind Sherry of Micah? "It does not go as well as I might wish."

"I am an admirer of Miss Austen's work myself," put in Lady Cecilia, and launched into an erudite discussion of *Pride and Prejudice*. "And Maria Edgeworth's *Belinda* is quite unexceptionable."

"At least the first volume is," remarked Sarah-Louise. "I found it dull going after Lady Delacour reforms. Although I did like the locked room!" She nudged Sherry with her elbow. "You must not listen to my sister, Lady Sherris! She will have you writing such dreary stuff as that Mary Brunton. 'The mind must be trained by suffering before it can hope for usefulness or true enjoyment,' indeed! Well, *I* have not suffered, nor do I intend to, and though I may not be useful, I certainly know already how to enjoy myself!''

"Rather too much so," observed Lady Cecilia disapprovingly. "Lady Sherris, you must pay my sister no mind. Tell us, what renovations do you plan for Andrew's town house?"

"Yes, do tell us!" Sarah-Louise chimed in. "Because even Cissy admits she couldn't live in that dreary old barn. Although we all did as children, of course. But it was not so ghastly then. Talk about your dreary mausoleums! If ever a place deserved to be haunted, that one does!" She opened her eyes wide. "Why, perhaps it is! Perhaps Mary walks there. Mary was Andrew's first wife, you know. Not that her death wasn't perfectly natural, because it was: she tripped over her own skirts and fell down the stairs. Which served her right in a way, because she was so very vain. But she was not a very obliging person, and she did not get

151

along well with Andrew, and so if she had the opportunity of—''

"Sarah-Louise!" interrupted Cecilia, looking very stern. The younger woman flushed guiltily and broke off. "I'm sorry!" she said quickly. "I fear I tend to chatter like a magpie. You must pay me no mind!"

"Indeed!" said Lady Cecilia angrily. "You show so little manners, Sarah-Louise, that one would think you went seldom into society!" Then it was Cecilia's turn to flush as she realized what she'd said—for this little party was a dress rehearsal for the larger betrothal ball that was being planned, at which Cecilia wanted to make certain that Lady Sherry wouldn't disgrace herself and them. "Not that *you* will need me to give you a gentle hint, Lady Sherris, as to how you are to go on! As if I would be so presumptuous! I will not stand on ceremony with you: I feared I might have to speak where I should not! But you are perfectly correct and unassuming in your manners—obviously a model of good breeding, my dear!"

A number of things occurred to Lady Sherry during this speech: primarily that Lady Cecilia had a very high sense of decorum and a disposition to think well of herself. Perhaps this was a characteristic of ladies of the very first distinction. Lady Cecilia put Sherry strongly in mind of Lavinia. Even with marriage, Sherry was not to escape this sort of quizzing, it appeared. Even as Andrew's wife, she would still be interrogated and have her every action criticized. Lady Cecilia, like Lavinia, would demand an accounting of her time.

"In other words," murmured Sarah-Louise as her elder sister's attention was attracted by a passing guest, "we are delighted to find in you nothing for which to blush. You won't furnish the tea tables of the *ton* with tittle-tattle, as Cissy had feared you might, not knowing you as I do. . . . She doesn't read your books, you see!

They're not elevating enough for her. Although if Cissy was elevated any higher, she's scrape her nose on the ceiling, I vow!'' She leaned closer. ''Tell me the truth! You don't read that Brunton female!''

''No,'' confessed Lady Sherry, who was beginning to like this prospective sister-in-law rather a lot. ''I am rather more prone to read things like *The Annals of Newgate,* I fear. Or *The Genuine History of the Life of Dick Turpin,* who—''

''I know!'' interrupted Sarah-Louise. ''Who rode to York, jumping over all the turnpike gates on the way. I wonder if that tale is true. What do you think about this Captain Toby person? Cissy will threaten to wash out my mouth with soap if she hears me say it, but I'm glad he escaped!''

Lady Cecilia turned back to them then. ''You are glad *who* escaped?'' she asked.

''Not glad!'' protested Sarah-Louise innocently as she nudged Sherry in the ribs again. ''How could I be? At least that horrid Buonoparte person will not escape his prison on Saint Helena. Oh, look, there is Andrew with James. I'll wager they've been playing at cards. Come, Lady Sherris, let me introduce you to my husband. Isn't he a handsome brute?'' Without giving Sherry an opportunity to answer, she maneuvered her up off the sofa and through the crowd. ''I thought you were in need of rescuing. Cissy can be a trifle overbearing!'' confided Sarah-Louise. Tactfully, Sherry refrained from comment. She felt as though she were being swept along in a small whirlwind's wake.

Sarah-Louise's James was indeed handsome, a tall man with carelessly arranged dark hair and a mischievous twinkle in his eye. The sight of their obvious affection for each other caused Sherry a pang of regret that she did not love Andrew as she should, yet had still agreed to become his wife. Not that she didn't love him at all, simply not in the manner she had since discovered it was possible to feel.

Oh, the deuce with it! Lady Sherry sipped champagne from a glass. She had been in love, and it was both unsuitable and uncomfortable. At least she would be more content with Andrew than if she continued to dwell beneath Lavinia's roof. Perhaps her efforts to make Andrew happy—and Sherry did mean to make Andrew happy—would distract her from her own heartache. Surely it must be better to settle for what love was available than to do without any love at all.

And so the evening passed in a confused impression of bare arms and bosoms and backs swathed in shades of blue and green, violet and primrose; of gowns of patent net and lace and ribbon, velvet and silk, satin and shot sarcenet, crepe and tulle over satin slips. And the gentlemen . . . Sherry saw shirt points so high they must surely cut their wearers' ears and every variety of intricately tied cravats from the Oriental and the Mathematical to the Ballroom and the Trône d'Amour. Countless times, she was introduced to some new person; she professed herself enchanted countless more. Throughout it all she maintained an abstraction that would lead Lady Cecilia to incline her turbaned head, setting atremble the long white feather thereto attached, and pronounce gravely that Lady Sherris was a female of unusual character but an excellent creature withal, not given to frivolity but distinguished for her accomplishments and possessed of a well-regulated mind; and Sarah-Louise to speculate merrily with her spouse not upon Sherry's intellectual resources but upon what had preoccupied her thoughts.

Lord Viccars had not failed to notice that his fiancée was in a very quiet mood. Since Andrew was feeling a little somber himself, he wished that she would talk more and consequently think less. Indeed, somber was an understatement. Andrew was prey to that attack of the blue devils common among bachelors whose days of freedom are about to end. He saw looming before him a settled life as clearly as if it were a painted picture upon which he gazed. He saw himself grown sedate, complacent, and prone to *embonpoint*; clustered around him were his wife, children, and even the family dog, all of whom would no doubt make demands upon the head of their household. They would require his time and attention and affection. The children would grasp with sticky fingers at his exquisitely tailored coat and breeches; the dog would enthrone itself on the drawing-room settee. As for his wife . . .

Andrew glanced at Lady Sherry then and felt ashamed. Anyone less grasping would be hard to imagine. Yet he could not rid himself of the suspicion that with marriage she would change into someone quite different from how she was now, someone grasping and greedy for the things of this world that his money could provide her, clothes and jewelry and the fashionable diversions of the *haut ton*; that with marriage a transformation would be wrought in Lady Sherry similar to that which had occurred in his first wife. There was something to be said in favor of such creatures as Marguerite, who wore their avarice on their sleeves as openly as more tender females wore their hearts and who gave good service for payment received.

With the thought of Marguerite, Lord Viccars experienced renewed guilt. He had been quite cavalier of late about his visits to his *petite amie*, had not even broken to her the news of his impending nuptials. No doubt she had heard the tidings by now. Among her acquaintances must surely be someone who read the *Morning Post*. He would call on her again, Lord Viccars promised himself, as soon as he had steeled himself to withstand her recriminations and her tears—and, yes, her wiles as well, because Marguerite would not give up a title and ten thousand pounds a year without putting up a good battle, and her weapons were not easily withstood. If only Sherry . . .

But to think of a reciprocation of passion in marriage was absurd. The highest relationship in love was mutual esteem. So Cecilia had always decreed, and Andrew couldn't doubt that his elder sister knew best when it concerned propriety. Lord, but Cissy gave a dull party! Sherry must be bored half to tears. Andrew himself wished he might be elsewhere. At Mott's in Foley Street, perhaps. Or flirting with some bird of paradise in the Argyll Rooms. Anywhere other than moving through these hot and crowded rooms, among people who would speculate among themselves as to how Lady Sherry had inveigled him into the parson's mousetrap as soon as they were out of earshot.

This evening must be even more of an ordeal for Sherry than it was for him. "I'm sorry about this. Cissy was determined to do all that was proper," he said, and patted her hand.

Sherry started at the sound of Andrew's voice and murmured some polite response. She, too, had been deep in thought. Indeed, so noisy were these crowded rooms that it was nigh impossible to do anything else. Sherry had forgotten that the most successful party was one in which several attendees came perilously close to being crushed to death. She had not appeared in public for some time. Not since the morning of Micah's abortive hanging, in fact. Sherry wondered what Micah would make of these fine ladies and gentlemen, what he would say to Lady Cecilia. Most likely, he would laugh as he laughed at all else. Given the opportunity, which in time he doubtless would be, Micah would laugh at Lucifer himself. She wondered where the rogue was now. And then it occurred to her to wonder whether there were others among this fashionable throng who had set out to enjoy the spectacle of a hanging several days past. If by exposure to the polite world she increased the risk of being recognized. And this train of thought recalled Sherry to the insurmountable-seeming problem that she faced: Ned, who grew more threatening daily and who must be paid off.

Lord Viccars paused in a smaller room where a game of piquet was underway. Sherry roused herself from her abstraction and watched the card play, which was for twenty-five pounds the rubber and ten shillings the point. She remembered what Micah had said about his gambling debts. Had he, too, played at cards? Or was he a more foolish plunger like the *beaux* at White's, who had been known to wager on the progress of a fly across a windowpane? Like the regent himself, who had once lost several thousand pounds betting on twenty turkeys racing against as many geese?

What difference did it make? Lady Sherry had her own debts to resolve, and soon. Now that Lavinia was known to be increasing and Sherry had been so foolish as to quarrel with her, Sir Christopher could not be persuaded to advance Sherry money, because Lavinia would wish to take her revenge by allowing Sherry to be married looking like a dowd. Or so it seemed to Sherry, who admittedly was not thinking clearly at this point.

Much as Sherry disliked to involve Lord Viccars in her troubles, there was no other solution now. "Andrew," she murmured as they continued their perambulations through the crowded rooms. He bent closer so that he might hear her. "I promise that I mean to make you very happy. And I wish you to lend me five hundred pounds!"

Chapter Eighteen

Exhausted as she was by her dissipations of the previous evening, Lady Sherry arose the next morning at her accustomed hour. She hoped to find her brother alone at the breakfast table in order to have a private word with him, to try to counteract if possible Lavinia's spite. But Lavinia was there before her. "Aha!" Lavinia said. "Sherris, you are late today. We had not thought to enjoy your company over the breakfast cups. But since you are here, I wish to hear all about your party. I hope you explained that illness prevented my attendance and Christopher's, or else it must have looked very strange, indeed!"

What Sherry recalled primarily about her party was that she had asked Lord Viccars for the loan of five hundred pounds. "It was well enough," she murmured as she took her seat at the table. "If you care for that sort of thing."

"If you care—" Lavinia arched her golden brows. "Sherris, you are hopeless! Do you not realize what a signal mark of honor Cecilia did by honoring you in that way? And you do not even know who was present! How can you know if you were a success or not if you do not even know who was present and who was not? I should have known, had I been there! Had I not been so ill!"

Clearly, Lavinia wished some comment on her illness. Sherry wondered belatedly if Lavinia had wished that her sister-in-law similarly stay home. It seemed a trifle absurd to refuse to attend a party held in one's honor simply because a member of one's family was increasing, but perhaps that was the way things were done in polite society.

Had she not already quarreled with Lavinia, Sherry might well have voiced that unkind comment. However, she did not wish to make matters worse. "I am sorry you are feeling poorly," she murmured. "Christopher, I understand you are to be congratulated."

Sir Christopher looked up from his plate on which were piled Scotch eggs with chopped anchovy and gravy, fried yellow-brown. "Don't know why *I* should be congratulated! Livvy did half the work," he said, and chuckled at his wife's embarrassed face. But he didn't mean to make her cross or to prompt any more of the strange fantasies that seemed to plague females who were *enciente*, so he engaged his sister in humorous reminiscences of their shared childhood.

Lavinia was not entertained by her husband's little stories. Although, to give her all due credit, Lavinia truly was in an enfeebled state of health. Attendant upon the discovery that she was in an interesting condition had come all the less pleasant side-effects of that state. So very queasy was Lavinia that she was breaking her fast this morn with only barley water and toast. And so she was not in charity with her fellow diners, who were setting to with good appetites while she exercised all her will power in an effort not to cast up her accounts.

Furthermore, she was not enjoying her husband's story of a childhood adventure in a blackberry patch. "Christopher, this is very bad of you," she said when he paused to take a mouthful of cheese toast. "You know I got up out of my sickbed only to hear about the party, and now you are monopolizing poor Sherris so she can't say a word! How I wish I could have gone! I hope you explained to dear Cecilia why I could not attend.''

Sherry spread orange marmalade on a biscuit. "What we should have done was postpone it,'' she said. ''Until you felt well enough to attend.''

"Postpone it? How absurd you are!'' Was Sherris being sarcastic? Lavinia recalled that this thankless creature had already called her a Polly Pry. All in all, Sherris had tried Lavinia's civility too high. "I do think I am entitled to a little sympathy!'' Lavinia added tearfully. "First I am awakened by noises in the night, and then poor Prinny is found missing, and then to have to miss your party, to which I was so looking forward—'' She sniffled. "I do think life is very hard!''

"There, there!'' Sir Christopher put down his cheese toast and patted his wife's hand. He wondered if he would have to spend the next several months listening to absurdities like these. Yet even if pregnancy did turn his usually lucid Livvy into an adorable cabbage-head, it was a small price to pay for an heir. "We'll get you another hound.''

"I don't want another hound!'' Lavinia protested, smitten by a vivid memory of the previous hound's less lovable qualities. "Nor do I want any more people breaking into the house. Sherris, that girl of yours—''

"Daffodil had nothing to do with that business,'' Sherry said, and set down her cup of chocolate into its saucer with a thump. "And well you know it, Lavinia. Those noises you claim to have heard were probably no more than—''

"Mice!'' shrieked Lavinia, who knew perfectly well that Sherry knew she'd heard no noises. Lavinia didn't want that intelligence made public, especially within the hearing of Sir Christopher. "Oh, never say so, Sherris!

160

My nerves cannot withstand these continual shocks. I keep teasing myself with thoughts of poor Prinny and what sad fate may have befallen him, poor thing.''

Sherry pushed away her plate. ''He'll turn up,'' she said.

''Turn up?'' echoed Lavinia. ''I should think he will not! That hound was valuable, Sherris. I do think you might show a little more sympathy for my grief. Yes, *and* the strain all this has put me under—in my condition! Strangers prowling about the house!''

Sherry could not argue with this statement. There *had* been a stranger on the prowl in Longacre House. Fiend take the man! ''I doubt that the dog was stolen,'' she said dismissively. ''He probably just ran away.''

Lavinia liked this theory little better. ''I have not the most distant guess why Prinny should do such a thing!'' she said icily. ''Surely you do not mean to suggest that he was unhappy here with us. That he was mistreated. I'm sure *I* never did such a thing. Indeed, if anyone can be accused of unkindness . . . Well, everyone knows poor Prinny spent most of his time with you!''

Carefully, Sherry set down the marmalade knife with which she had been toying and said, ''This is absurd!''

So it was. Sir Christopher was startled to hear his wife talking such moonshine. Who would have thought that that hound's disappearance would have put her in such a pucker? ''I had some interesting news this morning,'' he ventured in an attempt to restore the peace. ''That highwayman fellow has been captured. He's tucked away all right and tight in Newgate. There'll be no escape for him this time!''

''Micah!'' whispered Sherry. Fortunately, at that same moment Lavinia cried out, ''Christopher, surely they will not hang him now!''

Sir Christopher frowned. ''Highway robbery is a capital offense,'' he said in grave tones. ''The rascal should have thought of that before the first time he put on a black crepe mask and took up his pistols in order to rob an innocent traveler. He'll hang, puss, but he'll have a grand time of it before, what with half of London clamoring to pay him a last visit. The female half!'' He forced himself to chuckle and pinched her cheek. ''Confess; you'd like to visit him yourself, you sly minx! Not that I'd allow such a thing.''

''*I* visit—'' Lavinia stared with honest astonishment at her spouse. ''Good God! Christopher, you have windmills in your head.''

This pretty declaration quite wrung Sir Christopher's heart, and he pressed his wife's hand against his chest. Sherry thought uncharitably that if she was forced to watch her brother making sheep's eyes at his wife for another moment, she would become ill herself. So Micah had been recaptured? It served the wretch right for sneaking off like a thief in the night. As he would not have, had Sherry not told him to go away. She could not help but feel responsible for Micah's recapture. She must do something, but what? Sherry pushed back her chair and asked to be excused.

Sir Christopher assumed his sister was going to her book room, inspired by his news to work on the tale of her own highwayman. ''The scamp's red-haired doxy is still at large,'' he said helpfully. ''But it's only a matter of time before she's behind bars also, or so I hear from the officials at Bow Street, who have been given some very good information about the wench.''

Though Lady Sherry might have been expected to share Bow Street's interest in that unfortunate female, she didn't press her brother for further details. Sherry didn't care to hear additional comments upon that red-haired female's no doubt unfortunate fate. She withdrew to her bedchamber, to think and pace there.

Aunt Tulliver found Lady Sherry in that pastime when

she entered the room some moments later, clutching a newssheet, which she promptly waved in Lady Sherry's face. "I know!" said Sherry as she ceased her pacing at last and sank down in a chair. "He has been arrested. Just when I fancied I was doing a fairly good job of forgetting the wretch. And now he is back in Newgate. We must *do* something, Tully, but I don't know what."

"Nor do I, milady." Flushed and breathless from her rapid ascent of the stairs, the old woman fanned herself with the newssheet. "It'd be a miracle if he escaped again. I fear this time that pretty scoundrel *will* dangle in the sheriff's picture frame."

Lady Sherry shuddered. "Perhaps he may yet make a recovery," she suggested, though with faint heart. "I always wondered if that first escape wasn't somehow arranged."

"Fiddle-de-dee!" interrupted Aunt Tulliver, who had by now caught her breath. "Better you should think on whether he'll betray us if the right questions are asked— and what you'll say then!"

"Betray us? How can you think for even a moment that Micah would do such a thing?" Unfortunately, memory served Lady Sherry up just then with a description of Newgate Prison that she'd used for her book and the various means by which a prisoner might be induced to say that which he would rather not. Micah would have his breaking point, as did any man. With sufficient inducement, he would betray them to spare himself further pain.

Abruptly, Lady Sherry stood up, moved to her wardrobe, and began to rummage through its contents. "I must see him, Tully!" she said. "Where is Daffodil?"

Aunt Tulliver wasted no time in futile argument. It was perfectly obvious to her in which direction the wind blew. "Trying to turn a certain party up sweet," she replied. "Are you forgetting that Viccars is to call this evening? With a certain sum of money to pay a certain party not to let the cat out of the bag? By the by, what did you tell him was your reason for wanting such an amount?"

Sherry flung a shawl around her shoulders and placed a bonnet on her head. "I told him a clanker," she said gloomily. "Don't bother to tell me I should not have! Never mind that now. I must go to Newgate, Tully. If Daffodil cannot go with me, then I will go alone."

Aunt Tulliver sighed and heaved herself up out of her chair. "Aye. You'll walk up to the gate and ask to see Captain Toby, which of course they'll let you do without remarking the color of your hair. And landing you in just the kind of trouble we're paying a certain party to avoid! Adone-do, milady! Don't fly into a pelter now. We'll go to Newgate, all the same. I've a few words to say to that pretty scoundrel myself, and so I will, while *you* stay outside!"

So it was decided, after a show of some reluctance on Lady Sherry's part, but Aunt Tulliver was adamant about the terms on which this expedition would be conducted. The ladies slipped out of the house without attracting undue attention and set out for Newgate.

Lady Sherry had much with which to occupy her thoughts during the hasty journey through the London streets, and the sights that would ordinarily have caught her attention held little interest for her now.

They arrived in the neighborhood of the prison. There was Newgate Meat Market, the College of Surgeons, Surgeon's Hall, Bart's Hospital, and St. Sepulchre's. People crowded the narrow streets: fish and oyster and fruit vendors; hawkers of playbills and ballads and newssheets; Italian organ-grinders; kidney-pie and baked-potato men. "Wait here!" muttered

Tully. Lady Sherry paused in the shadow of a baker's shop. She stared up at the tall, gray-black prison building with its narrow windows and arched gateway. Newgate was the largest and oldest of London's prisons, dating back to antiquity. It was referred to in the annals of King John's reign. Lord George Gordon had been imprisoned here, had died here in 1791, singing the "ça ira."

Death again! Sherry sought to wrench her thoughts away from this extremely painful subject and from speculations upon what Micah's dying words might be and whether he would utter them from a scaffold or if he would succumb to jail fever first. She stared into the baker's shop at the servants and children waiting for the drawing of a fresh batch of rolls.

Consequently, Sherry did not see Aunt Tulliver's approach and gasped when the old woman clutched her elbow. "Tully! You startled me. Well, how did you find him? Is he well? Did he send me a message? Oh, do say something, pray!"

Aunt Tulliver was prepared to say quite a lot, once the opportunity was granted her, but she required more privacy than could be found in these crowded streets. "Hist! That one's fine enough," she said as she signaled energetically to a passing job-carriage and urged her mistress to climb aboard. "Short of temper and sound of limb."

"Short of temper?" Sherry frowned. It was very ungrateful of Micah not to welcome Aunt Tulliver, no matter how many female visitors he might expect to receive. "He wasn't glad to see you?"

"No, and why should he be? The rogue had never set eyes on me before." Lady Sherry looked even more bewildered by this remark. Aunt Tulliver leaned closer and spoke into her mistress's ear. "It makes no odds, milady! There's a resemblance, a definite resemblance, but an inch in a miss is as good as an ell!''

Lady Sherry drew back, ashen-faced. ''Do you mean—''

''I mean,'' said Aunt Tulliver with relish, ''that they've got the wrong pig by the ear!''

Chapter Nineteen

Marguerite stared at her companion. "I don't believe it!" she cried. "Lady Sherris? *Merde alors!* Is it true?"

Jeremy flicked shut his snuffbox and tucked it away in a pocket of his many-caped driving coat, in which he looked very fine, if a trifle overdressed on so warm a day. "What is truth?" he inquired grandly. "It lies in the eyes of the beholder. Many different interpretations can be put on almost anything. You look confused, my poppet. Consider this: Viccars ain't likely to marry a highwayman's wench."

Marguerite did consider this and found her companion's comments much to her liking. One small scruple still troubled her, nonetheless. "But if Viccars finds out I was telling him taradiddles—"

"He won't! Because you ain't." Jeremy removed a large and very elegant handkerchief from another pocket and applied it to his damp brow. "Lady Sherris did go to Newgate. Her woman went in to see that Captain Toby fellow in which Viccars has such an interest. That Captain Toby whose particular had red hair. *And* who ain't yet been caught. Seems to me it might well be Lady Sherris as any other red-haired wench that helped him escape. Not that you'll say so to Viccars. You'll tell him what you saw and let him figure for himself that two and two make four."

Did two and two add up to four? Marguerite's upbringing had not equipped her to deal successfully with accounts. She thought despairingly of the *post-obit* bills tucked away in her ormolu writing desk. "But I didn't see anything!" she protested. "Jeremy, I think you must be all about in your head."

"The suspicion is mutual," Jeremy retorted crossly. "Do you want my help or not? If so, you'll do as I've suggested. Lady Sherris did go to Newgate and she was seen. But if you've no stomach for the business, you may find another way to keep the wolves from the door. At all events, it's no bread and butter of mine!" He turned with a great flourish of his capes and prepared to make a highly dramatic exit.

Before he could do so, the door opened and Marguerite's maidservant peered into the drawing room. "Oh, ma'am, it's hisself!" The girl gasped. "I seen him comin' up the walk!"

This simple statement of fact put paid to Jeremy's dramatic aspirations. Jeremy had past experience with jealous patrons of beautiful females, and he did not care to have Lord Viccars find him in a tête-à-tête with Marguerite. "Remember what I told you!" he hissed by way of farewell. He fled with the maidservant down the hallway, into the kitchen, and out the back door.

Marguerite rushed to inspect herself critically in the pier glass that hung upon one wall. At last Viccars came to call on her, the brute. No doubt to give her her *congé*. Well, Marguerite was prepared for him. She gave her auburn hair a last tousle, made certain adjustments to her person—unlike Jeremy, Marguerite wasn't the least big overdressed—issued certain instructions to her maidservant, then stretched out languorously upon her settee.

Lord Viccars found her in this posture. He paused on the threshold of the drawing room and feasted his eyes on the spectacle presented by Marguerite. And quite a spectacle she made, with her sleepy eyes and tousled air *à l'abandon*, in a pale muslin gown that clung to her voluptuous body in a manner that made very clear the fact that she wore not a stitch of clothing beneath it. Lord Viccars checked a very strong impulse to rush forward and take her into his arms. No twinge of conscience prompted this forbearance, no reminder of his soon-to-be-married state, but a strong suspicion that, dared he be so bold, he would have his ears boxed. Lord Viccars had not seen his *petite amie* for some time. After all that had transpired in the interim, she would not welcome him back with open arms. Quite the contrary. Lord Viccars was prepared for her to raise the devil of a fuss.

Consequently, Lord Viccars was very surprised when Marguerite rose gracefully from the settee and walked toward him with outstretched hands. "*Mon cher* Andrew. You have come to me at last!" she murmured, and kissed him chastely on the cheek.

Surprised and also suspicious, Lord Viccars caught Marguerite's plump arm. "What's this? No tears, no recriminations?" he asked. "Or have you anticipated this moment and already found someone to take my place?"

"*Au contraire, mon chou,*" Marguerite said reproachfully. "I do not think I can do that. Nor do I wish to say *adieu* to you in such a way. Because of course it must be *adieu*. I know you have tired of my company and now wish me to move out of your house. I have already begun to pack." Sadly, she gestured toward a half-filled box. It was the only half-filled box in the house, but Lord Viccars was not to know that. "What is there in that with which to quarrel? *Hélas*, poor Marguerite has fallen in love, which is very foolish, because she is of the *demi-monde*." A tear trickled down her perfect cheek. "I do not wish that we should part on a quarrel. We did have some happy moments together, *n'est-ce pas*?"

Indeed they had. Lord Viccars wished they might have more. It was unthinkable, of course. He released the smooth arm he had been grasping, absentmindedly caressing, and walked toward the fireplace. "You know, then."

"Oui." Indeed she did know. Marguerite glowered at his lordship's well-tailored back. "You might have prepared me, *mon chou*. It was a dreadful shock. But of course you have been very busy putting your affairs in order." He turned to face her and Marguerite remembered to replace her frown with a sad smile. "Poor Andrew! I wish you every happiness, I truly do. I only hope you have not made a terrible mistake!"

"A mistake?" Lord Viccars had come to this Italian villa prepared to endure Marguerite's ill temper, to coax her out of the sullens if he must. Instead he had been met by smiles and sweet good humor, and it had left him nonplussed. Now, however, he recognized the signs of an imminent wheedle. "How can you say so?" he asked as he leaned against the mantelpiece and prepared to be entertained.

"Should I tell you?" Marguerite was the picture of charming feminine perplexity. "I should not . . . But *mon ami*, I think I must. You will not like it, I fear."

"What won't I like?" he asked with a hint of impatience. "Try if you can to talk without roundaboutation, Marguerite!"

Certainly she could talk without roundaboutation. But would it be to her advantage to do so? Marguerite moved closer to Lord Viccars, close enough so that he could smell her heavy perfume, but not so close that he could reach out and give her a good shake. "My poor, dear friend!" she murmured. "You have been so deceived."

Lord Viccars was not immune to that perfume, or to Marguerite's demurely downcast glance, or to her daring décolletage. She was very near perfection, he realized. "So I have been deceived," he responded. "Somehow you do not astonish me, my dear. I only wonder why you choose to tell me about your indiscretions now, at this point in our relationship."

"*My* indiscretions?" Marguerite opened her eyes wide and angrily stamped her foot. "Pray do not be such a pudding-head! I do not have indiscretions, Andrew. I have *affaires de coeur*, which are quite another thing." With an effort, Marguerite controlled her temper. "I was not talking of myself, Andrew. Here, the girl has brought your brandy. I think you had better drink it and sit down."

This sounded like an excellent notion. Lord Viccars accepted a bumper of diabolino, then settled himself upon a gilded and brocaded chair. In so doing, he was reminded of the jewelers' box that he carried in his coat pocket. It contained his parting gift to Marguerite. But he would not present her with that pretty bauble just yet. Lord Viccars had come here prepared to deal with a hysterical female, and it was curiously deflating to his ego that Marguerite refused to hang around his neck in tears. He had always known her affection was less for his person than his pocketbook, of course. As he had known their paths must part. He did not expect Marguerite to be so philosophical about the business, however. She was up to something, obviously. Lord Viccars was very curious as to what that something might be. "I am seated," he observed. "You had something to impart to me about indiscretions, I believe."

"I do not like to tell you this, Andrew, but I must!" Marguerite sighed. "I do not know how Lady Sherris can have used you in this cruel way. She is infamous beyond description! All things considered, I can hardly think she would make you a proper wife!"

Lord Viccars took another swallow of diabolino, thereby delaying his response. Marguerite referred to

171

Sherry's gaming debts, of course. Andrew experienced renewed amazement that Sherry could have gambled and lost five hundred pounds. No wonder she had feared to apply to Sir Christopher for funds to redeem her vowels. Andrew wished she had experienced a similar reticence as concerned himself. But she had not, and he felt honor-bound to help her, would take her the funds this very night and extort from her a promise that she would refrain from further play. How little he knew the woman he was about to marry! Andrew would have thought Sherry was the last lady to succumb to the lure of cards.

"How did you find out?" he asked.

Marguerite experienced a great relief that Lord Viccars had taken the news so well. "One cannot dispute the evidence of one's own eyes, *mon chou*!"

So one could not. Marguerite and Lady Sherry had met over the gaming tables, then? Lord Viccars's imagination boggled at the thought. "Good God, all of London must know!" he said. "Everyone but me. Are you sure of this, Marguerite? If I find out that you are libeling a perfectly innocent female—"

"How cruel you are!" cried Marguerite, before Lord Viccars could complete his ominous threat. "To accuse me of such unkindness when I only wish for you the best. And that female is *not* the best, Andrew, though I say so when I should not. But you will not believe me. Like all men, you see what you wish to see and then you belabor us poor females because you have been deceived." But why the deuce was she giving him such good advice? Marguerite wanted Lord Viccars to be deceived. In an effort to secure his cooperation, she burst into tears.

"The devil!" said Lord Viccars. Like many other strong men, he disliked to see a female reduced to tears. "What are you crying about, Marguerite? I'm the one who's been hoodwinked. Perhaps it's not so very bad. After all, it's early days yet.''

What Lord Viccars meant, of course, was that Lady Sherry's gambling fever might be nipped in the bud. But since Marguerite knew nothing of Sherry's supposed lust for play, she thought that Andrew was being very tolerant of his fianceée's profligacy. Or perhaps Marguerite had not made it clear just how low Lady Sherry had sunk in depravity? She could not be sure. This conversation was very hard going, and Andrew was proving very stubborn. Marguerite was getting a headache.

''Oh!'' she said, and pressed her hands to her throbbing temples. ''You do not understand. Lady Sherris . . . *Oh, la vache!* I know the truth, Andrew. One redhead is as good as another for you, even if it belongs to a highwayman's doxy!''

Andrew stared at his *petite amie*. Never had he seen her so overwrought. Then the impact of her words struck him. The highwayman! ''Captain Toby?'' He gasped.

At last he understood. Marguerite felt giddy with relief. She also felt a trifle guilty at thus maligning a perfectly innocent female. But it was too late now to make a clean breast of things. Much too late, thought Marguerite, remembering the *post-obit* bills in her writing desk. Sadly, crying all the harder, she nodded her head.

Lord Viccars stared at those auburn curls. He felt as though someone had served him a painful, upperhanded blow. He had not trusted Marguerite, exactly, but he had not thought either that she would set about intriguing with a highwayman right under his nose. Or not beneath his nose, because he had not been around much of late. He supposed this wretched business was partially his fault. Had he not been so neglectful, Marguerite might not have wandered so far astray. ''My dear,'' he said somewhat helplessly as he set aside his brandy glass and rose from his chair.

He was crushed, of course. Marguerite allowed herself to be enveloped in his embrace. She would provide him comfort now, in his hour of need, and he would be so grateful that he would pay off all of her wretched debts. But how strange. Lord Viccars was stroking her bare shoulders as if it was she who was in need of comforting. And, moreover, it felt very good. Marguerite shrugged off this puzzle and gave herself up to his caress.

Poor girl! thought Lord Viccars. Marguerite lived for pleasure and the good things of this world, and he was saddened by his realization of how far she'd been led astray by a handsome, feckless rogue—and here perhaps it should be explained that Lord Viccars had taken Marguerite's comments about Captain Toby's red-haired doxy to refer to herself. The human brain is a marvelous instrument, with great capacities for staunch beliefs and leaps of faith. But there are limits to human credulity, after all. Andrew had found it difficult to imagine Lady Sherry at the gaming tables. For him to comprehend the notion of her association with a highwayman was nigh impossible. Marguerite, however, was a filly of an entirely different color. Lord Viccars had long experience of her imprudence. But he had misjudged her. He had thought she sought to cut a wheedle. Instead she had confided in him for the first time in all their acquaintance, and he was touched.

Confided in him? Good God! Andrew had confided in Sir Christopher not many days ago, had passed along information that might lead to the arrest of Captain Toby's light-o'-love. Lord Viccars drew Marguerite closer, appalled by thought of so frail and fair a barque languishing in Newgate.

It must not happen. Marguerite must not be sent to jail. Andrew must prevent that happening somehow. But what was he to do? He would visit the tavern he had told Christopher about, Andrew decided, and try to find the fellow who had bragged in his cups that he knew precious all there was to know about a certain red-haired wench.

Nor would Lord Viccars tell Marguerite how close she stood even now to betrayal and the gallows. If he were to lose her, and in such a manner . . . Lord Viccars groaned aloud and buried his face in her sweet-smelling auburn curls.

Chapter Twenty

London was a city of many diversions: concerts and picture exhibitions, shops displaying every manner of goods, the theater. At Drury Lane this evening, a family party had been got up. Lady Childe and Sir Christopher were present, along with Lady Sherry and Lord Viccars and his sister Sarah-Louise.

It was not a happy gathering. Indeed, the entire party seemed to be under the influence of low spirits, with the exception of Sarah-Louise, who was very curious as to why everyone had fallen into the dismals. Not surprisingly, no one offered her enlightenment on this score. Lady Childe did not explain that her presence was occasioned only by a grim determination to see that Sherris should do nothing to jeopardize her prospective union with Lord Viccars. Nor did Sir Christopher voice his dislike of the theater in general, and especially of this theater, which had burned to the ground some time before and had recently been rebuilt. He was present only to keep his Livvy company—what a brave creature she was, determined to spoil no one's pleasure even if she was so indisposed!—and to bear her and his unborn heir to safety in case of another fire breaking out.

Sir Christopher's sister's motives were a great deal less noble; she had come to collect the five hundred pounds from her fiancé. And as for Lord Viccars, he was present because the outing had been his idea in the first place. Not the best of ideas, he thought now as he waited for the interminable evening to draw to a close. How he chafed at sitting through several hours of theatrical entertainment when so many serious matters required his attention. But his betrothal to Lady Sherry was a serious matter also. Andrew was marrying a very superior woman even though his heart was in the keeping of one of the carnal company. If only he had realized this sad state of affairs before he offered for Lady Sherry! He glanced at her red-gold curls and thought despairingly of his *petite amie*. The thought of Marguerite dangling from the gallows had concentrated his affections wonderfully.

Intermission came at last. The gentlemen excused themselves from the box. Lady Childe and Sarah-Louise embarked upon a desultory conversation about actors they had seen.

Lady Sherry did not contribute to this conversation. The smell of the theater was heavy in her nostrils, that suffocating combination of perspiration and stale cloth, theatrical makeup and burning candle wax. The theater was crowded, for the popular Mr. Kean was to appear as Shylock in *The Merchant of Venice* tonight, and Mr. Kean could reduce an audience to silence or tears or rouse them into a frenzy almost at will. Sherry glanced around at the neighboring boxes, which were filled with representatives of royalty and the Quality and the *demimonde*; at the wits and squires, *beaux* and bullies jammed uncomfortably together on hard wooden benches in the pit; at the abigails and journeymen and cits jostling for position in the gallery.

Everyone seemed very gay, thought Lady Sherry as she listened to the babble of voices. She wished she could join in that general mood. Sherry could not rid herself of the awareness that she had sunk herself quite below reproach. She almost wished she'd taken to the road herself rather than ask Lord Viccars for the money. And then to have to tell him tarradiddles as to why she needed it . . . Association with a highwayman had obviously not elevated the tone of Sherry's mind. Yes, and her willpower was little more commendable. Sherry could not keep Micah from her thoughts. Since it was not Micah in Newgate, who languished there in his stead? How had such a mixup come about? Surely someone must have realized that the wrong man had been arrested! But Tully had said there was a resemblance. Few people in Newgate would know Micah as well as they did. And where *was* Micah if not in jail? Surely he would not let another man hang in his place!

The gentlemen returned to the box then, distracting Sherry from these thoughts. Sir Christopher immediately joined in the theatrical conversation, allowing that his own favorites were Elliston the comedian and Grimaldi the clown. Frowning, Lord Viccars resumed his seat beside Lady Sherry. "You are very quiet this evening, Andrew," she murmured. "Are you angry with me?"

Lord Viccars frowned all the harder at this suggestion. Rather, Lady Sherry should be angry with him, he thought. But she was blissfully unaware of the alteration that had taken place in his sentiments. "Why should I be angry?" he countered irritably. "Forgive me if I have been neglecting you, but I have many things on my mind."

"Oh, no! Pray think nothing of it!" Sherry wished her fiancé would continue to ignore her, because then she wouldn't have to talk to him. Not that she disliked talking to Lord Viccars, but it was difficult to concentrate on commonplace nonsense when there were very important things to contemplate. Such as a certain sum of money. "Andrew, I do not mean to tease you, but did you bring the''—she glanced cautiously at the other members of the party—''er?''

The er? What the devil was Sherry prattling on about? Then Andrew recalled her gambling debts and his five hundred pounds. ''I have,'' he said sternly. ''But in return I must have your word that this will be an end to your—'' He, too, glanced at the others. ''You know! I am very surprised at you, my dear. Yes, and disappointed, too. But I do not mean to scold you! You will know better in the future, I know.''

Sherry did not respond but meekly bowed her head. She supposed she deserved to be catechized and sermonized in this odious way. Deserving a thing, however, did not make it easier to bear. Nor did Sherry relish her growing suspicion that the man she had contracted herself to marry was a crashing bore. How unfair she was! Andrew meant his advice for the best. And good advice it would have been, moreover, had gambling been her vice.

Lord Viccars interpreted his companion's silence as abashment. ''We'll speak no more of it!'' he said even as he wondered what life would be like shared with someone so submissive. Marguerite would have wept in such an instance or attempted to cajole him into a more accepting mood. Andrew would miss those cajoleries. They had had their price, of course. Many were the expensive baubles he'd fastened around that lovely throat. The throat that was now threatened by the hangman's noose. ''Has your brother said anything more to you about that highwayman?'' he asked with studied nonchalance.

''What highwayman?'' inquired Lady Sherry with equal offhandedness. Why was Andrew so interested? Did he suspect the use she meant to make of his five hundred pounds? But how could he? ''You mean Cap-

179

tain Toby? No, not a word. The man's been captured and will hang. I suppose there's little more to tell.''

Sarah-Louise had been blatantly eavesdropping on this conversation, which she thought very strange. Her brother and Lady Sherris were the most lukewarm lovers Sarah-Louise had ever seen. She was pleased to hear them mention Captain Toby, thereby giving her the opportunity to abandon the theatrical conversation, which had grown a trifle dull.

"Oh! Captain Toby!" cried Sarah-Louise. "What an interesting rogue, to be sure! We should have a new play about a highwayman, I vow. It would be vastly popular. Perhaps you should write it, Lady Sherris! The hero will be a very handsome fellow who ran through a considerable estate by gambling, then took up the profession of the road. He will be very gallant, never taking from his victims quite everything they own—none of this 'your money or your honor' business for our lad. Nor will he kill without good reason or ravish nuns. But he *will* console distraught widows, of course; females will flock around him like moths to the flame because of his handsome face. Eventually one female, jealous of the others, will betray him, which gives us an excellent opportunity to bring a gallows onto the stage. The tension will mount—ladies in the audience will swoon— and then, at the very last moment . . .'' She snapped her fingers. "Our hero will be reprieved!"

"Oh, bravo!" cried Lavinia, who had enjoyed this nonsense very well. "You should write it yourself!"

Sarah-Louise laughed. "I have not the discipline, as anyone can tell you; I am a useless creature, indolent as a butterfly. Oh, look, Andrew, there is Cissy.'' She wriggled her fingers at a nearby box. "She has snagged Grenville, the wretch. There will be no bearing her now that she has that feather in her cap. Even though she *wouldn't* have it if he were not a distant connection of her husband's family. Strange to find a man with such a history with a reclusive streak."

Talk of feathers in caps could not fail to interest Lavinia. As the daughter of a duke, she had a social position to maintain. "Grenville?" she echoed, craning her neck so that she might see into Lady Cecilia's box. "I thought Grenville died."

"Oh, yes!" Sarah-Louise chuckled. "I did not mean that his shade walks among us. Although if he could, he probably would; the old man had a positive lust for life from all accounts. Do not frown at me, Andrew. You know there is an eccentric streak, to put it no higher, in that family. We are not children here, and lust is definitely the correct word. It was well known that no serving wench was safe from old Grenville, not even the servants in his own house."

"Disgraceful," murmured Lavinia. Child she may not have been, but she had no liking for conversations as frank as this. "But there was some problem with the succession, was there not? The absence of an heir?"

Sarah-Louise nodded. "Old Grenville's son was killed on the Peninsula. The title has passed to the cadet branch of the family now, and I suspect old Lord Grenville must be turning in his grave. It's Cissy's belief the old man stayed alive as long as he did in an effort to prevent that disaster taking place." She glanced quizzically at Lady Sherry. "Perhaps you might be interested in his story. It is not as good as a moldering castle—although the family owns the next best thing, an ancient mansion near Cavendish Square—but very interesting, nonetheless!" Without waiting for an answer, she gestured imperiously toward her sister's box.

Truth be told, Lady Sherry had scant wish to make the acquaintance of the current Lord Grenville. She had been told before of stories that must fire her writer's imagination and had found them uniformly tedious. But

181

she supposed she must make a show of interest since Sarah-Louise obviously meant to be kind. Sherry prepared herself to be civil to the man who appeared in the doorway to their box. She glanced up—and stared.

He was tall and muscular, swarthy of complexion, with dark hair and eyes that were very green. His clothing was well cut and elegant in an understated manner, and he walked with the aid of a cane. This impediment was the result of a riding accident, explained Sarah-Louise, an accident that had kept Lord Grenville from coming forth sooner to claim his inheritance. Lord Grenville, she admitted, was something of an adventurer and had spent many years exploring exotic lands and strange climes.

Lord Grenville smiled. "You exaggerate," he protested. "The truth of the matter is that I am the black sheep of the family."

Sarah-Louise tapped his arm with her fan. "Whatever you may call yourself, sir, you tell a rousing good tale! Come let me make you known to Lady Sherris Childe, who will be very interested. But I warn you, be careful not to be *too* interesting or you may find that she has put you in a book."

He limped forward and bent over Sherry's hand as Sarah-Louise performed the formal introductions. "Lady Sherris," he murmured, "I am charmed. I have long been a great fan of your books."

The wretch! How dare he appear so brazenly in the box and speak to her, play off his games in front of a magistrate? Sherry tried very hard not to look confounded. "I did not know," she responded tartly, "that my little stories had such a wide readership that you might find them in even, er, exotic climes!"

He released her hand. "Oh, yes, Lady Sherris! I daresay you would be surprised at how very diverse your readership is. I am especially looking forward to your current novel, which I hear concerns a highwayman.''

A highwayman! Now he was so bold as to walk up to her and speak of highwaymen! Andrew interrupted them with a question, saving Sherry from having to make a reply. As unobtrusively as possible, she stared at Lord Grenville—also known as Captain Toby and Micah Greene. Her thoughts were in a whirl. She was relieved beyond measure to see Micah hale and unfettered by the shackles of the law, and at the same time she wished to box his ears. What did he mean, parading himself like this for all the world to see? Didn't he realize that he might be recognized? But perhaps in his very boldness lay safety. Who would expect a highwayman to pose as a peer of the realm?

Intermission ended then, and Lord Grenville returned to Lady Cecilia's box, and the members of Lord Viccars's party turned their attention to the stage in anticipation of enjoying Mr. Kean's performance as Shylock. Mr. Kean did not disappoint. He paced and declaimed; he was impulsive, animated, passionate; he transcended his small stature and sallow, ugly face and became the role that he played. His harsh voice cracked like thunder, turned gentle as a kitten's purr. His eyes were fierce, frightful, melting—it was said that small, ugly Mr. Kean could express as much in a few moments as most actors could in a night.

The audience responded with almost hysterical enthusiasm. Sarah-Louise clapped her hands and shouted as enthusiastically as if she'd been sitting with her servants in the gallery. Even Lavinia forgot about her queasiness and Andrew about his *petite amie*, and Sir Christopher conceded that this evening's entertainment had been a bit of all right.

Only Lady Sherry was lukewarm in her response, but this was not in response to any histrionic lack in the great Mr. Kean. Sherry's thoughts were still of Micah, and her attention was more for him than for the actors on the stage. What a rogue he was! No doubt he would lay claim to a fair portion of the Grenville fortune and then disappear. He could not expect to carry off the imposture indefinitely. Yes, and if Micah was here, looking for all the world like the peer of the realm to whose inheritance he'd laid claim, then who languished in Newgate in his place?

Chapter Twenty-one

Lady Sherry retired to her book room early the next morn, inspired by these recent developments not to put pen to paper on behalf of Ophelia and Captain Blood but to drop her chin into her hands and stare gloomily into space. In this pursuit she was interrupted by Daffodil, who entered the book room without so much as a knock. For this rudeness she may be forgiven: Daffodil's attention and energy were entirely taken up in trying to exercise some degree of control over a large, exuberant, and very dirty hound.

"Good God!" cried Lady Sherry, trying to fend off the beast, which seemed determined to knock her off her chair. "Wherever did he come from, Daffodil?"

"Dashed if I know." Daffodil gasped as she grasped the dog's plumed tail and yanked in an effort to persuade him against crawling into Lady Sherry's lap. "He turned up in the garden this morning. What's more, milady, Ned did not!"

"Yes, and I'm glad to see you, too!" Sherry tried, not entirely successfully, to fend off Prinny's great damp tongue. What advice had Micah given her about controlling him? That it all depended on the tone of voice? Sherry made her own voice very stern. "Oh, do get down, you wretched beast!" To her surprise, the dog obeyed her, left off his demonstration of affection, and strolled across the room to collapse upon the settee.

Lady Sherry then returned her attention to her abigail. "Why *should* Ned have been in the garden?" she asked. "He's not a gardener; he's a groom."

"I know what Neddy is!" Daffodil retorted irritably. "None better! Even though I would rather not. He should've been in the garden because he always *is* in the garden at that time of day."

Lady Sherry contemplated her abigail's pink cheeks. "I see," she said. "The pair of you enjoy a little stroll together around the garden before embarking upon the arduous duties of the day."

"Something like that, milady." Daffodil saw no need to explain that those gentle strolls were generally not strolls at all and took place in the gardener's shed. "But he wasn't there today, nor is he anywhere else to be found. No one's seen hide nor hair of him since yesterday. You'd given him the evening off, and he set out for that boozing ken he's partial to and never did come back."

"You're certain?" asked Lady Sherry. Daffodil vigorously nodded her head. Her source of information was unimpeachable, she claimed.

"Something's happened to him!" she added. "I know it. Neddy was mighty wishful of getting a hold of that money. He wouldn't play least-in-sight when he knew there was a chance of him getting paid."

Lady Sherry had to agree with her abigail's assessment of the situation. "It's early yet. Perhaps he drank more than was wise and is sleeping off a sore head. He may yet turn up, Daffodil. We'll wait awhile and see."

Daffodil nodded again, this time less vigorously. "And if he don't turn up, milady?"

Sherry sighed. "Then I suppose we'll have to tell Christopher."

Satisfied, Daffodil left the room and went in search of consolation from her unimpeachable source of information, namely the recently hired footman with the shapely calves. Lady Sherry contemplated Prinny, who was dozing peacefully on the couch. What a strange coincidence that Prinny should appear in one moment and Ned disappear in the next, as if one had turned into the other as in some fairy tale. This was not a fairy tale, of course, and the exchange—however desirable from Sherry's point of view—had not been so pat. Where could Ned have gotten to? Sherry could not think that his disappearance boded well. She wondered if a diabolic spirit might be at work against her. The thought of diabolic spirits recalled to Lady Sherry her current manuscript. In search of distraction from her unhappy thoughts, she reached for paper and pen.

Some time passed. The book room was silent save for the sound of Prinny's snores and the scratching of Sherry's pen. Then a tap sounded at the door. Definitely a diabolic spirit was at work, or else Sherry would not have been interrupted at a moment when she was at last at charity with her manuscript.

"Come in!" she called, assuming that it was Aunt Tulliver who interrupted. "You may help me to decide whether I wish to dispatch Barnabas by way of a particularly nasty poison or whether I prefer to bludgeon him to death with a blunt instrument!"

Aunt Tulliver made no comment. Lady Sherry set down her pen. "Or have you brought word of Ned?" she asked as she turned toward the door. It was not Aunt Tulliver who stood there, or Daffodil, but Micah. He was smiling. "Oh!" cried Lady Sherry, and then flung herself away from the table and into his arms, knocking over her chair in her haste. "You terrible, terrible wretch! To leave us like that! I feared that you'd been captured or were dead!"

Micah responded to this outburst in a most appropriate manner. His arms closed around Sherry. So very close did he hold her that Sherry could hear his heart beating against her breast. He bent his head and kissed her. His embrace was every bit as wonderful as Sherry remembered it, and more. When he would have released her, she put her arms around his shoulders and drew his face down to her again.

Prinny regarded these proceedings through one half-opened eye. He had been wakened from his nap by the sound of Lady Sherry's chair crashing to the floor. It was very bad of his friends to wake him, but he knew how exciting these reunions could be. Prinny supposed he should add his own little bit of welcome. He lumbered down from the settee and, tail awag, padded across the floor. When his friends continued to ignore him, he inserted his head between them and emitted a reproachful *whuff*.

Sherry was thus recalled to the present by a damp, cold canine nose. "I suppose we are to thank you for bringing the beast back. Or perhaps for taking him in the first place. Why ever did you? I cannot imagine that he facilitated your escape."

"Facilitated? Hardly." Micah brushed a stray curl off her cheek. "And I did not take him with me willingly. He gave me no choice in the matter. It has been most interesting, lying low in London accompanied by a great brute of a hound."

Sherry smiled, amused by the vision thus conjured. "I thought perhaps I had imagined you last night. That perhaps you weren't truly there at the theater. That perhaps there was a slight resemblance, which I magnified in my mind—that I had turned lunatic! But it is you who are lunatic! How dare you walk in here so boldly? Don't you realize what a risk you run? What if you are caught? I believe one can be hanged for impersonating a peer! Not that it will signify to you, since you have already been sentenced to that end. Apropos of which, just who *is* that man in Newgate?''

Micah left off scratching Prinny's ears, limped to the bookshelves, and removed the decanter. ''Ah! So you went to visit me,'' he said, and smiled.

Sherry accepted a glass of port. Never had she felt so great a need for a restorative. ''Tully went to see you,'' she retorted. Reason had asserted itself over emotion now, and Sherry didn't mention her own part in that fruitless expedition to Newgate. ''What are you calling yourself now? What am I to call you? Lord Grenville or Captain Toby?''

He moved toward the library table, glanced at the manuscript strewn there. ''Micah will do. You've been working on your book.''

Sherry watched him. How she had worried about this man. Now she was made cross to see him sound in body, if not in mind. She supposed gloomily that she might have trusted herself to fall in love with a madman. ''Micah, what the *devil* are you up to?'' she cried. ''When you were introduced to me as Grenville, I was so startled I almost gave you away.''

Micah's attention was on the manuscript. ''You would not do that.''

How sure he was of her. Sherry conceded that he had reason. She could hardly kiss a man as she had Micah and then turn him over to be hanged. ''Perhaps not,'' she said. ''But others might. Surely this Grenville person must be known to someone.''

''I shouldn't think so. He's been out of the country.'' Micah gestured toward the manuscript. ''If you want my advice—''

''I don't!'' retorted Sherry. What good to her was the advice of a man of obscure origins and doubtful morals, who had abandoned a career on the high toby to embark upon an imposture that would allow him to squander yet

189

another fortune, and this one not his own? "What have you done with Ned?"

"Ned?" Micah raised his brows. "Who is Ned?"

"You really don't know, do you?" Sherry sank down onto a chair. "Ned is my groom, and now he's disappeared. I can almost be grateful for it, since I had to borrow five hundred pounds from— But never mind that now! The wretch knew that we had hidden you here and demanded to be paid off."

Micah was frowning now. "You mentioned none of this. And now this groom has disappeared? With five hundred pounds?"

"No. That is one consolation, at least." Sherry wondered what Andrew would say if she returned his money and claimed to have been mistaken about her gambling debt. He would probably think that *she* was a lunatic. "That is what makes it so very strange. Ned knew I was to have the money from—er, last night. But he has not shown up to claim his prize. One cannot help but fear foul play."

Micah sipped his port. "One might say that he deserved to meet with foul play."

"One might!" snapped Lady Sherry. "I, however, am neither an impostor nor a thief, and though I would be perfectly happy to never set eyes on Ned again, I wouldn't wish him a penny of the worst of any ill wishes on my part. Oh, let us not quarrel! I do not mean to rip up at you, Micah, but all this has been a trifle much to bear!"

If Micah was angered by Sherry's unflattering assessment of his character, no sign of it appeared on his swarthy face. "I should think all this has been hard on you," he said. "You should have told me the man was blackmailing you. I would have gotten you the money to buy him off. It seems a fair enough exchange for the safety of my neck."

And where would Micah have gotten the money? From whom would he have stolen it? More than a table's width separated them, Sherry realized. They stood on opposite sides of the law. True, her own recent actions had not been entirely aboveboard, but those minor transgressions had been fraught with guilt, an emotion to which Micah would be alien.

"You got the money from Viccars. He's not the man for you, you know." Micah tapped Sherry's manuscript. "He doesn't have an ounce of adventure in his soul."

Sherry suspected that this assessment of her fiancé was uncomfortably close to the mark. Micah was a shrewd judge of character. Such astuteness must be a great asset to him in his adventurer's career. "I suspect I've enough adventure in my soul to do for both of us," she said dryly.

"My love." Micah moved around the table and caught her by the wrist. "You don't know what adventure is. You would like to, I think, but you're afraid. And so you write your books. If you marry Viccars, you will continue to long for adventure. But you will not mention your longing to him, for fear he would be shocked—and you're correct; he *would* be shocked—and he will not supply it to you, and you will both be unhappy, which will be very sad."

Sherry thought this encounter was very sad. "You seem to know a great deal about Lord Viccars," she said gravely. "Yet you have barely met."

"I've known a hundred like Viccars." Micah stroked his thumb against Sherry's waist. "They are no more adventurous even when they travel abroad."

Almost Sherry believed that Micah *had* traveled abroad, so sincere was his voice. She reminded herself that it was folly to trust the rogue. But trust him or no, Sherry wanted very much for him to kiss her again.

There was at least that much adventure in her soul. She pushed back her chair, stood up, and touched her fingers to his swarthy face, his dark curls. He pressed his lips to the back of her wrist. Prinny, who had been watching this exchange with a somewhat jaded eye—Prinny had no great appreciation of affection lavished on any other than himself—sighed and resumed his nap upon the settee in anticipation of more of the same.

Nor was Prinny mistaken. For a time, the book room knew no other sound than the lovers' breaths and sighs. Then a tap came at the door, and Daffodil entered the room without waiting for a response. "Coo!" she said, upon witnessing her mistress caught up in a highwayman's embrace. No wonder Lady Sherry had called the rogue a flirt. But what was well and good for the maid was not equally so for the mistress. Daffodil didn't think she approved. "Begging your pardon, milady, I'm sure! And yours, my fine gentleman. Milord Captain Toby, is that what we're to call you now? And if I may suggest as shouldn't, you might be wishful of leaving before her highness returns to the house!"

Micah nodded, finding this an excellent suggestion. He had already been informed of Lady Childe's absence before he mounted the stairs. "We'll meet again soon," he said as he clasped Sherry's hands.

She shook her head. Oh, why in this of all moments did she have to remember that Micah had been so discerning as to call Lavinia a prune? How she would miss him. But honor decreed that she must either break off her betrothal or banish Micah from her life. And common sense informed her that there was no future for her with a highwayman. Sherry did not wish to cause damage to Andrew's heart such as that which had already been done to hers. "We must not meet again," she said. "Must I remind you that I am to be married soon?"

"Married?" Micah arched his brows. "What has

passed between us does not signify, then? I had not thought you such a coward, my love. Or such a peagoose! I'll find my own way out. But be warned: We'll talk of this again!'' Before she could speak, he strode from the room.

Lady Sherry stared woefully after him. ''Oh, the devil!'' she cried, then repaired to the settee and gathered up a startled Prinny in her arms.

Daffodil surveyed her mistress's stricken posture and the tears that streamed down her face and dripped onto Prinny's startled head. ''Here's a pretty kettle of fish!'' Daffodil sighed. ''I don't blame you, milady, for being moped. And I don't like to tell you that things have gone from bad to worse. But they have, milady, so buck up, do! Neddy's been kidnapped! Three men bundled him into a carriage and drove him off!''

Chapter Twenty-two

Lady Childe was in fine fettle, having felt in sufficient trim to sally forth and enjoy a comfortable and catty coze with her two bosom bows. Neither Lady Throckmorton nor the Countess Dunsany had thus far produced offspring of her own, and so Lavinia was privileged to receive their envious congratulations with good grace. To receive also their congratulations on the fast-approaching nuptials that would remove the disruptive Lady Sherris from Lavinia's house. To that house Lavinia returned then, in anticipation of sharing a cold collation with her spouse. Sir Christopher had recently fallen into the habit of returning to Longacre House at midday to ensure that all was well with his adorable little wife.

They met in the dining room, where they enjoyed a tête-à-tête. No sooner did Lavinia realize that Sherris and Aunt Tulliver were not putting in an appearance than she dismissed the servants, saying that she and Sir Christopher would wait on themselves. And so they did. Lavinia sliced her husband's roast beef for him, and he popped hothouse grapes one by one into her pretty mouth. During these proceedings, a great deal of nonsense was uttered, as can be imagined. Lavinia flirted outrageously with her spouse, who in turn loaded her with caresses and declared himself the most fortunate fellow in all of London—nay, in all England, if not the world! And now she was to provide him with an heir, who would, of course, have her good looks and personality, who would be a pattern card of perfection, no doubt.

His Livvy had recovered her spirits, and Sir Christopher wished more than anything to withdraw with her abovestairs for a resumption of those most pleasurable activities that had already led to the getting of an heir.

He cleared his throat, then broached the suggestion. "Would you care to retire to our room, my dear? For a spot of . . . you know!"

Lavinia stared. "Really, Christopher!" she said in shocked tones. "How can you mention such a thing to me! God bless my soul, it's the middle of the day! What would the servants think?"

Sir Christopher didn't give a damn for his servants just then. His ardor had been sparked by Lavinia's sighs and smiles, his passions enflamed by the uninhibited manner in which she had allowed him to feed her grapes. Now he was not to be put off by any missishness. "I don't give a button about the servants! They ain't paid to think!" he announced, and took his wife roughly into his arms.

Some women might have thrilled to such treatment and to the knowledge of their powers to excite thus. Lavinia was not among them. She thought only that Christopher was messing up her pretty gown. "Oh, do be careful!" she cried crossly. "You'll have the cloth off the table and the dishes in our lap. For heaven's sake, Christopher, do stop *pawing* at me! I have no intention of allowing you to ravish me in my own dining room, and this wretched chair is hurting my back!"

Not astonishingly, these harsh words had a dampening effect. Sir Christopher released his wife and sat back in his chair. "I beg pardon if I have offended you," he said stiffly. " 'Twas not my intent."

Of course it had not been his intent. Despite her instinctive dismayed reaction to the notion of pursuing such activities in broad daylight, Lavinia knew her spouse had not intended to offend. As for what he had intended . . . Well, Lavinia had no objection to such activities when set about in the proper manner, undertaken in the privacy of the marital bed under cover of night. Not that she had the words, or boldness, to express these feelings. "There's a time and a place for everything," she said.

So there was, and this obviously wasn't it. Intending to return to his magisterial duties, Sir Christopher pushed back his chair. But before he could rise from the table, the door was flung open and Lady Sherry stepped across the threshold. "Christopher," she said. "I must speak with you!"

There was in Lady Sherry's appearance much upon which to speculate. Her face was ashen save for the splotch of hectic color that burned in each cheek; her red-gold curls were disheveled, as if she'd run her fingers carelessly through them not once but many times. There was a manic glitter in her eye. And another time, Lavinia might have remarked these details well, might have speculated on them with relish across the teacups with the ladies Throckmorton and Dunsany. But today Lavinia did not accord her sister-in-law a great deal of attention, because Prinny accompanied Lady Sherry into the dining room.

Lavinia's emotions at this first sight of her pet were complex. "Oh, my God!" she cried. "When did *he* come back?" Any further questions Lavinia might have had were forestalled by Prinny himself. The hound was no sooner made aware of his mama's presence in the dining room than nothing would do for him but to lick her face.

Lavinia wanted her face licked no more now than she

ever had and sought discreetly to push the dog away. Since she had kicked up such a dust about the beast's disappearance, she could hardly reveal her disgust of him now. Then a reprieve presented itself to her. "The baby!" She gasped as the dog tried to crawl into her lap.

"Prinny! Get down from there at once!" snapped Lady Sherry, who, it must be confessed, had not only been aware of Lavinia's dilemma but had observed the reunion with a certain perverse delight. To Lavinia's amazement, the dog obeyed and flopped down on the floor at Sherry's feet. "He appeared in the garden this morning," Sherry continued. "Apparently he thought better of having run away and decided to return home. We must all keep a closer watch on him to make sure the wanderlust does not come upon him again. In your condition, Lavinia, it is not good for you to be upset!"

In Lavinia's condition, it was not good for her to be baited in this manner. Impotently, she glared. Feeling as if she had somewhat evened the score between them, Sherry turned to her brother. Was she doing the right thing? Sherry didn't know. There seemed no other course of action open to her now. If Ned had been kidnapped, it was for a reason. Sherry couldn't doubt what that reason was. Had Ned not claimed that others would buy his information if Sherry did not? Sherry had thought he referred to Lavinia, but apparently the groom had strewn his lures further afield. Nor could Sherry delude herself concerning Ned's loyalty. He would not only let the cat out of the bag; he would shout the news from the rooftops if by so doing he could prevent damage to his own precious skin.

Christopher was frowning, and Lavinia looked as though her curiosity had been aroused. It would accomplish nothing to delay the moment further now. Sherry took in a deep breath. "Chris, I must talk to you," she said. "Alone, if you don't mind."

Sir Christopher didn't mind. He was concerned about his sister's distraught appearance and out of charity with his wife. "Livyy, if you will excuse us?" he murmured with a pointed glance at the door. Lavinia flushed, but she voiced no protest, merely pushed back her chair from the table and exited the room with great dignity. Lavinia's lack of comment did not deceive Sir Christopher; he knew she was in a snit. He also thought that it served her right. This interruption of their tête-à-tête would not have occurred had Livvy acceded to his request and accompanied him upstairs.

Too, he was genuinely concerned about his sister. "You look like the devil, Sis!" he said bluntly. "What's amiss?"

Sherry walked to the door and closed it firmly after nudging Prinny out into the hall. Then she turned back to her brother. "Chris, I'm afraid I'm in the devil of a fix!"

How serious she made it sound. Sir Christopher could not help but be amused. But he knew how females took these little crises to heart. "It cannot be so very bad as that!" he said kindly. "Come, sit here beside me and tell me all about it, and we'll decide how best to fix it up all right and tight!"

Lady Sherry sat down on Lavinia's abandoned chair and plucked a grape off the plate. "I don't think it *can* be fixed up all right and tight!" She sighed. "It's much more likely that you'll be visiting me in Newgate, Chris!"

Sir Christopher still failed to grasp the seriousness of the situation. Indeed, he chuckled. "You and Viccars had a lovers' quarrel, is that it? You'll patch it up, I promise. Why, Livvy and I quarreled any number of times, and look at us now!" It occurred to Sir Christo-

198

pher that he and his Livvy were currently not on the very best of terms, and he continued hastily. "And if you don't patch it up, crying off ain't a hanging offense yet!"

Lady Sherry did not immediately respond. Or if she did, it was in too low a tone to be audible to Lavinia's keen ear, which was currently applied to the dining-room door. And, for the record, Lavinia was not half so misled as her spouse. She knew perfectly well that Sherry's trouble was serious. What she did not know was which of a number of grievous sins Sherry had committed. Lavinia thought it behooved her to find out.

In this undertaking, Lavinia was not assisted by Prinny, who took advantage of her stooped posture to try to lavish further caresses on her face. Lavinia's attempts to prevent him doing so further interfered with her attention to the confidences underway in the dining room. "Oh, get away from me, you wretched beast!" she hissed, and swatted at the hound—ineffectively, as it turned out, because hers was not the tone of voice in which Prinny understood commands.

Lady Sherry, meanwhile, was having an equally unpleasant encounter. Though Lavinia was experiencing difficulties in hearing Sherry's confidences, Sir Christopher had not, a circumstance that caused him to wear a dreadful scowl. Amiable creature that he was, Christopher took very seriously his responsibilities as concerned the law. He respected the law immensely, be it in need of reform or not. And now to discover that his own sister had committed an appalling number of criminal acts . . . He looked at her with severe approbation and expressed a conviction that she had windmills in her head.

"I think I must have." Lady Sherry sighed. "But I meant it for the best. And now, with Ned's disappearance, and Viccars, and Grenville . . . I am at my wit's end, Chris. I am sorry to involve you in all this. I am sorry to have involved myself in it! But I didn't know what else to do."

"There, there, don't cry!" Sir Christopher pleaded as he wished he had had his luncheon elsewhere. "You did right to come to me. You should have done so sooner! After that fellow first accosted you. 'Pon rep, how could you ask Viccars for a loan of money? What must he have thought, Sis?"

How could Sherry have *what*? Lavinia by this time was seated plump on the floor with her ear as close to the door as permitted by the eye she had affixed to the keyhole. She had given up attempting to fend off Prinny's demonstrations of affection for the moment, deeming it better to endure his wet tongue than to miss what was going on between her husband and his sister.

"Viccars?" That word, at least, was clear and spoken by Sir Christopher. "This is a bad business, Sis. Viccars had a bit of information about the highwayman's doxy, which he passed along to me. Seemed to have a notion you'd be pleased if the rascal was brought to justice. Seemed to think you might wish a word with him."

"Good God!" responded Lady Sherry faintly. "Andrew thought that?"

"Seems that Viccars had wind of some jackanapes who talked whilst in his cups," added Sir Christopher. "And not of cabbages and kings. Well, puss, this is a fine pickle you've gotten yourself into. If that fellow was to tell what he knows—"

"I know." Sherry sighed. "That's why I decided to buy him off."

"You should have come to me." Sir Christopher's voice was stern. "There was no need to be bringing strangers into the business. Not that Viccars is a stranger, but you know what I mean."

"I do know." Could Sherris be weeping? Lavinia

200

applied her eye to the keyhole once again. "But I hated to involve you, Chris. A man in your position. And Lavinia . . ." Her voice trailed off.

"There, there!" Sir Christopher took his sister into his arms and awkwardly patted her. "We'll see this thing through somehow. Blood's thicker than water, after all. Don't fret your head about Livvy, because I'll deal with her."

So he'd deal with Lavinia, would he? In that moment, Lavinia felt strongly like bursting into the dining room and demanding a full explanation of the queer remarks she'd overheard. It sounded very much like Sherris had become involved in some disgraceful escapade the nature of which Lavinia had no clue, save that Lord Vicars was concerned. Could it be . . . ? Stricken in the act of rising by a dreadful suspicion, Lavinia clutched at the doorjamb for support. Surely Sherris had not anticipated her marriage vows! Surely Andrew was not so lost to common decency as to connive at such a thing!

Surely she was being foolish. Lavinia drew a deep breath. This was her home. She had a right to march into the dining room and demand an explanation of the rudeness that she had so keenly felt—the rudeness that had caused her to suffer an upheaval of emotion so intense that she must take to her bed. Chris would be sorry then that he had been so cruelly rejecting; anyone with a grain of proper feeling must be. Lavinia adopted an expression so martyred that anyone who glimpsed her must be guilt-stricken, whether they had previously made her acquaintance or not, and laid her hand upon the doorknob.

The knob turned, but the door did not open. It was locked. Lavinia could have wept with vexation. But tears were useless when there was no one to see them. Nor would it accomplish anything to kick the offending door. And so, what was she to do?

Caught up in indecision, Lavinia hovered in the hallway. Prinny watched anxiously. He would have leaped to console his mistress, if only he could have been certain that it was consolation she sought; the expressions that flitted across her pretty face were myriad and diverse. It was difficult to determine whether she was furious or morose. If his mama was unhappy, Prinny could not leave her uncomforted. He gathered up his courage and pressed close.

Alas, this act of affectionate condolence was one unpleasantness too many piled on Lavinia's plate. She cursed in a most unladylike manner and gave Prinny a smart slap. Prinny yelped, less in pain than in surprise. "What the devil?" ejaculated Sir Christopher from behind the closed door. Lavinia didn't care to be discovered in so ignominious a position or to be accused of manhandling her hound. She fled.

Sir Christopher glanced out into the empty-seeming hallway and then back at his sister. "This is a grave business. I won't pretend that it's not. If you don't wish to marry Viccars, then you needn't—indeed, you shouldn't, if the only reason you betrothed yourself to him was to lay hands on five hundred pounds. But you must be the one to explain it all to him, mind. And as for this other business . . . I just had word this morning that your Captain Toby escaped from Newgate sometime yesterday."

"Escaped!" Lady Sherry gasped. "But he was never there! I mean, it wasn't him! Oh, never mind that now."

"I'll do what I can, but in return I'll expect you to testify." So saying, and by so doing inadvertently proving the old saw that eavesdroppers heard no good, Sir Christopher closed the door. Lavinia emerged from the closet in which she'd hidden herself and tottered toward the stairs.

Chapter Twenty-three

Lord Viccars had not been idle. He was resolved to rescue Marguerite from the shadow of the gallows, and therefore had repaired with his faithful valet and coachman to the tavern of which he had apprised Sir Christopher, where a certain fellow who talked more than he should was said to spend a fair amount of time. It was not the sort of tavern Lord Viccars might have enjoyed visiting under other circumstances, not one of the flash cribs around Haymarket that were frequented by pretty horsebreakers and young bloods or one of the brothels near Piccadilly that were much patronized by swells. It was, in Lord Viccars's opinion, a low, vulgar place, and he was glad he'd followed his coachman's advice and ventured there in clothing a great deal less elegant than his usual.

Nor was his visit a short one. Much time elapsed, and much ale was quaffed, before Lord Viccars's quarry appeared, causing much consternation to all concerned, for of course Lord Viccars could not fail to recognize Lady Sherry's groom. Ned's memory proved to be equally excellent, and Lord Viccars was hard-pressed to manufacture an adequate explanation for his presence in such a place. Then Ned proved to have a suspicious streak and was not easily lured outside. But finally the fellow was knocked unconscious by the faithful Briscoe, trussed up by the equally faithful Williams, and tossed into the nondescript carriage that had been hired for the evening's excursion, it being agreed that no good purpose would be served by advertising Lord Viccars's position in the world via the crest emblazoned on his own coach. And then the conspirators encountered their first dilemma. Having caught their quarry, what were they to do with him now? They could hardly take him to Lord Viccars's rooms in the Clarendon without arousing more attention than all of the occupants of the menagerie in the hotel garden combined.

The matter occasioned some discussion. Williams put forth the suggestion that they should repair to Lord Viccars's town house, which was empty save for a caretaker and his wife, where they could interrogate their prisoner without fear of interruption. But Lord Viccars was not enamored of this suggestion. He had drunk a great deal of ale, and consequently was not thinking too clearly, and voiced a strong determination to avoid as long as possible an encounter with the shade of his first wife. Williams and Briscoe did not argue; they, too, remembered that spoiled and strong-minded lady well.

This conversation continued for some time until Williams diffidently pointed out that it might be prudent to leave the scene before someone recalled that Ned had last been seen in their company. On this point, at least, all agreed. Williams and Lord Viccars repaired within the coach, while Briscoe climbed up on his box and took up the reins. Still they had no destination in mind. "Oh, the devil with it!" Lord Viccars, whose ale-induced high spirits were fast being replaced by a sore head, groaned. "We'll take him to Marylebone!" Williams and Briscoe thought this an excellent suggestion. Ned's opinion was not asked.

Thus it came about that Marguerite's maidservant was knocked up in the middle of the night and granted admission to Lord Viccars and Ned. Not that it was so easily accomplished as that, because the startled woman did not recognize Lord Viccars in all his dirt, thought she was on the verge of being molested, and hysterically threatened to call the watch. Lord Viccars managed to identify himself to her before this disaster could transpire and told her not to waken her mistress but to return to her own bed. The woman didn't argue. She knew on what side her bread was buttered and out of whose pocket her wages were paid. She retired to her bedchamber after a quick detour to the kitchen for a quick nip of the cooking sherry as a restorative to her shattered nerves. Briscoe and Williams took their departure also, to return the hired coach and then retire to their own cots.

The fair Marguerite, meanwhile, slept through all these stirring events and did not rise from her bed, as was her custom, until noon. Then she roused and stretched, splashed water on her face and drew a brush carelessly through her curls, slipped into a peignoir and descended the stair in search of tea and toast. But before she could break her fast, she was distracted by a familiar voice issuing from her drawing room.

Viccars? Here? Marguerite moistened her lips, pinched color into her cheeks, tousled her curls, and contemplated returning to her bedroom for her false eyelashes made of mouse skin. But her curiosity was too great. She loosened the ties of her peignoir and stepped across the threshold. "*Mon chou!* But what is this? Why is that man trussed up like a chicken for the pot?"

Viccars spun around. He had slept the remainder of the night on the sofa and had woken with the devil of a head. Consequently, he was feeling very cross with Marguerite, whom he held responsible for all his woes. To have gone to such trouble for her, and then for her to disavow all knowledge . . . "Don't play the innocent with me!" he snapped.

Marguerite failed to see how she could be accused of playing the innocent when her breasts were largely exposed by her peignoir. So exposed, in fact, as to wring from Lord Viccars's captive a glassy-eyed stare. Perhaps he referred to her question. Marguerite supposed she should not doubt her own eyes' evidence. There *was* a man trussed up on her couch, and there was Viccars dressed up like a groom. It was true that no person truly knew another, evidently. Had Marguerite known of her *inamorato*'s proclivities before this, she might have contrived to keep him better entertained. *"Mon Dieu!"* she murmured. "You scold me for gambling, which is nothing compared to this!"

Lord Viccars scowled. His conversation with Ned had thus far availed him nothing, nor had his threats. The groom was as close-mouthed as an oyster. Lord Viccars wished that his *petite amie* shared that trait. He was prevented from telling her so only by the introduction of a fourth person into the drawing room.

Jeremy paused on the threshold, a vision of sartorial elegance in skintight inexpressibles, an exquisitely cut coat worn open to display a rose-colored waistcoat and a snowy cambric shirt, spotless, wonderfully made boots, a wide-brimmed glossy hat, and a white-thorn cane. He raised his quizzing-glass to better take in the startling scene before him. "Viccars. Your servant," he murmured, and executed an elegant bow.

Had Jeremy been his servant, Lord Viccars would have without preamble turned him out into the streets without a reference. This intelligence he managed to convey in a single scornful glance. "I blame you for this, Jeremy," he said bitterly. "You encourage her." He turned away from them, intending to resume his interrogation of Ned.

Jeremy raised a quizzical eyebrow. Marguerite shrugged, an act that brought even Jeremy's supercilious attention to the neckline of her peignoir. But he was considerably more interested in discovering why Lord Viccars was acting like a man who'd gone off his hinges. To that end, he strolled forward and gazed down at the man trussed up on the couch. "Damned if the poor fellow don't look deuced uncomfortable!" he observed. "Perhaps if you was to untie him, he might prove amenable to whatever it is you want him to do."

"Don't act as if you don't know what this is about!" Lord Viccars responded bitterly. "What's to prevent him from making a run for it if I do as you say?"

Jeremy smiled and withdrew a very wicked-looking sword from his cane. "This," he said, and proceeded to use the sword to such good end that Ned was soon unbound. Ned sat up, chafed his wrists. "Now," continued Jeremy, "suppose you tell his lordship here what he wants to know."

Ned gazed unhappily on the sword that Jeremy had failed to sheathe. "I know what I know, and I'll tell what I know, but only for five hundred pounds!"

That sum sounded familiar, Lord Viccars thought. He supposed it must have been the amount he last paid out for Marguerite's gambling debts. In exasperation, he grasped her arm and gave her a shake. "Let us have done with this charade! Have you forgotten that you took me into your confidence, Marguerite?"

She had taken Viccars into her confidence? Marguerite couldn't recall doing such a foolish thing. Surely she could not have told him the extent of her debts! But if not, then why was he so cross? With perplexity, she stared at his lordship's captive. Could the man be one of her creditors? Marguerite didn't think she'd seen him before, and certainly not across the gaming table, because such a bizarre occurrence she must surely recall. "*Ma foi,* Andrew!" she cried. "I do not know this man. Nor do I know what you are talking about!"

"Perhaps that's true." Lord Viccars valiantly elevated his gaze from Marguerite's neckline. "But he certainly knows you."

Ned, too, had been staring at Marguerite's neckline. Now he looked hastily away. "I don't know her!" he protested. This gentleman had already demonstrated a nasty quick temper, if not some degree of lunacy. Ned didn't like to think of how Lord Viccars would react to the suspicion that Ned had known his ladybird, for such she obviously was, in the biblical sense. "Never set eyes on her before!"

Was ever well-intentioned man forced to deal with such stubbornness? "The devil!" snapped Lord Viccars, and released Marguerite's arm. "You know the highwayman's doxy. You bragged of it, not once but several times!"

At least this much of the conversation Ned understood. "Aye. That I did. And I'll sing like a canary bird—for five hundred pounds."

"Ah." Jeremy crossed his elegant legs at the knee. "We seem to have reached an impasse. No one in this room has five hundred pounds at hand. At least I don't, and Marguerite's never had so much put by in all her life, and it's plain as a pikestaff that Viccars here ain't so plump in the pocket or he'd have already bought you off. And yet we're all very curious now about what tune you'd sing, my boyo, was you so inclined." He fingered his sword lovingly. "Was I you, I'd cut my losses before you come to worse grief."

Ned swallowed. This stranger's cool logic and icy gaze left him very impressed. "Five hundred pounds!" said Lord Viccars suddenly. "Of course! That's why Lady Sherry wished to borrow the money, to buy you off!" He frowned. "But why should she? For my sake, I suppose. What a loyal creature she is. I am not worthy

208

of her." He turned his frown on Marguerite. "And neither are you!"

Poor Marguerite was, at this point, very confused. She couldn't understand what she had to do with Lady Sherry—unless Andrew meant to set up a *ménage à trois*. Not that Marguerite was adverse to such a proposal. A female in her line of work couldn't afford to be a prude. But still, one could generally tell which gentlemen would make suggestions and which would not, and she would have been willing to gamble that Lord Viccars would not. *"Chacun à son goût!"* she murmured.

Everyone to his own taste, was it? Marguerite preferred a highwayman to an earl, apparently. Lord Viccars's pride was stung. "I cannot let you hang," he said stiffly. "No matter that you hold me in low esteem."

"I hold you— *Merde alors!*" So startled was Marguerite by this statement that she flew up out of her chair to clutch at Lord Viccars's sleeve. "Have you windmills in your head, Andrew? You must, to think such a thing. It is you who are getting married, not me!"

"My marriage has nothing to do with it!" retorted Andrew with admirable masculine logic. "You need not try and tell me you have been faithful to me, Marguerite."

"Eh bien! Now you slander me!" At his slur upon her character, Marguerite's eyes flashed. "I *have* been faithful to you, Andrew, or as close as makes no difference, and if you do not believe me, then I must ask you to leave my house!"

Lord Viccars did not believe Marguerite. How could he, when she had already confessed to him her liaison with a highwayman? He might well have stalked out of the house, vowing dramatically never to return. Two things prevented him from taking this action: he recalled that the pretty little Italian villa was not Marguerite's but his; and Jeremy chose at last to intervene, in tones convulsed with laughter. "I believe that you are laboring under a delusion, Viccars," he interrupted. "The worst fate that can befall our Marguerite is that she'll land in debtors' prison. Unless the law is changed so that a person can go to the gallows for not paying her debts." He moved the sword closer to Ned's face. "I think it's time, my pretty bird, that you began to sing for us."

Ned thought so, too. He didn't care for the manner in which the gleaming sword inched closer and closer to his unprotected throat. "I'll talk!" He gasped as it came closer yet. "I saw her riding hell-for-leather with that Captain Toby fellow on her horse, and then I saw them coming out of the gardener's shed. And *then* I put together what I'd seen and what I'd heard, and figured I could buy a nice little tavern for myself if only I was to lay my hands on the ready-and-rhino. That's all! I swear it! Can't blame a fellow for trying to get ahead!" Perspiration stood out on his brow.

Jeremy contemplated the gleaming tip of his sword. "That lets out our Marguerite. She can hardly stay mounted on a nag, let alone ride anywhere *ventre à terre* with anyone clinging to her skirts." Silence greeted this remark. Marguerite looked bewildered—Jeremy thought he would have to tell her not to let her mouth dangle open in that unattractive manner—and Lord Viccars like a man who'd received an unexpected reprieve. "Oh, my darling!" he cried, and drew Marguerite into his arms. "I have been absolutely sick with fright. I confided in Sir Christopher when first I heard of this braggart." He gestured toward Ned. "Which I certainly wouldn't have done if I'd thought it was you he would arrest. And then you chose to confide in me, or so I thought—"

It occurred to Lord Viccars then that the mystery was not altogether cleared up. With some reluctance, he put

Marguerite away from him. "What *were* you trying to tell me?" And then he blanched, stricken by the realization of which red-haired female of his acquaintance had access to a gardener's shed.

Jeremy could not refrain from comment, being of the temperament that liked to rub salt in wounds and pull wings off butterflies. "In other words, it ain't Marguerite who looks to dangle from the gallows but Lady Sherry," he said, and availed himself of a pinch of Martinique.

Chapter Twenty-four

Lady Sherry spent a restless interval pacing her book room. When she needed advice most, she thought irritably, neither of her confidantes was at hand. For this, she could only blame herself, having dispatched both Lavinia and Daffodil to learn what more they could of Ned. Curse the wretch! Sherry's position would not be half so bad save for his avarice. Save for her decision to witness a certain hanging! But there was no time now to waste in contemplating might-have-beens. She must act. In what manner she was to act, Sherry wasn't certain, however. She applied for inspiration to the decanter on the shelf. Christopher had said that he would take care of everything, and Sherry had no reason to think that he would not. Christopher had also said that she must testify against Micah in return. Sherry didn't think she could bear to do that. But she had given Christopher her promise, and she could not go back on her word.

And then a thought struck Sherry: If Micah was not captured, she need not testify against him. Scoundrel though he might be, Sherry could no more testify against the man who'd held her in his arms than she could fly to the moon. The man whose bare chest she'd caressed with her fingers, who . . . There was no time for these thoughts either. Christopher would not take immediate action against Micah. He would first try to puzzle out this mystery of two highwaymen with the same name.

As he had sternly informed Sherry, one didn't clap a peer of the realm into irons without being damned sure first that one could prove him guilty of a crime. Sherry had time to issue a warning that might prevent Micah's arrest.

She withdrew a shawl from her wardrobe, flung it around her shoulders, and covered her bright curls. Then she scribbled a note, lest Daffodil and Tully think she, too, had been kidnapped. If only Christopher had not demanded that she give him Lord Viccars's five hundred pounds. Sherry hoped she would not have to offer anyone a bribe. She poked her head out into the hallway but saw no one, and so warily descended the steep backstair. If only she could slip out of the house with no one—particularly Sir Christopher—the wiser as to what she was about.

Sherry thought she had made good her escape when she became aware of heavy footsteps padding after her down the sidewalk. Sherry paused, then turned reluctantly, expecting to find her brother in irate pursuit, or, even worse, an officer of the law who would press upon her metal handcuffs that closed with a snap and a spring.

Not Sir Christopher, or any officer of the law, waited to accost Lady Sherry. Sherry gazed without pleasure on Prinny's large, white furry mass. Aware that she did not look happy to see him, the dog gave his plumed tail an apologetic wag. "Oh, very well!" Lady Sherry sighed. "I suppose you have developed a taste for adventuring. What's more, I don't have time to take you back to the house!" She took hold of his collar. Prinny licked her hand.

Through the London streets they walked, Lady Sherry and the hound. She had no interest today in the colorful array of humanity that thronged the highways of that city of domes and towers and pointed steeples, or the narrow streets that wove among palatial residences and slums. She was oblivious to the racket of hooves and wheels and stagecoach horns, to street vendors and musicians and market carts. Prinny was a great deal more curious about all these exciting sights and smells, but he was discouraged from exploration by Sherry's brooding manner and her restraining hand.

Their stroll was not without direction. Bloomsbury, Cavendish Square—here among these older buildings was the address that Sherry sought. But she had no notion which it was. She glanced at Prinny. "If only you could talk!" But of course the hound could not, even with the best will in the world. Sherry then stopped a hot-potato vendor and asked if he knew the neighborhood. The man allowed that he did. He also knew which was the ancestral home of the Grenvilles. Lady Sherry was practically standing on the front doorstep.

Oh, no. It couldn't be. Sherry gazed up at an ancient stone mansion that might well have graced the pages of one of her books. It was three stories high, with large bay windows glazed in quaint patterns and a high-pitched, red-tiled roof. Square towers that were exaggerated bays rose a story above the building's main mass. Various familiar adjectives presented themselves to Sherry as she stared up at the great, dark forbidding pile. In that list, 'moldering' and 'haunted' were foremost. But she could not stand there gaping. Sherry walked to the front door.

No one answered her summons. The house seemed deserted. Sherry wondered despairingly if Micah, like Lord Viccars, had chosen to dwell elsewhere than in the ancestral home. Surely not. A rogue bent on impersonating a peer would neglect none of the accouterments of the rank. Nor, most likely, would he know how a house of this size should be run. The servants were no doubt taking their leisure in another part of the house. Very well, Sherry would roust them out. Since no one had come to the front door, she would go to the back.

There, too, she received no answer. Sherry glared with impotent fury at the locked door. It is very frustrating to rush *ventre à terre* to someone's rescue and then find them away from home after all. Sherry might have abandoned her mission then; she knew nowhere else to look for Micah, and this expedition had come to seem like less than a good idea, but Prinny had a more forceful way with doors than she did. The hound realized that Lady Sherry wished to gain entrance to this old building—why, he couldn't imagine, but Prinny had long since decided that the ways of humans were incomprehensible to the canine brain—and he himself wasn't averse to a good tussle with a rat or two. This house looked as if it might harbor any number of rodents. Prinny shrugged out of Lady Sherry's grasp and leaped in abandon at the door.

"Oh!" Lady Sherry had thought for a moment that the hound meant to run away. How she would explain that occurrence to her brother and his wife, Sherry couldn't say. But the door opened inward with a creaking groan of wood, and Prinny did not set off down the street but strolled inside. Sherry could not let a dog upstage her as regarded courage. Nor did she wish to seek him in the dark corridors of the old house. She hurried after him and caught at his collar. Behind them, the door swung shut, putting Sherry strongly in mind once more of ghostly specters and the like. She wondered if Lord Viccars's ancestral home was as eerie a place as this. A pity, if true; Sherry's stories would no doubt have benefited greatly from being written in such a malevolent atmosphere. Minus such touches as cobwebs, she decided as she brushed one from her face. And well-lit by candles, as well as swept. Sherry didn't care to think what crunched on the cobbled floor beneath her feet. It sounded suspiciously like small animal—or rodent—bones.

A candle first, Sherry decided. She pushed back her shawl as if that act would make it easier for her to see. Impossible in this gloom to determine if anyone was living in the house. Not that Sherry could imagine Micah in such a setting. But she had not imagined him either as a peer of the realm. "The kitchens, I think," she murmured to Prinny in the tone of one whistling while passing through a cemetery. Still, it was logical to assume that one would find candles there. If the rats hadn't gotten to them. Unlike her companion, Lady Sherry experienced no pleasure at the thought of rats. She drew closer to the hound.

The kitchens were not difficult to locate. With relief, Sherry stepped into the large, low-ceilinged chamber, walked across the stone-flagged floor. In the dim light, she could make out spits and implements for roasting and grilling and a huge fireplace in which a man could stand erect.

Where was the logical place in which to keep candles? Sherry moved to an ancient sideboard, rummaged among chafing dishes and graters, pot racks and dripping pans. A quick search revealed candles in a drawer along with a tinderbox. Sherry released Prinny and lit a candle, tucking another in her bodice for good measure, as well as the tinderbox. The old place was drafty; Sherry cupped her hand around the flame of her candle, then almost dropped it as a rough curse shattered the stillness of the old house.

Holding the candle in trembling hands, Sherry spun around. There at the kitchen table a man was seated. He had been sleeping, Sherry thought, and Prinny had awakened him with an enthusiastic caress, because he was glad to be reunited with his old friend. Unfortunately, his old friend did not appear to share the hound's joy. "Get down, curse you!" he snarled.

It was the proper tone of voice in which to issue commands; Prinny dropped dejectedly to the floor. But it was not the voice that Sherry associated with that face. And now that she moved closer, even the face was not the same. The features were broader, coarser; the eyes were more hazel than green. And the pistol that was pointed at her was very wicked-looking, indeed.

"You're not Micah!" Sherry gasped. If it was not an especially intelligent observation, she may surely be forgiven. Although this was not the first time that Sherry had gazed into the muzzle of a pistol, the occurrence still caused her considerable distress. Tully had said the man in Newgate had the look of Micah, she remembered. "You're the highwayman who escaped from jail!"

He grinned and indicated with a wave of his pistol that Sherry should take a chair. "And you're Micah's peculiar. The red-haired doxy everyone's so monstrous eager to meet." With the pistol still trained on her, he reached for the jug that stood on the table, lifted it, and drank. Then he wiped the back of his hand across his mouth. "Fancy you playing right into my hands like that."

A number of thoughts, in this interval, passed through Lady Sherry's mind. She thought of all the ladies over the centuries who had been given a choice of surrendering their jewels or their honor and who had often lost both in one night. Although this brigand who looked so much like Micah had made no threats upon her virtue, Sherry was aware that her situation was very grave. It seemed very likely that either this person would shoot her or she would accompany him to Newgate. But Sherry's story-telling instinct did not desert her in this mo-

217

ment of great peril. If she was to go to the gallows, she would at least have some questions answered first.

"Why did you become a highwayman?" she asked, resolutely ignoring his ominous comment about her playing into his hands. "Or is it a family tradition, so to speak? If you *are* a highwayman! I suppose I should ask you that. Between you and Micah, everyone seems to be somewhat confused.'

Her host drank from his bottle again. "You're a queer one," he replied. "But I don't see as what harm there is in telling you, seeing as you'll have no chance to snitch on me. Aye, I took to the high toby." He grinned. "*Captain* Toby, if you take my meaning, ma'am. And a rum-paddler I was, too, until I got careless and had to hop the twig."

Sherry understood this to mean that Captain Toby had had to make a sudden departure from the scene of his activities. "You were in the military?" she asked.

"Aye." The smile faded. "I was with Wellington in the Peninsula. At Salamanca and Cuidad Rodrigo. At Victoria and Pamplona and Toulouse. At Waterloo. And nary a scratch of a wound did I have, though three horses was shot out from under me. I said then what I say now: I'll die damned hard and bold as brass—but not yet. As for why I went on the pad, 'tis simple: I was poor as a church mouse."

There was something queer about this tale, this situation. If Micah had sufficient money to pose as a nobleman, then why was Captain Toby so poor? Perhaps Micah's charade was being financed by highway robbery. "And so you took to the road," Sherry prodded. "It seems a great deal of risk to take for so little gain. For the theft of a few pounds, you could hang."

"Dance the Paddington frisk?" Captain Toby laughed. "Not I. Though Micah damned near did so in my place. I should have let him, curst interfering meddler that he is." He looked at Sherry appraisingly. "But he'll meddle no more, I think! Not since *you* saw fit to pay a call on me!"

Sherry didn't like the sound of that. "What do you mean? Micah would be very angry if you were to harm me, I think."

"Harm you?" Captain Toby looked indignant. "I haven't harmed a woman yet. At least not in the way you mean. No, ma'am, I wish you no ill. But it's time for me to shove my trunk, if you take my meaning, before I make a renewed acquaintance with the constables, and I'm out of twig. It hasn't seemed exactly the right time to refurbish my purse by going back on the road. And old Micah's proving damned unreasonable about the matter, saying I should turn myself in and take my medicine so as to let *him* off the hook."

Sherry followed these disclosures with considerable interest. "So Micah isn't a highwayman?"

"Old upright Micah on the scamp?" Captain Toby threw back his head and guffawed. "We may be related, ma'am, but we ain't such close kin as that. Mayhap it has to do with me being born on the wrong side of the blanket and him on the right."

Sherry didn't think it was altogether upright of Micah to pass himself off as Lord Grenville, but this hardly seemed the moment in which to quibble about such details. "So you are, er, illegitimate."

"No need to mince words, ma'am. There's many as would tell you I was a right proper bastard, was you to ask. Which you won't, of course, having seen the wisdom of keeping dubber mum'd." He paused, listening. "Hist! What's that?"

Sherry heard it, too, a distant banging noise as if someone was assaulting the front door. Was it Micah? Sir Christopher and his constables? If only Sherry could gain possession of Captain Toby's gun. If only Prinny would choose this most opportune moment to fawn upon Captain Toby as he did upon everyone else. But Prinny had lost interest in the conversation and had gone off to hunt down rats, and Captain Toby gave no indication of the sort of carelessness that would enable Lady Sherry to take possession of his firearm. Instead, he grasped it all the firmer as he pushed himself away from the table and yanked Lady Sherry out of her chair.

"Wait!" she pleaded as he dragged her across the stone floor toward the huge fireplace. "You said you meant me no harm."

"Nor do I mean to preach at Tyburn cross!" retorted Captain Toby as he pressed a certain stone above the fireplace. "You'll find your way out soon enough—but not so soon I won't have cleared out! Go on, get in!"

Lady Sherry stared at the dark opening revealed by a section of the wainscoting that had swung aside. She was looking at a secret passage of the sort about which she had written so many times. But writing about a secret passage and exploring one were two entirely different things. Sherry had no desire to step into that dark, dank, and no doubt rat-infested space.

She hesitated. The shouts from outside had grown louder, as if the persons who desired admittance were following Sherry's path around to the back door. Prinny added his barks to the melee from somewhere in the house. "Oh, please, don't make me go in there!" Sherry begged Captain Toby. "I promise I won't say a word about you to anyone!"

Captain Toby was not so green as to believe this promise. "When pigs can fly!" he growled, and pushed Lady Sherry through the opening, so roughly that she stumbled to her knees. Behind her, the panel slid shut, plunging her into the darkness of the tomb.

Chapter Twenty-five

Sherry lit the candle that she'd had the foresight to tuck into her bodice and tried to recall what she knew about secret passages. She reviewed priest's holes and hides in pit and chimney, entrance via flues and trapdoors, and medieval subterranean drains that could be used as exits in case of emergency. But the dark space in which she stood seemed to be very deep. Sherry stepped forward to investigate and discovered a narrow, winding passage in the thickness of the wall. She supposed she should not be surprised to find such a passage in a house as old as this. She wondered where it led. One thing was certain: She was not going back into the kitchens. Sherry gathered up her skirts and tentatively began to mount the stairs. At least the passage led upward, instead of down into some clammy, rat-infested drain.

She would not think of rats, not now. Sherry wondered why she'd never thought to use rats in any of her books. As an inducement to terror, rats surely ranked with ghostly apparitions and ominous noises and lights seen flickering at midnight in ancient houses' abandoned wings. This ancient house appeared to be entirely abandoned. Sherry hoped its appearance was not deceiving. She was in no frame of mind to deal with homicidal monsters or avenging shades. How many times she had written about a setting such as this: a delicate heroine exposed to supernatural danger and shattering alarms; of clanking chains and haunted chambers and even once a globe containing human ashes that had been discovered in a haunted maze. The heroine of that particular tale had been able to see visions. Sherry wished she shared the trait. Despite the number of Gothic thrillers she had written, Sherry had never created an atmosphere so macabre as the one in which she now found herself.

Furthermore, the candle stub was rapidly burning low. Sherry hoped she might find an exit before it burned out and plunged her again into the dark, and she was reduced to screaming lunacy. Captain Toby had meant her no harm? Perhaps he was under the impression that Sherry wouldn't mind rats nibbling at her toes and bats jousting with spiders for the right to nest in her hair.

At this horrid thought, Sherry almost did scream aloud. She decided she would rather deal with ghosts than make the acquaintance of the rodent population of this house. And then she heard faint voices, as if wish had fostered thought. Sherry turned as quickly as she dared on the narrow step and peered back into the darkness through which she had come. She saw nothing but heard a scampering sound as if tiny—or not so tiny— rodent paws scurried away from the light. Certainly Sherry was not going back down the narrow steps to investigate! She turned back and continued to mount the stair.

She came to a landing. The voices seemed louder now. Despite her dislike of cobwebs and their creators, Sherry leaned closer to the wall. What was this? A latch? Sherry lifted it and a section of the wall slid creakily aside, and she found herself standing in a narrow opening at the back of a cupboard filled with clothes. Ancient clothes, Sherry decided as she gingerly pushed aside the garments and slid onto a shelf. She was careful to keep her candle as far away as possible from the rotting material.

Sherry moved to the front of the cupboard. Definitely the voices were louder now. Sherry recognized one of them as Captain Toby. Without thinking, Sherry pushed open the cupboard door and stared into the door.

It was a large room and so brightly lit that Sherry squinted in the sudden light. Here at least King Cobweb did not reign supreme, not in the corners of the ceiling that displayed the twelve signs of the zodiac, or in the chimney piece that was a network of carving displaying the judgment of Solomon, or the mantelpiece lush with monkeys and birds and fruits. The mermaids and dolphins and arabesques on windowhead and wainscoting and plasterwork seemed freshly scrubbed, as did the intricately glazed windows in which clear panes contrasted with stained glass. The heavy oak furniture—delicately inlaid with pearl and hardwoods of different colors, and carved with intricate animals and flowers—gleamed as if recently polished.

As did Captain Toby's pistol, which he was brandishing in a very menacing manner at the cupboard door. "Damned if you ain't a plaguey one!" he snarled. "I thought I'd done for you at least upward of an hour. So there's an opening to the passage in that closet, eh? Mayhap both of you might wish to explore. Here, my lad, up with you!" He moved aside then, allowing Sherry to see Micah, who was sprawled in a chair.

At first she thought that he was drunk. Of all the ill-advised times to overindulge in the grape! Then she realized that the amount of liquor required to reduce a man to such a condition would most likely have also put him in his grave. "What have you done to him?" she cried as Captain Toby dragged Micah to his feet. And what had he done with the people who had been hammering at the back door not many moments past? No doubt

223

when they had received no answer they had simply gone away.

"Climb down off your high ropes!" Captain Toby grunted. Perspiration stood out on his brow as he sought to balance Micah's weight. "I told you I was wishful of going to ground for a while. Lord Law-Abiding here was going to queer my pitch, so I had to put out his lights. Now, ma'am, don't nab the bib! It ain't permanent. I've no quarrel with old Micah here. To tell the truth, I'm kind of fond of him! I just dosed him up with laudanum."

Sherry had no inclination to nab the bib—to weep, in a gentler parlance. She was far too angry and indignant to find solace in her tears. This scoundrel Captain Toby had abused not only her but Micah as well. Sherry was so furious that she would find relief only in physical violence.

Well, and why not? Captain Toby was severely hampered by Micah's body, which he had slung over his shoulder like a sack of meal. But she had no weapon. Sherry looked anxiously about and encountered the gaze of a pair of green eyes. Micah wasn't unconscious! Sherry could have wept with relief. What was he frowning at so intently? Sherry followed his gaze to the display of ancient weapons that hung upon one wall.

Dared she? Sherry sidled toward the weapons. "And just where do you think you're going?" Captain Toby demanded suspiciously. "Oof!" he added as his burden came to life suddenly and kicked him in the stomach. Sherry hesitated no longer but yanked a broadsword down from the wall and applied it to the highwayman's head. Captain Toby collapsed with a groan.

Some few moments passed then as Sherry helped Micah to disentangle himself from Captain Toby and broadsword. "Oh, Micah!" she cried. "Are you all right? You look so pale. I didn't kill him, did I? Although it would have served the wretch right! Which reminds me, I came to warn you. I told Christopher everything! I had to! And now you'll go to jail and it's all my fault!'' She burst into tears.

This pretty speech had a reviving effect on Micah, who was not half as ill as he looked, having previously relieved himself of a considerable amount of the laudanum by the simple expedient of sticking his finger down his throat. ''Don't cry, my brave darling!'' he murmured as he offered her, in lieu of a handkerchief, his sleeve. ''It will be all right!''

Sherry cried all the harder. She didn't see how anything could ever be all right again. Before she could say so—indeed, as if to bear out her apprehensions—the door burst open and a group of people spilled into the room. Sir Christopher and Lavinia, Jeremy and Ned, Lord Viccars and Marguerite. ''Aha!'' said Sir Christopher. ''Caught you red-handed, you rogue. Good for you, Sis! Although you might better have left the business to Bow Street!''

''I didn't!'' protested Lady Sherry as she left off wiping her damp face with Micah's sleeve and instead clasped him to her breast. ''He's not! Christopher, you must listen to me. It's *that* man you want!'' She pointed to Captain Toby, who was clutching his abused head and muttering beneath his breath. ''That's your highwayman! And this—'' She glanced at Micah. ''Well, I don't know who he is!''

Micah removed himself, with reluctance, from Sherry's breast. ''Grenville,'' he said with a little smile. ''At your service, ma'am. If you arrest me in this devil's place, Sir Christopher, you'll be repeating a mistake for which I already damned near hanged!''

Impatient as he was to carry out his duties, Sir Christopher was a fair man, and there remained the to-do attendant upon the mistaken arrest of a peer. He looked

225

at the man sprawled out upon the floor and then at the man whose sleeve Sherry clutched. There *was* a definite resemblance between the men. "Then let's have the straight of the story without circumlocution!" he said judiciously.

Sherry could not bear to listen to the tarradiddles Micah spun for her brother's benefit. She released him and turned toward Lavinia, who was looking daggers at her. Who was that scantily clad female hovering near Andrew?

Andrew. Sherry had an apology to make to Lord Viccars. *And* a few choice words to say to Ned. She walked across the room. "Andrew, I am very sorry and I did mean to make you very happy, but it seems fairly obvious that we should not suit!"

"Not suit!" Lavinia had withheld comment already for longer than seemed humanly possible and could no longer refrain. Anyway, Christopher was too preoccupied with Lord Grenville to overhead and scold. "Sherris, have you become a bedlamite? Rubbing shoulders with highwaymen! Paying off servants to keep your secrets! And now, to *not* marry Viccars! Sherris, this is altogether displeasing! You have sunk yourself quite below reproach. Not to mention the rest of us, you wretched girl! How ever will we wrap *this* up in clean linen? I never was so shocked by anything in my life!"

No one made an immediate response to this tirade. Jeremy had wandered across the room to better hear the exchange between Sir Christopher and Lord Grenville, and Ned was deep in silent lamentation of his lost opportunities, his presence in the chamber attendant only upon Lord Viccars's firm grip on the collar of his shirt. In his turn, Lord Viccars looked embarrassed, and Lady Sherry abashed.

Less prey to polite or servile scruples, Marguerite contemplated Lavinia, who was dosing her shattered nerves alternately with vinaigrette and fan. Much as Marguerite might resent her rival, she rather admired Lady Sherry for taking up with a highwayman. Too, Lady Sherry had just broken off with Marguerite's protector, which left her feeling very charitable toward her.

"*Ma foi!*" she said, therefore, to Lady Sherry. "What a cat that one is. If she was forever ripping up at you like that, then it is no wonder you kicked over the traces, *ma chérie*! I wish you would tell me all about it!" She turned a speculative gaze on Captain Toby.

Sherry had no notion of this female's identity—save that she certainly seemed to know Andrew well—but there was no doubting her good heart. "Thank you," Sherry murmured, for want of a more appropriate response.

Lavinia gazed somewhat less appreciatively upon Marguerite, who had been so eager to witness the outcome of these perplexing developments that she had merely flung a cloak over her peignoir before rushing out of her house. "And who are *you*?" Lavinia snapped.

It was meant as a rhetorical question, perhaps, but Marguerite chose to respond. She explained very kindly to Lavinia that she was Lord Viccars's *petite amie*. Lavinia gasped, fell back, and fanned herself all the more vigorously.

Startled as she was by Marguerite's outspokenness, Sherry could not help but be amused by Lavinia's shocked expression. She met Lord Viccars's apologetic eye. "Now I know we should not suit!" she said frankly as she gave him her hand. "You should have told me your heart had been bestowed elsewhere. Christopher has your five hundred pounds and will restore it to you. I can only say I'm sorry for all the trouble I've put you to." She turned toward Ned. "And *you* may look for a new position straightaway. Don't ask me to give you a

227

reference; you may be grateful that I don't have you thrown into jail!''

Ned might have thanked Lady Sherry for her kindness then—certainly he should have done so—but the opportunity was denied him. The mention of five hundred pounds brought Captain Toby to his feet, in his hand the sword-stick that he had plucked from Jeremy's limp grasp. ''I'll just have that five hundred pounds, my covy!'' he said. ''Or the rest of you may watch this fashionable fribble get his throat slit!''

Clearly, Sir Toby meant business. No argument was raised. Sir Christopher handed over the requested sum. The others moved away as he backed toward the door, drawing Jeremy with him, sword tip still pressed to that ashen individual's throat.

He pushed Jeremy away from him and opened the door. ''For the record, Micah here ain't never taken to the road in his life. He was arrested in my place and so I felt obliged to interrupt his hanging. But since I *don't* intend to adorn the gallows in my own turn, I suggest you all—''

The highwayman's suggestion was never completed. Prinny pushed past him and into the room. From his mouth dangled a very large rat. Lavinia was of far too delicate a constitution to endure such a shock. She swooned.

''Mon Dieu!'' cried Marguerite, into whose arms Lavinia fell. Meanwhile, Jeremy was feeling none too well himself. He scrambled for possession of Lavinia's fan and vinaigrette. Prinny, the cause of all this confusion, failed to understand why his friends refused to appreciate him for showing them his prize. Perhaps they failed to realize that it was quite the plumpest of all this old house's rat population that dangled from his jaws. Prinny decided that he would never understand humans. He sighed and collapsed upon the hearth.

Sir Christopher and Marguerite being engaged with ministering to Lavinia, and Ned to Jeremy, Micah took advantage of this opportunity to speak with Lady Sherry. "A neat-enough ending," he murmured as he drew her down beside him in a chair. "They'll never catch Toby now, not in the maze of old drains beneath this house."

"You must be glad of that." Sherry was feeling very shy. "No matter how richly deserved, one wouldn't wish to see a member of one's family hanged!"

"I suppose not." Micah stroked Sherry's arm. "Tell me, what do you think of the house? I purposely didn't have most of it tidied up because I didn't know what you would like."

"What I would like." Lady Sherry stared at him. "Surely you don't mean to . . . I mean, it isn't yours!"

"My foolish darling, of course it's mine." Micah's smile was warm. "I tried to tell you I wasn't a highwayman, but you wouldn't listen, if you will recall. This house *is* mine, along with the title. I was en route to claim both when I was arrested in Toby's place. I hope you will not be too disappointed. Toby told me a great many of his adventures, and between us we must surely have enough imagination to fill in the blanks. What a jolly time we shall have, my darling. Or should I say, Ophelia will, and Captain Blood?"

Could it be? Dared she believe? "You can't mean that—" Sherry murmured, then broke off, aghast at the audacity of her thoughts. "Er, I would be happy to give you what advice I may about your house. And I would be pleased to have your advice about my book, Mi—Lord Grenville!"

"Peagoose!" responded Micah. "It's not your advice I want!" And then he proceeded to kiss Lady Sherry so thoroughly that any doubts she retained about the nature of his feelings were laid forever to rest. Indeed, so thor-

229

oughly did Micah perform this pleasurable task that it caught the attention of the other occupants of the room. *"Très bien!"* said Marguerite admiringly, while Lord Viccars looked embarrassed again and Sir Christopher fond. Ned and Jeremy ignored the incident altogether, the latter pondering how this adventure might be put to the best use and the former lamenting the loss of five hundred pounds. Lavinia, who had just recovered from a swoon, threatened to succumb to another. "Christopher!" She gasped. "How can you just stand there and watch your sister being *compromised*?"

"Compromised?" echoed Micah, who had taken Lavinia in dislike. "This is nothing, ma'am. If you had a notion—after all, I did spend several days in Lady Sherry's book room . . ."

Here Lady Sherry felt obliged to add her own wicked comment. "Reading *The Giaour*!"

"Reading *The Giaour*!" added Micah with a fond glance at Lady Sherry. "And—but I won't make you blush! There's nothing for it that I can see but that I must marry her to save what's left of her good name!"

"Oh, Micah!" Sherry whispered as Lavinia sputtered with outrage, torn between horror at the notion of illicit goings-on beneath her roof and profound curiosity as to just what those goings-on had entailed. "Are you *certain* you wish to marry me?"

"I have no choice," Micah replied manfully. "You have been closeted alone with me while I was without my shirt!" Marguerite giggled, Lavinia gasped, and the gentlemen remained tactfully silent while Lord Grenville kissed Lady Sherry yet once again.

And so our adventure draws to an end, with Lady Sherry in happy prospect of union with the lover of her choice and Lord Viccars reunited with his; with Lavinia's horror at the goings-on beneath her roof being soothed by Sir Christopher, who had in mind some goings-on of his own when they returned to Longacre House and never mind if it *was* the middle of the afternoon; and Prinny snoozing on the cold hearth with his plump prey clutched between his front paws. It was an adventure that would be long remembered by all even peripherally concerned: by the ladies Throckmorton and Dunsany, who would long speculate with a silent Lavinia on how Lady Sherris had made so sudden and so brilliant a match; by the ladies Cecilia and Sarah-Louise with regret and relief; by Williams and Briscoe, who by tacit agreement with their employer never discussed the events of a certain night; by Sir Christopher, who recalled with fondness the afternoon when his Livvy had been persuaded to broaden her knowledge of conjugal affairs. Daffodil, too, would remember the business that led her to break off altogether with Ned, who was no sooner turned off from Lady Sherry's employ than he was hired by Jeremy, who had discovered in himself a sudden desire for a new groom, and which in turn led Daffodil to console herself in the arms of the strong-sinewed footman whom she was eventually to wed.

Aunt Tulliver continued in Lady Sherry's employ until her death many years later of nothing more dramatic than a peaceful old age. Marguerite continued as Lord Viccars's *petite amie* for many years, until his second marriage, at which time she passed without regret from being a *femme entretenue* to the proprietor of a most exclusive bordello.

After their marriage and a prolonged and very blissful honeymoon abroad, Lord Grenville and Lady Sherry took up residence in the family's ancestral house. Although Lady Sherry did not emulate her sister-in-law by turning out a prodigious number of progeny, she did continue to write novels, and *Ophelia and Captain Blood* remained a very popular edition for several years. Prinny resided with them and enjoyed himself immensely, terrorizing the rat population and his surrogate mama when she came to call. Once they no longer had to dwell together beneath the same roof, Lavinia and Sherry discovered that they liked each other very well.

As for Captain Toby, the rogue who set in motion this whole tale, no word was ever heard of him again. Although there were certain periodic rumors of a brigand who plagued the Continent for some years thereafter, who never offered harm to a lady, and who . . .

But such speculation is pointless. Suffice it to say that Captain Toby graced no English gallows under his own or any other name.

True romance is <u>not</u> hard to find... you need only look as far as FAWCETT BOOKS

TAF-43

27 million Americans can't read a bedtime story to a child.

It's because 27 million adults in this country simply can't read.

Functional illiteracy has reached one out of five Americans. It robs them of even the simplest of human pleasures, like reading a fairy tale to a child.

You can change all this by joining the fight against illiteracy.

Call the Coalition for Literacy at toll-free **1-800-228-8813** and volunteer.

**Volunteer
Against Illiteracy.
The only degree you need
is a degree of caring.**

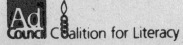

Ad Council   Coalition for Literacy

LV-3